DEATH

of a

WHALER

NERIDA NEWTON was born in Brisbane, and has since lived in Malaysia, South Africa and the United Kingdom. Her first novel, *The Lambing Flat*, won the Queensland Premier's award for an emerging author, and was shortlisted for *The Australian*/Vogel award, the Commonwealth Writers' Prize for the Asia/Pacific region (first book) and One Book One Brisbane. In 2004, she was named by the *Sydney Morning Herald* as one of Australia's best young novelists. Nerida resides in Brisbane with her husband and son.

DEATH
of a
WHALER

NERIDA NEWTON

ALLEN&UNWIN

First published in 2006

  This project has been assisted by the Commonwealth
Government through the Australia Council, its arts

Queensland **Australia Council** funding and advisory board and the Queensland
Government for the Arts Government through Arts Queensland.
Arts Queensland

Allen & Unwin
83 Alexander Street
Crows Nest NSW 2065
Australia
Phone: (61 2) 8425 0100
Fax: (61 2) 9906 2218
Email: info@allenandunwin.com
Web: www.allenandunwin.com

National Library of Australia
Cataloguing-in-Publication entry:

Newton, Nerida, 1972–.
  Death of a whaler.

  ISBN 978 1 74114 791 9
  ISBN 1 74114 791 3.

  I. Title.

A823.4

Set in 12/15pt Bembo by Asset Typesetting Pty Ltd
Printed in Australia by McPherson's Printing Group

10 9 8 7 6 5 4 3 2

To Vida, for the joy passed.
To Oliver, for the joy to come.

ONE

Byron Bay, 1956

Through this thick oozing stench, the town. Not much. A grilled brown mark on the edge of the farm-lands, scratched out between the ocean and the rainforest. Buildings huddled together against a road, their backs or sides to the sea. Except the pub. The pub wide open to the elements. Sand on the verandas. The bargirls complaining that their hair is sticky because of the sea salt that blows in. The old blokes straddling the stools, their thongs hooked under the rails, sitting with their backs to the glare.

The whalers huddle over their beers, don't speak much. They are out of their butchers' garments, they've rinsed their galoshes of the dark blood and the soft, foamy fat that hardens like gum in the patterns of the soles.

The afternoon turns lilac and a half moon brightens into focus. The wind picks up and slices through the bar. The smell with it. The bargirls wipe the wisps of hair out of their eyes and wrinkle up their noses. The old men turn to look at the whalers as if they were responsible for this, this easterly. The industry. It's the way forward, people had said. The stink of cut flesh and guts unfortunately just part and parcel. A small price to secure the future of the town. They're less sure now, the people. Now that the clothes on their washing lines smell of it, and their fruit and milk taste permanently sour. What choice? they say, clucking their tongues. It was this or the death of us.

Byron Bay, 1962

A freak accident, it was one of those things that happen in a split second followed by months of disbelief. The knife, for example. Flinch had only just picked it up a second earlier. A big knife, more like a sickle. He was holding it with both hands.

It happened on the second last day before the station shut down. Some people mumble that they had it coming. Something like this was inevitable. Nay-saying the hobby of choice in the town by then. At Nate's funeral, a few of the drive-by tourists huddle together, stare unrelenting at the whalers. As if it's a usual part of the weekend spectacle. Before the priest has finished the sermon, the whalers are mumbling curses under their breath and a flick knife is pulled from a pocket.

Death seems bigger in some places. On the flensing floor with its torrents of blood it looms huge and formidable even in the harsh, stinking midday. In the graveyard under the circling grey skies it is smaller, subdued. Nate inside the coffin in his Sunday best lies with his arms crossed over his chest. It's a makeshift box, the cheapest coffin available, made from what looks like driftwood, or someone's old veranda boards. Lazy workmanship has left slits through which the worms and the ants will crawl. Nails in the lid already rusted as if sea-worn.

The priest holds his hand up. Flinch notices the rest of the men are standing with their fists clenched. The priest slaps his Bible shut and nods. The coffin is lowered into the ground.

Nate in a box that sounds solid, thick with his presence, when the clumps of earth are shovelled over it. Flinch thought it would be sandy earth, fine granules like on the beach, the same soil that is all around the bay, washing up then out to sea and back again with the tides. But here in the graveyard it is more like clay. It sticks to the sides of his only pair of dress shoes. Later, he will scrub it off with an old toothbrush.

Mumbled prayers and last rites gestures completed with a sigh that echoes the apathy of routine. The priest makes his way towards the out-of-towners, shaking his head, and they all leave soon after.

The knife that killed Nate could slice through blubber like it was butter. Had already many times. An old knife, but a good one still, kept sharp by the boys on the floor and on the boats. And the blood. Nobody noticed a man bleeding when they were all covered in it; it was on everyone's hands, on their clothing too, all over their faces. And he didn't cry out. Not initially.

They'd brought in the whale, hauled her onto the tray. She was a huge one, swollen with pregnancy, though the gunner couldn't tell that when he shot her. She'd been heading up the coast to birth.

The harpoonist had hit her hard, dead-centre, but the head of the weapon hadn't exploded, so her death was a long and violent one. She'd struggled at first, raged against them, dragging the boat askew more than a few times, streaming a red wake. She had thrashed against the harpoon, the boat pulled along like a dog on a chain. The men on the deck had to hang onto the masts or they would have been flung into the water, worse still onto the whale, been drowned in her fury. Flinch was in the crow's nest, crouched down inside it, so much sweat behind his knees that it trickled stinging into his jocks. He'd stayed, fingers clinging to the edge, acorns for knuckles that cracked when he tightened his grip, nails worn through nervous chewing to red, wet stumps. Flinch was the whale spotter. It was how he spent his days.

A struggle like this was a rare thing and Flinch thought they should have known then that this was a catch to be wary of. They don't battle them like they used to in the old days. No white water, no boats smashed into matches, no 'thar she blows!' Just a quick shout from Flinch when he's spotted them through the binoculars and an easy turn into the path of the whale. The harpoon usually explodes on impact and then death is immediate. Pools of blood stain the surface like oil spill. The men strap the dead whales to the side of the boat by their tails, cutting the flukes off so they don't act as rudders and slow the boat down. Then a rubber pipe inserted, the air pumped into the body just the same as inflating an inner tube, so that the carcass floats. Makes it easier to drag back to shore. Sharks like abandoned corner-store mongrels steal alongside, hungry for a piece of the kill. Unable to gnaw through blubber, they wait until the whale is dead then attack the lolling tongue, the vulnerable flesh.

It's mechanical, technical, a process. Harpoon them, bring them in, slice them up, extract the oil, package the meat onto trays, snap freeze. Flinch had heard that most of the whale meat went to England as pet food, and he used to find it hard to believe that the massive animal dying in front of him would be eaten by someone's poodle in London a month later. The jaw bones, baleen the colour of sand hanging like a bristly curtain, are saved for museums and biologists, or used as attractions at curio shops up and down the coast. Schoolboys stand in the hollow remains of the open mouths and have their photographs taken.

This whale played out her last moments in the ocean like some fat old diva, theatrical throes then a sudden unexpected resignation. She had long stopped struggling when they dragged her onto the onshore ramp. Exhausting herself with the battle while still in the deep blue, she had stayed afloat the rest of the way in. She looked dead, though her sides swelled and dropped once or twice very slowly. They had to put hooks into her to get her onto the tray, then back to the meatworks where they could work on her properly.

She was rolled onto the floor on her side, her belly exposed for the first cut. And Nate, at his end, had taken his carving saw to start on her tail. He was standing over her, right next to her, when she let out a massive groan and with a sweeping blow knocked him straight back into Flinch and they had crashed against the railing. The knife lodged between Nate's shoulder-blades, slipped into his flesh as if into a sheath.

He slid off it slowly, his eyes wide and lips pale. He dropped to his knees and stayed propped there as if praying, the blood trickling thickly down his back.

Flinch cried out loud, he thought he was screaming but he was mouthing the words, like some beached fish, his mouth open and shut. Eventually a sound like a squawk, Nate keeling over onto his face into the sticky pool around the whale.

The police absolved Flinch of blame straight

away and nothing more was said. There were enough witnesses. And Flinch, young Flinch with the one leg shorter than the other, wide-eyed and clumsy and as awkward and soft-hearted as a child, had grown up in this town. Nate was a drifter. Men die in this business, that's not unusual. It just usually happens at sea. Even the fishermen of the smallest fish drown, knocked overboard by waves, hitting their heads on the way down. Sometimes they wash up, swollen with the water they've soaked up, flaky and soft and white, their ears and the soft apple of flesh in their cheeks nibbled by crabs. Other times the whalers and the other fishermen help the local cops look for them. They drag fishnets between the boats. It's easy when they're floaters, but not all of them are.

Nate's family didn't make it to his funeral. The priest said he would send a letter to an address they found in his belongings. It wasn't a complete address. Just the name and postcode of some small town none of them could point to on a map. Under the address there was one word. Eleanor. No last name. No indication of whether she was a wife or a mother or a girlfriend.

Flinch didn't realise how little he knew about Nate until he was dead, and then the questions filling his throat rose so often that they grew stale and tasted of bile. They'd spent every night together drinking, indulging Nate's love of tiny glasses of cold beer, Flinch's standard of a nip or two of rum. More often than not they were the last to leave, occasionally hurled by management onto the grass across the road, where they'd lie on their backs and philosophise in the way they could only when they were utterly drunk, the connections in their logic loose and flexible, the truths they found startling and profound. Flinch, stumbling back to his bed in the old pastel house, would try to remember those truths until the morning, sing them like a mantra until he fell asleep, but when daylight rolled around they were gone.

Nate was the first person with whom Flinch had spent any decent amount of time talking. The old stories again and again about the biggest whales, the difficult catches, the harpoonist who was so hung-over one day he blew up a rowboat that had swept loose of its moorings. Comfortable words. Stories worn and traded like old coats. Putting them on after a drink or two and recognising each other in them.

But these stories give Flinch no comfort now. They are cold and misfit, threadbare without Nate to weave his part. The questions Flinch wants to ask him now are the type the one bored police-rounds reporter asked him after the funeral.

Who was he? Where did he come from? Why was he here?

And there are the other ones, the ones that have stayed with Flinch, the ones the reporter asked with a glint of malice in his eye and his pen poised, but which Flinch didn't answer then, and can't yet.

You were holding the knife that killed him, weren't you? Can you live with the guilt? Will you ever forgive yourself, Flinch?

NATE

The pain first. But it is brief, a second, and then it is something beyond that, a chill that shudders through me so violent I lose control of my bowels and a scream gets stuck in my throat. My body's confusion at being forced open, at the intrusion of the blade. My brain is in a thick fog until I realise with a jolt, with a perfect clarity that sears straight through me — it is a knife in my back. I have been stabbed and it is the tip of the knife that I feel up against a rib, scraping the bone.

I feel him behind me, my friend. Flinch is touching me on the shoulder and I am propped up against him, as if I were his puppet, the knife is his hand inside me. The knife exits and I feel it slip through the flesh, through parts of me that have been severed, and I think I land on my knees, at least I'm lower now. I'm staring right at the whale, right into her side, her blue-grey skin, its barnacles and crevices filling up with her blood.

Then I fall I feel I fall for a million miles until my cheek is against the flensing floor and I'm lying in blood, but it is not mine and I tell myself this because surely if it is not mine I will be alright. I tell Flinch 'I have lived through worse, believe me' but he is looking at me pale-faced and doesn't seem to hear.

Hands on me, someone rolls me onto my side. I see the knife that has fallen from Flinch's hand and as shadows fall over me and move away the sun catches the blade and it flashes a wicked bright wink at me. He is here still, Flinch, he is next to me. I feel cold, I tell him and he nods and I can see that he is crying. Nothing new. I've seen him cry before. Old Flinch a soul too soft for his own good. Easily moved by the most subtle and strange events. Lost children. Red sunsets. Fresh roadkill. God knows.

A voice tells me that a doctor has been called, the police too. They should call Eleanor, I think. If it's that serious.

At the thought of her, fear pulses through me and I try to call to Flinch but my heart is in my mouth like a huge lump of meat and I choke on the taste of it. I can feel my blood being pumped through the vessels in my brain, the cold place in my back where I am severed, the whole mess of my insides leaking out of me like a sack sliced open its contents spilling onto the ground.

Eleanor, I yell to Flinch, but all that comes out is a gush of thick red blood. Bubbles at the side of my mouth. You have to let Eleanor know!

The pain has numbed but now the fear is enveloping me, weighing me down like a cold wet blanket. I struggle against it, try to wrench free. I am exhausted but I kick and I use my elbows. It is no good, my struggle futile. As soon as I move there are more hands on me and the voices telling me that I must stay still.

Stay still!

I can tell that they are scared I might die. But I will not stay still and I lunge in Flinch's direction and that's when the others block him from my view and take him away.

Eleanor Eleanor Eleanor Eleanor.

The memories of her are sucked to the surface like a leech draws blood to the skin. My head feels bloated with them. My entire body, numb just before, is now singing with the thought of her like a string pulled taut.

I need her and the desire is extreme enough to make me retch.

And then I see her as if she was before me. Blessed or cursed with an optimism that was ridiculed in our house, and though she quickly learned to hide it from them she shared it with me and her eventual freedom became our secret focus. I am with her under the spiked branches of the lantana bushes in our backyard, where we carved a hiding hole. It took us the three full days of a Labour Day long weekend, with only the carving knife from the kitchen and my pocket-knife as our tools. The earth under the bush was hard so we stole blankets from neighbourhood clothes lines and carpeted our dirt floor with them. From the local dump we took some cushions from a flea-ridden couch that had been abandoned there. We itched and scratched like mongrels after every secret meeting in the lantana, but the red welts were worth the temporary escape. Every child hides but some children have more reason to than others.

The constable is bending over me. He is pallid. Milky and green and damp with sweat. I've had a run in or two with him but nothing serious. I know he thinks I'm odd and I guess I am. He's a good bloke. He probably hasn't watched too many men die and I know I'm bleeding onto his hands.

'The doctor is coming,' he says when my eyes flicker. 'Hold on, son.'

God knows I haven't been much of a son to anybody, but then again I've never had much of a father.

I wonder how long it takes for a man to die.

TWO

Now here he is, driving up towards the lighthouse — that white, ocean-side phallus perched on the highest rock on the easternmost point of a continent that is, for the most, parched. Fringed on this side by rain-forest, it slides into the ocean on the white sand of ground-down coral reefs. This coastline bulges towards the tropics, its fat man's belly sagging between the Coral Sea and the Tasman and into the depths of the Pacific.

The ute is chugging its way up the hillside, farting black smoke and grit from its muffler. Flinch crouches forward over the steering wheel as if the shift in his weight will make a difference to his chances of making it up the winding road. But the old girl spits and dies a groaning, shuddering death and rolls backwards a few metres before he catches her, slams his good foot on the brake and his other onto the wooden block that he's attached to the clutch with string and masking tape. He lets her roll back onto the thin strip of sand at the side of the road. The rubber pieces of his thongs wet between the toes, slippery with sweat. He skids on his short leg as he gets out to check the engine.

He has to pound his hip against the bonnet to get it to open. No easy feat for a lopsided man on a hill. The latch jiggles apart and Flinch props the bonnet up with the broomstick handle that he keeps in the tray for the regular occasions on which he has to fiddle with some part of the greasy old engine. His shaggy fringe in his eyes as he leans into the car.

This wind is roaring around the headland, bellowing with its mouth wide open. Vast, stinging waves of sand ripple up the open stretch of Tallow Beach and gulls stall, flapping, midair. The wind gusts in towards the point, making thin work of the streaky clouds. It has been born in those damp islands to the east, where hurricanes drop in like distant relatives who visit at the same time each year and cause the expected havoc. The wind isn't up to shredding palm trees when it arrives at the bay, but Flinch can smell the intention on its breath and he hates it anyway.

Flinch has never been good with cars. Never claimed to be one of those men who can slide under a vehicle and reach their hands into its guts and tinker around until an engine bursts to life. He wishes he could have learnt to be handy with a screwdriver but it just never came easy to him as it did to many other boys. When he grew old enough to mow lawns with the stinking, spluttering two-stroke, work the cantankerous washing machine, strike up the outboard motor on his barnacled little dinghy, he would watch bolts rust and smoke stream from cracks and not know how to go about fixing these things. His mother, by that time expert at seeking out the cracks in Flinch, would bemoan the fact that there was not a real man about the house to look after things properly. At first, feeling her manicured nails prying at pieces of him, Flinch tried. He oiled things, got grease in the crevices of his knuckles. Burnt his forearm on the outboard motor when he tried to fix it before it had cooled. Wore that scar like a badge. He made sure his mother could see it when he went to the fridge for butter to soothe it. The first three letters of the motor brand seared into his skin.

'Put it away,' she had said, without looking up.

Finally, unable to fix the internal mechanics of either his equipment or his relationship with his mother, he gave up trying anything more.

Flinch has learnt what he's had to do to keep the ute running for the past few years of its life — a progressively longer list of band-aid solutions to ensure she will get him most places around the bay as long as he doesn't push her too hard or too long. He calls her Milly and talks to her, urges her up inclines and flatters her into chugging awake on cold mornings. A bottle of fresh water and a big container of oil, both of which he keeps in the tray of the ute along with the broomstick, solve a lot of the problems but he recognises that there's nothing he can do right now. This is something new.

The wind dies off for a moment. Sky mumbles something about rain.

Flinch staggers to the side of the road and pushes himself up on the toes of his good foot so that he can see the ocean over the banksias and scrawny seaside scrub. The sun finds a gap in the clouds and the heat on his back is instant and scorching. The ocean glistens in the afternoon light. There's a deep gutter fairly close to shore that will be vacuuming surrounding schools of fish and passing them through it with the force of the tide, and he can see the gulls hovering and diving into the black water then flying off, each mouth filled with a shimmering fish.

Turning his back on the ocean, he returns to the car and leans against the bonnet. The heat of the metal sears the backs of his thighs through his shorts. Crickets whirr in the scrub. The sun like a white noise itself. He slumps against the tyre, shades his eyes like a salute. He could wait hours on this road before somebody passes. And it would take him an hour to walk back to town. Hobble down the hill and limp through the streets to the mechanic's garage, dragging his bung leg like a parody. Some medieval town fool.

Or. The black water, the gutter. In his mind an abundance of fish, shiny whiting with golden fins. He feels that itch for the tug of the line on his finger, anticipates the tease of the catch as the reel spins, the line singing with pleasure.

The rod is in the back of the ute, wedged under a deflated spare tyre, next to a foul-smelling canvas travel bag. He dislodges the rod and slams the tray door closed with a thump, recoils from the odour, stumbles, almost falls backwards down the hillside behind him. Cusses again at the balance that eludes him even after years of willing himself to stand upright on freshly scrubbed decks.

Sweat-soaked by now, the rod slippery in his grip, he decides the best way down the incline to the shore is to sit down and slide. He removes his thongs and slips them between his fingers, over the palms of his hands, shoves his reel under his armpit and lowers himself onto the loose gravel of the hillside. He propels himself forward by pushing himself along with his hands. Still muscled in his upper body, the days of hauling his own body weight up to the crow's nest with the aid of only one good leg have stayed with him. Strong as his nostalgia.

He leaves his rod and thongs at the base of the hill, concealed in the stiff grey shrubbery, and makes his way to the damp sand. The ocean rough and churned russet from the wind and a gnashing tide. Smooth rocks and shells in the dazzling thousands along the shore. A decorated beach. It's a moody stretch. One day naked and clean as a fresh white sheet, other days like it's vomited up the entire contents of its watery belly, stinking dead fish and sea-weed, rotting coconuts, lost fishing nets, an entire tree with its root system intact. Mutton birds with broken wings floating on the breakers.

One thing the short leg is good for — the uneven weight means extra pressure when he puts his right foot down. When he walks barefoot on the damp sand tiny bubbles erupt, reveal the location of ugaris. He finds a couple of big ones, wiggles deeper into the sand until he feels them under his toes, hard and smooth as pebbles. He smashes them on the sand further up the beach. The gulls hear the shells shatter and hover over him.

As the tide recedes he draws the flesh of the ugaris through the water and waits. He only wants one today and soon enough he sees it, the tiny white head, all gaping mouth and pincers. He is patient. The next wave rolls over and wets him where he squats. And the next. The angry white head flails in the rush of water, stretches out of the sand. When he sees a gap in the breaks, he takes precarious steps towards the worm, moves to the side of it and places the flesh of the ugari almost underneath it, careful not to touch. The worm grips the flesh, ready to drag it below the surface. He waits. There is the split second, as the worm arches for a greater tug on its meal, when it relaxes the hundreds of legs that otherwise act as powerful anchors to the underground. Flinch is quick. In that second, he pinches the worm and pulls it out of the sand. It's a good one. Thick as Flinch's little finger and as long as he is tall, knotting into indignant coils and offering a sharp bite to Flinch's thumb. The perfect bait.

He returns to the scrub where he has hidden his fishing rod. Surfers leave all kinds of things unattended on this beach while they are in the ocean. Some mornings, when the swell is best here, the soft, dry sand is a gallery of surfer paraphernalia. Tubs of wax, shoes, bottles of soft drink, abandoned clothes, thongs, bicycles, boards. But Flinch is precious about his rod. He always hides it somewhere. Under logs. Up trees.

Flinch settles himself behind the shrubbery, rolls his squirming bait in the sand to allow more grip. He squeezes its head off between his nails. The head is the best bit. If the fish don't take it, they're not out there.

From up the beach, wisps of a conversation and laughter. It's always been his instinct to hide from strangers, like some ill-treated family mutt. He squats low behind the shrubs, tucks his shrivelled leg beneath him so that he can lie flat and watch.

A woman and two men walk up the beach towards him, apparently looking for shade. They settle just near him, spread bright sarongs underneath the boughs of an acacia. Without even looking around, they strip down to nothing, and run laughing into the water. The men are fit and lean and young, and they move with the kind of ease that reminds Flinch of horses. The woman last in the water, lithe and brown as a seal. When she dives Flinch can see her buttocks above the water for a second, a bright white flash, like an unripe peach.

Near the shore, large dumpy water is ricocheting off the sandbar, behind which is the gutter streaming fish. The gulls still crying and cussing overhead. The men catch the waves as they curl under and break and they swim with them to shore, race back for the next set. The woman tries to bodysurf once, but she misses the crucial moment and is dumped by the wave — Flinch sees one foot then the other appear above the rush of white foam — before getting up, spluttering, long hair over her face and a piece of seaweed laced around her throat like a mermaid's necklace.

She calls to the men and they wave at her, and she heads in towards the beach. The men seem unconcerned by her nakedness, unfazed by it. How do men become that way, he wonders. He remembers his first and only experience with a naked woman; if anything, the whole incident had left him more curious and confused and excited than before.

As with all of Flinch's poignant moments, he remembers the smell of water. With her it was stale water, the kind left in vases or jars that has turned mouldy with the remnants of seaweed or the stems of dead flowers. Bovine and much larger than he was, when she clutched him to her chest that time his nose had lodged in the crook of her armpit, and he could smell her damp odour and talcum powder, a cocktail which at the time seemed both erotic and needlessly intimate.

She seemed to be always hiding something, tucking a brown paper bag into her satchel, fingering something in a pocket, concentrating so hard on it that her eyes glazed over. Flinch had recognised her straight away as another outsider, and avoided her. To schoolyard bullies, the only thing more attractive than one freak was two. If you grouped, you inherited the joint playground inadequacies of the entire gang. You weren't just a cripple then, you were also a nutter, loser, spaz, retard, dago, wog, coon, crybaby. She was teased cruelly in that way only teenagers understand, but she resisted by fondling the things in her pockets, crept off into some place inside herself. Flinch saw her retreat there, and some part of him was envious.

In his last year at school, there was a dance. Not much by most high school standards. The community hall decorated with tinsel left over from Christmas and lights covered with blue cellophane. The class of 1958 had, predictably, decided on an underwater theme. Dry fishing nets had been borrowed from the local fleet and, still smelling vaguely of the ocean floor, hung around the walls of the room, cardboard fish with shocked expressions woven between the nylon. When Flinch leaned against one, it felt gritty, and grains of sand fell to the floor beneath it. Flinch wore an eye-patch, pinned a cardboard skull and crossbones to his terry-towelling fishing hat, and tied his left leg to a block of wood.

He spent most of the early part of the evening against a wall sucking on a bottle of lemonade, watching the other kids dance. Then she entered the room. She was wearing a bikini top, massive breasts oozing out from under each cup, and a long silver skirt. Above her waist she wore a leather belt, to the back of which was pinned a cardboard cut-out of a dorsal fin. Flinch could see that she'd taken great care in making it. It was covered with the silver aluminium lids of milk bottles, each shaped and placed like a scale. Flinch estimated that to cover the fin she must have been collecting those lids since the theme had been decided at the beginning of the year. Over two hundred pints of milk had been consumed to decorate it.

When she stood in the entrance of the hall, the light flooding in around her, Flinch thought she looked like some great sea goddess arisen from the depths.

It wasn't long before the other kids started taunting her, laughing and pointing at the layers of flesh folded on top of one another over the waistband of her skirt. *Bring out the harpoon!* someone cried. The boys made a game of picking the silver caps off her fin and she had spun, her fists clenched, and swiped at them, making contact with two of them. She was on top of a third, beating him around the head, before a teacher managed to drag her off. Flinch had seen her eyes, seen something rise up within her and watched as she had come out of her secret place to defend herself. He was filled with admiration.

Ten minutes after she was sent home he found her crying quietly behind the woodworking shed, and half an hour after that he found himself squashed against her, enveloped by the expanse of her naked flesh, tilting his head right back as she bent over to kiss him wetly on the lips. He walked home later with shimmering aluminium scales stuck to his forearms.

The naked woman stretches out face down on the sand and Flinch, on his haunches now, rocks forward to peer through a gap in the shrubbery. Her ribs visible, rising almost imperceptibly, damp hair clumped to one side, the soft cushion of her breasts spread against the sand. She's no local. Flinch, scratching absent-mindedly at the familiar ache in his groin, guesses she's a leftover from the festival. From one of the hinterland communes.

The first group of newcomers had wandered into town — sandaled or bare-footed, some cloaked in orange, others in white like high priests or vestal virgins, some bald, some as hairy as apes, beards and hair down to their waists — the same month as the whales had started to appear in numbers again out in the bay. They had set up in and around Nimbin, first, where they had a festival, the beating of drums a pulse throughout the valley for an entire year. Flinch had heard stories of the festival while he was in one of his temporary jobs, at the meatworks. The farmers who dropped off their cattle and pigs for slaughter leaned over the fences of the stockyards, tipped their hats back, wiped their hands on their overalls and had a good chuckle with the butcher. There had been a friendly competition. Aquarians versus locals. A tug of war. The Nimbin team were national champions. District heroes. Farmers' sons used to shoving bulls around with their bare hands, tossing hay bales into lofts, riding the bucks out of difficult horses. All beef and beer gut.

The competition had been reported in the local newspaper because it was attended by the Deputy Prime Minister, the man in the black suit demanding progress. He'd been a dairy farmer from around here, once. A fact he liked to remind the voters, the little people, when they complained about the degradation of their land and livelihoods.

During the tug of war, a tightrope walker had sprung with feline agility onto the taut rope and walked the length of it, as if circus entertainers were nothing out of the ordinary in rural communities. The boys from the Nimbin team had been taken by surprise but despite this, and despite being outnumbered, they had won anyway. There was mud on the faces and clumped in the long hair of the Aquarians, but it all ended in laughter.

There were other stories, too. Rumours whispered among the ladies chattering and nodding like pigeons outside the church after the Sunday service. Of both men and women walking around topless in broad daylight. Of songs sung at dawn by thousands of people. Drumming that never ceased. Of a midnight concert. A grand piano on a platform in the middle of a cow paddock at night, reflecting a full moon. The pianist pounding out Mozart and Bach and Lennon and Dylan. One farmer claimed to have seen a silent sea of people wandering across his property in the pitch-black of night, candles and lanterns bobbing in the darkness like buoys on the water. People living in the treetops like apes. A woman dying to the sound of a chant that was intended to heal a venomous snake bite. Rasputinesque monks preaching from soapboxes. A jumble of images from tall stories. Flinch could not decipher the fact from the fiction, hence the whole festival became half-myth in his mind.

Mostly the Aquarians were students, but the ones still here appeared to have forgotten that they were due to return to university courses; pack up their pot, shave off their long hair and apply for jobs at the beginning of the new year. Flinch hears some of the townspeople whisper about them in the grocer's shop as if their arrival is some unspeakable disease. *Hippies*, they hiss, in the same tone reserved for when someone's son has gone to Sydney under the suspicion of being *ho-mo-sex-ual*. The old biddies love an opportunity to be appalled. This is a town of blokes, loves, darls, fishermen and their wives, battlers, farmers, good decent clean-living folk. On the whole.

Flinch doesn't know what they are doing here, why they chose this place. On the main street, planks of wood barricade the windows and doors of shut-down businesses. The weatherboard houses rot in the heat and salt spray, white lace curtains stain brown and yellow. Behind the curtains, the old stayers, peering out through the tears in the lace. But the newcomers seem unaware of the slow disintegration of the town. Perhaps they just don't care. Or perhaps, Flinch suspects, they are blind to what he sees. A town coloured with memories of what used to be here.

The woman rolls over and sits up to gather her loose curls into a low knot at the back of her neck. She swivels around to reach for a scarf and Flinch, the backs of his knees sweaty with crouching, slips forward and clutches a branch to catch himself. It breaks off with a loud snap. The woman looks up and catches Flinch's eye. She smiles and waves at him. Flinch, horrified, scrambles back up the hill on hands and feet like a lame dog. It is only when he reaches the ute that he realises he has left his fishing rod at the base of the hill. His penance for peeping.

THREE

Flinch is used to penance. Childhood lashings and countless small moments of rejection have moulded him perfectly for the regret he now bears like a hunchback's lump. His mother Audrey, fattening his guilt with stories of her own failed attempts at happiness, left him in no doubt that he was the bane of her pitiful life. That he represented everything that went wrong with who she should have been, if only she had been given the chance she believed life owed her. Over the years she had become convinced that the very purpose of Flinch's existence was to remind her of how pointless life can be when one is pushed hard up against the odds.

But Flinch has always secretly believed that there was more to it than that. He decided early that there was only one way to find the purpose of his existence, his destiny, and that was to take to the seas.

Water, after all, has never left Flinch alone.

It has been with him since he was conceived in a grimy clawfoot bathtub in a small guest room above the pub. As soon as he could understand, Audrey let him know that he was an ugly child. He had been squashed in the womb, then bruised on the unforgiving bones of her pelvis as she shoved him out into the world, amidst her screams and a torrent of water that the midwife claimed she'd never before witnessed. His face was red and swollen down one side. He had a black eye. And of course there was the leg. Though its inadequacy was not so pronounced at first, and wouldn't be until he finally stood up to walk at the age of three.

All his life, Flinch has lived in a small pastel house near the top of the headland. Little more than a worn weatherboard shack perched above the ocean, a long walk from the town. The house is noticeably lopsided, leaning away from the sea-wind, as if scared to look down over the cliffs due to a fear of heights. It had been owned by the lighthouse keeper. An insomniac, he had stayed awake through the night, dutifully checking the light rotating in the lighthouse, and during the day he had painted the house: azure, then lemon, then violet, then dull orange, then, finally, candy pink. When the lighthouse keeper grew too old to manage his post, Audrey, out of work at the time, had presented herself on his doorstep and told him she would be his carer. She was seven months along,

Flinch sloshing around inside her. The lighthouse keeper, hard-hearted and unmoved by most things, was fearful of God and pregnant women, and didn't have the stomach to turn her away.

When the lighthouse keeper died (a broken heart, Audrey sniffed, seeking melodrama, but the boys in the pub said it was too much whisky and excessive masturbation), the pastel house was overlooked by the executor of his will, whether accidentally or on purpose it was not clear, given its derelict condition and the general view that it should be pulled down. The lighthouse keeper's only relative, a second cousin, had never shown up to stake his claim. So the pastel house became theirs.

The surrounding cliffs are dotted with temperamental feral white goats that scale the rocks and ridges, teetering precariously above the ocean, eating everything they come across. They wander frequently into Flinch's backyard, eat the sheets off the washing line and devour whatever they can find in the stinking compost heap. Flinch has an uneasy relationship with them. They have been known to head-butt small children when apple cores or crusts aren't offered quickly enough for their liking, but will also observe Flinch knowingly from a few metres away and he can't quite detest them.

Audrey had allowed the place to stay pink, although gradually the paint flaked, and large patches came off in powdery clumps. By the time Flinch was ten years old, the house looked like an old woman who knew her age and, with a sigh of relief, was letting herself go.

From the pastel house, Flinch can see the ocean in all directions. When he was young, and had learnt to run in his lopsided way, he would chase the wind down the cliffs towards the ocean, and dive, hoping to be swept up above the sea, the way the gulls were scooped up, effortlessly. It never worked. He once broke his nose, and another time cut himself so deeply above the eye that it bled for days. So he compensated by looking out as far as he could over the ocean. He tried to see all the way south to Sydney and north to Cairns, but had to content himself with counting the ships and yachts that wound their way up around the point, sails bubbling and blistering in the wind.

From his vantage point, Flinch learnt to read the ocean. He knew that when it bristled like fur on a cat's back, there was a current that would bring tailer down the strait in July. When it curled like a scorpion's tail, it made for good surfing at the Wreck and the dolphins would be out playing in the breaks at the headland. When it rolled fatly and looked as if it had the consistency of dough, then you could dive under the water at Wategos Beach and it would be so clear you could see tiny silver fish darting between your fingers.

Between May and October, the whales came, spraying white water into the air like big old steam trains, rolling over the waves and then disappearing until the next year. The days Flinch spotted the whales were his favourite days. Sometimes, on those days, the ocean seemed to settle right down, as if the slap of the whales' tails had made it see that rough water simply made no sense.

Flinch never forgot the pleasure watching them had given him. But when he started whaling, there were days when seeing a whale brought to shore, its slow, thick death, made him feel like a god. Other days, it made him feel smaller than a grain of sand, and as worthless. Often it depended on the length of time on the water. The heat of the sun. The glare alone could make him delirious. Delusions of grandeur rose up from his stomach in much the same way as seasickness. From the same place.

When he left school at fifteen, he headed down to the jetty to try his luck on the trawlers. He leant against a pylon to watch them come in. The sea teased into a frenzy by a wild wind, the stiff arms of the boom masts asplay, the boats rocking and tipping like drunkards on their way home. The fishermen threw coils of rope as thick as Flinch's thigh onto the docks. The men swung themselves off the ship with the ease of gymnasts and Flinch, hobbling around them, that one skewed hip raised like a question, tried to catch someone's eye. Little chance, with caps squashed so hard over brows. He could only just make out the odd glow of a cigarette or an unshaven grey jowl.

'Mate?' he said finally to one of the men crouched over a net, having dismissed 'sir' as too formal and 'excuse me' as too tentative.

'No, son.'

'What?' said Flinch.

'Not for you, son.'

'But—'

'No.'

The fisherman stood up. He towered over Flinch, all sinew and gristle. The orange hair of his moustache streaked with grey. Smelling of mint and fish scales and fags. A faded tattoo of a mermaid with exposed breasts on his inner arm. 'It's not for you, son.' Like a growl.

'How do you know?' asked Flinch. 'The leg's not a problem.'

The fisherman crossed his arms and shook his head. 'How d'you reckon you're going to stand up in rough seas and haul a catch on only one good leg?'

'I'll manage. The other one doesn't get in the way.'

'Sure.' With a smirk and a snort.

'Really.'

The fisherman sighed. 'Persistent little bugger. Alright, you got one day.'

And that was it. Flinch found the element of his destiny. Although he spent that whole first day face over the side of the rollicking trawler, throwing up his breakfast and mumbling small prayers for land. He felt consumed by the sea, that day metallic grey and ripped to shreds by an unseasonably cold tempestuous wind. The wind not strong enough, though, to remove the stench of the fish as they died, the mass of squirming silver bodies as they were dumped on board. The horror of it. All that accumulated panic in scales and fins.

'Comin' back?' asked the fisherman, when they deposited him green and shaking on the docks.

'See you tomorrow,' belched Flinch.

The fisherman turned a raw pink and roared with laughter. 'Rotten bugger. See you tomorrow. What's your name, since I'm gonna have to write you in the logbooks?'

'Flinch,' replied Flinch.

'Flinch, eh? Nickname?'

'Dunno,' said Flinch. 'It's what my mum calls me, anyway.'

The fisherman didn't respond, but knew that the boy in front of him wore the name because he looked like a dog about to be slapped. Always blinking and squinting. That leg cowering underneath his torso.

'Guess it'll do then,' said the fisherman. 'Flinch.'

Unlike his schoolyard experiences, out on the sea he slotted right in. Instinctively knew not to talk much. When he did, he made the kind of quiet observations that would bring about a smile and a nod from the others. Became known as a good little worker. A battler. It made him feel as if he was a soldier who had been injured during a heroic act rather than the unfortunate recipient of a common enough birth defect. At night, feeling the sway of the ship and the churn of the water while lying in his bed, the room rocking about him, he would reach towards his short leg and pinch his toes. He did this for the same reason he imagined old soldiers fingered the scars of bullets. To remind themselves of who they were.

When he heard that the whaling station was looking for a new spotter, it seemed an opportunity for promotion, in a way. From small fish to big ones. He'd spent four years on the fishing boats by then, now a permanent shade of red-brown, wrinkled beyond his nineteen years and with the furrowed brow of a man straining under the necessity of hard labour. He presented himself at the station in a new blue shirt, buttoned up to the collar, with a stance he imagined was plucky, chest out and arms hanging out from his sides as if there were apples under his armpits. The captain of the main whaling boat looked him up and down and, seeing the salt-abraded skin of Flinch's young face and smelling fish even through soap, decided the leg was not important and hired him.

His first day on the job he spotted more whales than they'd hauled in weeks. When they harpooned the first one it didn't die immediately. It ploughed straight down dragging the boat bow-first towards the water before the captain wheeled it around. The whale then reared skywards and Flinch saw for the first time but not the last the whale's lip line in its permanent grin, the white underside of the lower jaw riveted with dark crevices, its massive unblinking eye looking straight at him. He crouched down in the nest and clung to the mast and when the crew called out to him to praise his keen sight he was pleased that they couldn't see he was crying.

Cutting the whale up was worse. After a few months of squatting nauseous and teary in the crow's nest after each sighting, Flinch grew used to spotting, to the swift shuddering kick of the harpoon as it was shot, the thud of the impact, but he never quite got used to the slaughter onshore. The way every whale looked different was more noticeable once they were out of the water, on their sides, slowly being crushed under their own weight. The lifetime of battle scars, tears and holes in fins and tails, the odd jigsaw pattern of an old shark bite, the broad patches of shining black and white on the bellies. The age of them, the size of them, like ancient monoliths. Occasionally barnacles were stuck to the whales as if they were just big old abandoned ships. Flinch had watched the live molluscs open and close as the whales were sliced up, tiny, hairy mouths, their inner flesh like tongues. Their outrage at their own small deaths.

After the accident, Flinch found he could re-member with an uncanny and disturbing accuracy the minutest details of each whale they'd hauled that year. Still tests himself before he allows sleep to settle upon him at night, recounting each sea outing until that very last one. Every night for the past decade. He has heard of prisoners of war trapped in isolation chambers who recited the multiplication table in order to preserve their sanity. This ritual of his is nothing more than that.

Scared of the curse he must have inherited from Audrey, that cancerous decline of a life via a series of misfortunes, he has never returned to the sea. He figures that water as his destiny is therefore also the element of his inevitable downfall. He can still read the ocean with more accuracy than the local radio station's weatherman, but he is content to throw a line in from the shore. Gets wet only up to his thighs. More often than not, reels in a flashing silver fish to fry up for his breakfast.

He listens to the tide times announced nightly on his radio, and feels the same dull yearning usually reserved for lovers long lost.

FOUR

So many of the roads of Byron Bay are named after poets. Lawson. Tennyson. Wentworth. Somerset. Keats. At the time of their naming, an ill-informed council official in Sydney took it upon himself to maintain what he thought was a theme, though the bay itself was not named after the irascible poet but his grandfather, a vice-admiral and admired predecessor of Captain Cook. Better known as Foul-weather Jack. Cook named the bay after Captain John Byron during a period of fortuitous weather and successful landings. This was long before he grew sea-weary and became stranded on unforgiving reefs, before he became tired and desperate much further north. Those majestic northern shores and inlets still wear his mood and despair in their monikers. Thirsty Sound. Cape Tribulation.

Cook, sighting impenetrable swampland and some unusual mountainous formations through his telescope, did not bother to drop anchor in this bay. He could not have known that the headland and rocks around which he sailed formed part of the world's oldest caldera. Remnants of the rim of a gigantic volcano, now extinct, encircling a core that has over the millennia been whittled down to a solitary rock mountain much further inland. Still visible from the ocean, its nomenclature reveals nothing of its fiery past. Now simply a functional caution to sailors about the reefs they are soon to encounter once they spot it through their telescopes. Mt Warning.

The goats that hassle Flinch and eat his laundry are falsely rumoured to be descendants of a goat from that same ship. Daisy. First goat to circumnavigate the globe twice. Once with Byron, once with Cook. A goat with sea legs, providing an endless supply of milk, buckets of it spilt in rough seas. She avoided, somehow, becoming the victim of the crew's desire for fresh meat. Awarded, on her return to London, a silver collar engraved with a Latin couplet that had been composed for her by Dr Samuel Johnson. The collar buckled around her neck by Sir Joseph Banks. She became the well-travelled pet of the Cook children, and spent the rest of her years grazing on the family's lush lawn.

Long before Cook sighted the coastline, the northern and southern clans of the Bundjalung people, the Minjangbal and the Arakwal, called the bay Cavvanba. Meeting place. Where mother land lay resting in the ocean, they recognised the shape of her body and named the headland appropriately. Walgun. The Shoulder. This name for twenty-two thousand years. A place of ceremony and burials, of dancing and ritual. Miles of beach were swallowed once during that time by a rising sea that never subsided, drowning the ancient ceremonial sites forever. Later, the light-house was erected on top of the meeting place for men's business, a boat ramp built over the midden that used to exist at the pass.

Flinch remembers a class excursion from his child-hood, one taken during the term they learnt about Australian history, about Australia being discovered by men in bright red coats. His school textbook showed a picture of angry Aborigines throwing spears, with one or two lying wounded on a beach. A few white men sat offshore in a small boat, rifles aimed. The artist had drawn a grey smudge above one of the guns to indicate that it had been fired. Their overenthusiastic teacher had thought that taking the class to see how the local Aborigines lived would help bring history to life. So the class had taken a rickety bus up to Woodenbong, the housing commission camp well out of town to which most of the local mob had been relocated. The children were led past run-down weatherboard shacks, mostly abandoned, one burnt out. No doors, just gaping holes at the entrances. At the end of a scratched dirt path, in the shade of a large tree, women in torn housedresses sat on the ground. They looked up as the children approached and Flinch felt that he was trespassing. The starched collar of his school shirt, too tight because Audrey refused to buy a new uniform every year to accommodate his pubescent growth spurt, cut into his neck and he sweated as he hobbled towards the women.

'See, children,' the teacher had said, stopping the class a few metres away from the group. 'Watch the native women at work.' Flinch wondered why they had stopped so far away, as if the women might suddenly get up and attack them with spears, as the angry Aborigines in the textbook drawing had done.

A few silent, awkward moments, the women staring at the children and the children staring back. The class was ushered away. They were almost at the gate when an old man emerged from one of the houses. Flinch, dragging his limp leg behind him at the end of the line, stopped.

'Hello,' said Flinch. Then, to be polite, 'Thank you for having us.'

A low wailing sound came from the man's mouth and he started to shuffle his feet in the sand, pound the ground with his walking stick. The sound was like a chant, steady and repetitive. More instrument than voice. Like a wire vibrating in the wind. Flinch was unsettled by the song. Only later, trying to recreate the sounds himself, did Flinch realise that though the singing was the songman's own, the lyrics were fragments of common Christian hymns. The ancient rhythm trapped and subdued by the words like a bird thrashing itself against the bars of a cage.

The landscape of the region, the wild sea, yawning horizon, swamps and hillocks, draws people like ants to honey and most end up just as stuck. Farmers and workers talked themselves into staying even when their crops continued to fail and houses were taken apart room by room for firewood. Very few picked up and left for more promising or proven pastures. They persisted. This grit part of the culture of the bay, borne like a battle scar. A working man's credo ingrained quickly in those who arrived in the town. Try something until it fails then try something new.

First it was logging. Beyond the swampland were the massive rainforests, solid with thick red cedar. The Big Scrub. The crash of the massive trees as they fell resounded through the valleys. Logs were shipped down three separate rivers, out to the sheltered natural ports and across the oceans to faraway cities. Trees were ringbarked to cut the sap supply to the upper branches, severing the main artery they depended upon to live, causing the bark to tighten around the slit. Like solid ghosts, these trees stood pale and naked, gravestones of their own deaths. The loggers called them vertical firewood. Widow-makers, when the large dead branches fell. The land was left stripped and empty. The forest, unable to regenerate at the rate of its destruction, dwindled to a few clumps of trees. The loggers looked for something else to do.

The dairy farmers moved onto the bald hills. They brought paspalum grass with them and spread the seeds until the hills were carpeted, rich and green. The message was passed down from the Minister for Primary Industries, loud and clear, hollered into the ears of the hinterland families with their little herds of cows, their veggie gardens, their chook sheds and their one snuffling farmyard pig. It was stretched over banners and screeched through loudspeakers. GET BIG OR GET OUT. The butter factory was a lucrative venture for longer than any other industry in the region. Became the biggest dairy producer in the southern hemisphere. It was something to be proud of, stamped onto the sides of all of their products. Gone were the days of mere subsistence living. This was progress.

When they ran out of land, many of the local farmers couldn't compete with the bigger farms further south and they headed to the hills, but their fat cows slid off the steep inclines around the valley. The banana growers moved in.

Subtropical fruit attracts subtropical pests and diseases. The fruit growers couldn't sew the holes in their nets fast enough to keep the bugs and bats from gnawing at their produce, turning it rotten and brown in the sun before it even had a chance to ripen. Men and women in straw hats ran from tree to tree, beating the scavengers off with broomsticks, shaking the trees until the leaves fell off. A farm of any scale was out of the question.

The local butcher, squinting at the sea, decided that if the land would not provide wealth and prosperity for the town, then surely the abundant ocean would. He put to use the town's old tram track and engine and a large flat trailer, and extended his present meat works by adding a large corrugated iron shed. Though the little engine that towed the haul was nicknamed the Green Frog, he wanted no such whimsy attached to his serious modern enterprise. So *Byron Whaling Company* was painted in large square-shaped letters along the side of the new shed. In black.

The whaling company closed two days too late for Flinch. Two days earlier and Nate would be here now. Or would probably have moved on, knowing Nate. He was a fidgety fellow, Flinch had always thought. Even sitting on a stool at the pub he scratched and belched and swivelled in his seat. He twitched his mouth, pursed his lips frequently and sucked his teeth. Chatted incessantly, but in a good-natured way, and he listened to Flinch with an intensity that sometimes unnerved him, to be studied so closely. Nate stood out among the other blokes, content to rest their elbows on the towels that served as beer mats and a have cold drink or several before going home to their families and a night in front of the white static of a radio that crackled out murder mysteries and local storm warnings. The only time Nate sat still was when he had a book in front of him. Flinch had noticed early on the private daily ritual, on the way back into shore after the catch, Nate's back up against the mast, a book open on his knees. Nate angular, knees, elbows, cheek and jawbones, the sharp edge of a hardback, and like an anchor he didn't budge, not even in rough seas, unless it looked like his pages were going to get wet. Flinch had learnt to shake his shoulder gently when they were nearing the docks so that he didn't get yelled at by the captain. Nate walked a lot, even at night. Sometimes Flinch woke to find him asleep in the old dinghy on the lawn in front of the pastel house. He took to leaving blankets and a ham sandwich in it just in case. It was one of the habits he had to break in those shadowy months after Nate's death.

As he drives down the main street, Flinch wonders what Nate would have thought of the place now, all empty streets, the silence that has descended on the town and the odd old bastard crying quietly into his beer. The dairy factory shifted to Lismore, causing a landslide of lay-offs. Padlocks on the gates of the produce plants, dust collecting on the machinery.

He pulls up beside the recently deserted hardware store and is peering through the window when he steps back to see her reflection.

'Ah,' she says, 'it's the Peeping Tom!'

Flinch, caught doing nothing unsavoury, feels he may as well have been and is suddenly hot and itchy all over.

'No, I'm not, no, it's a, it's the, I need a screw. I mean, some screws and a screwdriver and this used to be...' Sweat on his forehead, dripping into his eyes.

The woman laughs. 'I'm just teasing,' she says. 'Sorry.'

'Oh,' says Flinch. It's the woman from the beach. The naked woman. Only now she's dressed in a long flowing skirt and a light green top embroidered with floral patterns. Flinch notices that she's not wearing a bra. Or shoes. A mesh bag slung over her shoulder. She is straining against it, one hip cocked sideways to bear its weight. Her hair blowing around her face, getting tangled in the beads she's wearing around her neck. Damp and warm in the midday heat, giving off a sweet, overripe scent like the hot-pink frangipani in Flinch's cliff-side garden.

'Are you okay with that bag?' asks Flinch.

'Yeah, I'm fine,' she says.

She is just standing there and smiling at him, and Flinch can feel all of his inadequacies, the stump leg, the crooked angle of his hips and the bend in his neck that compensates, every chink and crease in his awkward body.

'But is that your car?' she says after a moment. 'I could do with a lift, if you're not too busy.'

'Oh,' says Flinch. 'Right. Of course. Yeah.'

'What's your name?' she asks.

'Flinch.'

'Flinch!' the woman says. 'Wow, cool name. A bit out there, hey? Weird.'

The woman throws her mesh bag in the tray of the ute, and climbs into the front seat, sidling close to Flinch so that he can see small beads of perspiration on her upper lip.

'Well, nice to meet you, Flinch. I'm Karma.'

Karma sings with the kind of unabashed enthusiasm that Flinch has otherwise seen only in drunks. It makes him uncomfortable. He winds down the window and warm salty air rushes in and fills the cabin. Karma sings louder so that she can hear herself over the coughing engine of the ute.

'Towards Nimbin, right?' Flinch asks, almost yelling.

Karma smiles and nods. She stops singing and hums for a while instead.

As they head towards the hinterland hills, over winding roads that are mostly sand and gravel, the haze of the ocean air dissipates to allow clear-cut views of the distant mountains. From lush paddocks, black-and-white cows lift their heads and stare blankly at them as they approach, the ute belching and gagging her way up the range. Small creeks full with the previous night's rainfall bubble through gullies, wash pebbles and small green frogs onto the road.

Flinch tries to sneak looks at her while he drives, with his peripheral vision tries to gauge when she's looking out the window so that he can catch a glimpse of her. She seems to him so unconcerned. With anything. While he leans forward when they go up hills, his hands slippery on the steering wheel, Milly grumbling and threatening to give up halfway, she sways from side to side to the tune she is humming. She doesn't seem worried about being in a car with a skewed little man she has only just met. Her trust in him, in human nature, is quite beyond him and he is astounded and suddenly feels responsible for her. Carelessness is a concept Flinch has never understood, having struggled all of his childhood to keep his head above the flood of Audrey's anguish and self-pity. Now heaving around the weight of his guilt, lifting it when he walks and dropping it briefly when he pauses, like an anchor. He decides she is either stupid or enlightened but he is unsure which is more likely.

'Did you go to the festival?' she asks him suddenly.

'Um, no. Don't come to the mountains much.'

'Oh, baby, you don't know what you missed.' She winks. Flinch blushes hot red. 'You would have loved it, man. It was just all about joy.'

Flinch nods quietly. He wants to tell her that joy is something he doesn't deserve, but she is almost aglow with a quiet enthusiasm and he decides that that particular story is too long to tell now anyway.

'Where are you from?' she asks him.

'From?'

'Yeah, like, where did you come from?'

'Oh, right. Well, here. Grew up around the bay. Never been anywhere else, really.'

'Cool. Why would you, I guess.'

They drive from the baking paddocks into a gully, its cool wet shadow.

'Turn here,' she says.

A driveway near-hidden by brush and long grass, barely wide enough for the ute. Next to it, a timber letterbox, the words *Nim Eden* in white letters on the side, a small rainbow painted over them. The gully is swamp and rainforest, thick dark green and rank with the smell of mud and decaying foliage. Gnats swarm into the car, fly into their eyeballs, up their noses. Flinch wipes his face with the back of his hand and mashes several black spots into the corners of his eyes. The wheels of the ute churn in the mud. Flecks across the windscreen like sprayed paint.

A low-running creek trickles across the path and soon after the rainforest gives way to an open field, a sudden exposure to the glare of the day after the dank tunnel of ferns, palms and cedar.

'Pull up over there,' says Karma, pointing to a large fig tree, branches sprawled against the sky. 'It's dry and shady. It's on higher ground.'

Flinch slows the ute down to a crawl and Milly moans and whirrs and sizzles. Flinch knows she's probably overheating. He's a bit surprised she got them this far without more of a protest.

The field they've arrived in backs into the dark shade of a casuarina grove. In front of the grove are tents in all shapes and sizes. Sturdy round yurts. Lean-tos made of sheets of bark and palm fronds. A large rectangular room made up of hay bales and roofed with corrugated iron. Dome structures.

There is an entrance way of sorts. An arbour covered with multicoloured rectangular flags. On either side of it, two long bamboo poles with bright pink and blue streamers that flutter in the breeze. Strung up in the highest branches of the casuarina trees are a number of large banners, painted with different slogans.

No war.

Protect and love the Earth, it's the only one we have.

It will pass, whatever it is.

It is midafternoon, the commune quiet. People lie in hammocks that are strung between trees, sleep on hessian sacks in the shade. Nearby, a man leans against a hay bale, reading and smoking from a hookah.

A group of women huddle around a table outside a yurt, cutting up vegetables. Dirty-faced naked children chase each other around a garden of wilting lettuces, throw clumps of mud at each other. To Flinch, the people here look as if they are somehow shipwrecked. Marooned inland. Unkempt and unassuming, with nowhere to go, nothing urgent to do.

'C'mon,' says Karma, getting out of the ute. 'Come and meet everyone.'

'No, I'm right,' says Flinch quickly. 'Not today.'

'Oh, come on,' she says. 'You'll like it here, I can guarantee it.' Flinch looks over at the commune. Two young men in flowing white trousers are walking towards the car, laughing and talking. 'It's paradise, you'll see.'

If he thought Milly could do it, he'd start her up and floor it now, speed off and leave them chewing on his dust. But he knows she'll need to cool down a bit and he'll probably need to get out to top up her water anyway.

'Okay.' With a deep sigh.

He swings his good leg out and pulls the other one around with his hand to hurry the process. Tries to swallow down the reluctance, knowing what's to come. The stolen glances at his leg and torso, the cautious curiosity, uncertainty at how far the impediment spreads, monosyllabic words spoken slowly, even when people are trying to be polite.

One of the men rushes towards Karma and picks her up. Flinch can see their tongues as they kiss open-mouthed.

'Hey, baby, we were just going to start looking for you.' Eyeing Flinch when he says this, the suspicious sideways glance.

'No, it's cool,' says Karma. 'Flinch gave me a ride. The store up the road was out of rice so I managed to catch a ride to the bay, and Flinch drove me back.'

The young man lowers her to the ground. He's shirtless, hard muscle, deeply tanned to the waist. Evidence, Flinch guesses, of long hours labouring in the sun without a shirt or hat. Something the local fishermen would never do, be seen without a faithful terry-towelling hat or a cap, their skin bronzed exactly to the edges of rolled-up flannel shirtsleeves.

'Where did you meet Flinch?' Asking her, looking at him. An inspection that makes Flinch feel like he's being pressed against a cool hard surface.

'By the hardware store, hey, Flinch?'

'It's not there anymore, but,' says Flinch.

'Hey, you hungry, Flinch?' The other man steps forward and places a hand on Flinch's shoulder. Leaves it there, waiting for the response. It's a gesture that Flinch finds off-putting. Among the fishermen, no matter how much you admired a man, no matter how good a friend you were, you didn't touch him except to knock his cap off as a joke, punch a shoulder affectionately.

'No,' Flinch says quickly. The hand stays there.

'Sure? There's plenty of food around today.'

'Yeah, I'm sure.'

'Okay, then. Thirsty maybe? You could come hang out with us for a while in any case, relax a little after the drive.'

'No, I'm good, thanks anyway.'

The man takes his hand away. 'Well, thanks for dropping Karma home. I'm Matt. This is Jed.'

The muscled man. Jed flicks his chin up, an acknowledgement not impolite, but not welcoming. Matt fiddles with the hair at the nape of his neck, rolling it around his finger. It is shoulder length, clumped in cocoon-shaped dreadlocks. Oily at the roots.

'I have to head back,' says Flinch. 'Nice to meet you blokes.'

'You're welcome any time, mate. Come back and visit. We're having concerts every night at the moment. It's wild.'

'Yeah, maybe another night. I have to get back.'

As he turns around to get into the driver's seat, he hears Karma laughing and the two men talking in low voices. Milly has cooled down enough and he decides to take the risk of not checking the engine. He just wants to leave. He begs her quietly from between pursed lips and finally the old ute rasps to life. He waves as he drives off.

'Come back, won't you, Flinch?' he hears Karma call after him. 'We'll be expecting you!'

A few miles out of Nimbin, as the sun is setting, Milly finally breaks down and refuses to turn over, and no amount of water, oil or apologising will bring her round. Flinch is not unprepared for this, though he wishes he was closer to the bay. He removes the front bench seat from the cabin and puts it into the tray. He keeps a worn blanket rolled up in the back, for days when the chill gets to him after an afternoon fishing thigh-deep in the ocean. It smells mouldy and has a large hole in it where one of the goats has chewed through it, but it will do for the night.

In his fishing bag he keeps a bottle of rum, ostensibly also to warm him up on cold days, but more often than not consumed even on humid evenings. It's still half full. Flinch offers thanks for small mercies.

He lies in the back of the tray, wide awake. Overhead the stars punctuate the solid, dark prose of night. They sharpen and blur as Flinch sucks down the rum, focusing on one bright point until all others disappear, then shutting his eyes and starting over. In the distance there is drumming and an indistinct chanting. He would like to go back, he thinks. Would like to see what it is like, so many people living to-gether, all trying to make a new world out of the wilderness. Matt and Karma were both welcoming to him. He has already decided he would stay away from Jed. Years of quiet observation have nurtured in him an accurate gauge of others' dislike and discomfort, feelings he knows best from a childhood with Audrey, later because of his leg, and after that because he'd killed a man and allowed that fact to become a feature of himself, like others accept a big nose or bright red hair. Some people notice his wariness, that guilt, immediately and look away politely, walk away quickly, not trusting what it might be that made him that way.

He rolls over on the bench seat and pulls the blanket up over his shoulders. From the direction of the commune, a loud gong sounds. The drumming resumes. They were friendly, Flinch decides, insistent even. But he hasn't had a proper friend since he buried Nate. He wouldn't know where to start.

FIVE

Although Flinch doesn't make a conscious decision to return to the commune, over the next few weeks he tinkers with Milly's engine, better equips her for a long drive. He washes his mouldy blanket and hangs it out on his rusty old clothes line to dry in the ocean breeze. A goat chews a second hole through one corner of it.

Occasionally he sees a few of the hippies in town, or on the beach. He looks for Karma among the small groups of women with flowing skirts and long hair, but he doesn't see her again.

A cake tin that he keeps in his sock drawer holds all of his accumulated wealth. Money he saved from working on the boats, a very old penny that he'd found on the beach one day and thinks might be worth something, and the bullets that he'd retrieved from some of the whales. They'd been lodged into the blubber, metal cylinders as long as his hand, from

Russia, Japan and England, remnants of the times they had escaped the flensing floor before they met their fate at the end of the harpoon. At the bottom of the tin, he keeps bits and pieces that once belonged to Audrey. There wasn't too much left after she passed on. A blue sapphire ring that he suspects is fake. A pearl necklace. A pale pink scarf that still smells of her, that suffocating combination of hairspray, musk and cigarette smoke. A single photo of Audrey as a young woman, on the beach, smiling in a way that Flinch never himself witnessed.

The money is starting to run low. He is a good saver and he gets by on very little, but he hasn't worked much since the accident. A token job here and there when Milly needed repairs or when he needed new fishing line. One season picking fruit. Another cracking macadamia nuts. A month fencing paddocks. A few weeks repairing fishing nets.

Where Karma is living, at the commune, they don't even have real money. They have made up their own currency. During the car ride to Nimbin, she had taken some stuffed paper out of her skirt pocket to show him. 'It's a concept we carried on from the festival,' she said. 'We call them Nimbungs. Nobody gets greedy over Nimbungs.'

She explained that everyone got the same wage whatever they did during the day, however they worked, and people donated as much as they could afford towards the meals. Nobody went hungry.

'But don't people store them up?' Flinch had asked. 'Don't they save?'

'What's the point?' Karma had responded. 'Everything good about living at the commune is free. Music. Philosophy. Poetry. Knowledge. Love.' She had winked but Flinch wasn't sure why. He thought she might have a tic of some kind.

The concept of Nimbungs struck Flinch as strange, but not as strange as receiving someone's love for free. Flinch had never been given love for free. He had to pay for even the slightest brush up against it from Audrey by first swallowing her bitter tales of defeat and depression. With the fishing blokes, well, that wasn't love. More like respect. Mateship, maybe. He thinks he might have loved Nate. He never had a brother, but that's what he imagined he would have felt if he had.

He still talks to Nate. Lately more than ever. Last week, in the grocery store, he found himself discussing the unseasonal heat, asking Nate if he could remember a year like this one. The whole conversation without realising he was talking out loud. His thoughts interrupted by someone nearby coughing. Then the furtive glances of the other shoppers. A mother had hurried her child past him.

There are still the nights, too, merciless dark stretches, when he feels he is strung out on a rack, pinned down by sorrow. The agony of being the one still here. He spends some of these nights in the dinghy on the lawn, under a blanket, looking up at the sky, at the moonlight glazed across the ocean, grey clouds silhouetted silver. He tries not to, but inevitably he ends up asking himself questions, each one as white and hot and urgent as the next. Why did Nate have to come here of all places? Why did they have to work that day? Why couldn't he have picked up the knife later, instead of standing with it clutched in his hand like some keen butcher?

He wishes all kinds of different fates for himself and for Nate.

'You are doomed, my pet,' Audrey had told him when he was eleven. Home from school with a bout of chickenpox, all itch and fever and headaches. Fresh out of a cold bath, Audrey had him by the arm and was roughly dabbing calamine lotion on his pox spots as he stood shivering.

'Hold still, boy.' And, 'Honestly! Why didn't you get this at preschool like every other bloody kid? I tried to expose you to it. Made you play with that Greerson kid when she had it, even. But did you? No.'

He remembers the sighing, the lipstick-stained cigarette between the fingers of the hand around his arm.

'You are doomed.'

'What, Mum?'

'Call it a family curse.'

'Mum?'

'I need a drink.'

He had followed her into the kitchen. The familiar routine, the kettle boiling, the aroma of coffee, Audrey reaching to the top of the fridge for the whisky, with her sharp nails flicking the radio on. She had sat down at the kitchen table, had a long slurp of the coffee. The smell of the steam coming off it had made Flinch feel nauseous again.

'I don't think I'm doomed, Mum.'

'What would you know?'

The radio in the background blaring Perry Como. *Wanted, someone who kissed me. And held me closely, then stole my heart…*

'I got a B for my assignment in social science last week.'

'Yeah, well, that'll see you through life, won't it.'

Exhaling smoke. Wet rattle in her cough.

'Come here, boy.'

He had moved to her lap and put his arms around her neck.

'Now listen. Some are lucky, some aren't. You and me, we're the ones who aren't. Doesn't mean you can't give it a go, pet. But just don't get your hopes up, okay?'

Flinch had nodded but hadn't taken much notice. He had been focusing on drawing comfort from her warm body, trying to eke it out of her and into himself as if by osmosis.

Lately, Flinch has been taking more from the cake tin than he's been putting back. He knows he will soon need to find another job. He's been careful to build himself a reputation around town as a hard worker. Uncomplaining. Honest. Meticulous. He can't move fast because of the leg, so he's always depended on his ability to be careful. Listen. Watch his mouth.

He stuffs his wallet with a few notes. Coins in his pockets. Irons a shirt and drags a wet comb through his mop of hair. He looks at himself in the long oval mirror in Audrey's room. Sees what he always sees. Some sort of joke of a man. A cartoon figure, all just angles and sharp pointed bits crammed against each other on one side. A human accordion, half played. He takes the shirt off and folds it neatly on the bed. Digs his old blue singlet and checked flannelette shirt from the bottom of a pile of dirty laundry. May as well go fishing first.

He slams the door to the pastel house harder than he means to. Takes a deep breath of sea air. A goat eyes him suspiciously from a nearby patch of grass, a piece of orange twine hanging from its mouth like a string of spaghetti. The day is dazzling in its clarity, the ocean like shot silk. The glare is brilliant, yet Flinch can't help but stare, squinting, into its depths, the coral blue blending into azure, to navy, to black. Even from the pastel house, he can see sea turtles bob to the surface, their shells like glistening barrels, and huge manta rays rippling like dark cloaks among schools of fish.

He revs up Milly and heads to Belongil Beach. It's a good beach for finding the odd gutter, though Flinch doesn't like to wade too deeply into the surf.

On this beach, sharks still patrol the back waters, having somehow retained a group memory of the bloody offal and off-cuts that used to filter down to the sea from the meatworks. It doesn't seem to worry the surfers, though Flinch keeps an eye on the waters for a steely fin just in case.

In the wet sand, Flinch digs a little hole and puts his right foot into it. This way, he can stand evenly. Both feet touching the ground with the same weight, at the same time. He can feel normal, though he knows that digging a hole to feel normal isn't normal. He tries not to think about it too hard.

It takes him a few hours standing thigh-deep with his line in the surf, his knees and that hip aching, his neck creaking when he moves it. He snaps the line once and loses the sinker, has to struggle through the soft sand back to his bait box to string up a new hook. But in the end he has a canvas bag full of fish. Gleaming bream, whiting, dart and flathead. It won't feed the thousands, but it will be enough for about ten or so people.

He hopes Karma will be impressed, anyway.

The desire to visit her had risen in him almost imperceptibly, gaining momentum as the weeks had passed until returning to the commune seemed an inevitability to which he had simply resigned himself. Surprised at his own willingness to leave the safety of the pastel house, he had lain awake recent nights examining the urge as a surgeon might, trying to dissect what it was about her that could lure him out of his isolation. Eventually he decided that it wasn't her, exactly, that he wanted to see. It was that she represented to him the commune, its essence, and in that environment lay the promise of acceptance. He could be new there. To her. Disown his past.

He smells like fish gut and he is covered up to the knees in a soft, damp layer of sand, but he doesn't even return to the pastel house to shower. Just empties the bag of fish into a styrofoam esky, throws his rod in the back of the ute and drives towards the hills.

Once over the range, the road winds through lush paddocks, cows hemmed in with barbed-wire fences, through clumps of red cedar, pockets of rainforest that spill onto the road, twisted grey roots exposed, gigantic fern prongs arching over from the escarpment above. Farmhouses the exact size and shape of one bedroom and a kitchen dot the paddocks, smoke rising from their crooked chimneys. The wind breathes on the tall grass on the hills and the land looks like it is moving, like a gently shaken rug, all ripple and gloss.

Flinch misses the entrance to the commune twice but eventually he notices the letterbox amid the overgrown grass. He follows the road in. A few days of rain have made it even more difficult to negotiate than last time and the ute slides off the track, bumping over exposed roots and into potholes more than a few times. Eventually, the field. He pulls up in the same place that he dropped Karma off the last time, and

Milly lets out a long whistle that sounds like a sigh. He moves the esky full of fish to the cabin of the ute so that it is shaded, takes a deep breath and heads towards the commune.

He hobbles past the tents, yurts, open-roofed rooms made of hay bales. One large tepee has two open sides and inside it a group of women sit on cushions on the ground, stringing beads. In a hay-bale house, two men and a woman are leaning against the walls, eating a lunch of beans and rice and arguing vehemently. In another corner, a woman is nursing a baby, both breasts exposed. In the casuarina grove, hammocks are strung between the trunks and a man and woman sleep naked. Nobody pays attention to Flinch. He is used to standing out, and he is surprised to find this lack of interest liberating. Nobody asks him if he needs help and nobody looks at him as if he doesn't belong exactly where he is.

There seem to be fewer people here than he re-members from the last visit. Maybe they are starting to leave, heading back to more prosperous places. He thought it might happen eventually. Karma said it was paradise, and he's never heard of a paradise that stays that way.

He remembers the fish and decides he had better look for her, or Matt, so that he can give them the catch. He is pleased that he thought to bring something for them for dinner. At the pastel house, dinner is part of a small routine that he relishes, because it gives him a focus, something that has to be done regardless. He makes his meal as he listens to the news on the radio at six pm, mainly for the tide times, then eats at six-thirty pm, before retiring with a book and more often than not a nip or two of rum. Lately he has been using the photograph of Audrey as his bookmark.

He wanders around the commune maze for fifteen minutes before he realises that he will have to ask someone where Karma and Matt might be. He decides to approach the women who were stringing beads.

When he finds his way back to the tepee, the women have stopped beading and are sitting cross-legged in a circle, eyes closed, holding hands and humming. Inside the circle is a wooden crate, on the top of which is a little pot filled with sand and numerous multicoloured sticks of lit incense. The scent of lavender is overwhelming and, to Flinch's nose, a little sickly. He stands at the entrance, clutching the canvas flaps with his hand so that he can rest his leg. He doesn't know whether he should interrupt. He is still trying to decide when the incense finally gets to him and he sneezes loudly.

A few of the women open their eyes. One stares at him disapprovingly and he takes a small step back.

'Can we help you, brother?' says another.

It takes Flinch a moment to realise she is addressing him.

'Er, yeah. I'm looking for Karma.' His throat feels itchy and his voice comes out with a croak. He clears it. The disapproving woman sighs loudly and starts to look a little menacing. 'Or Matt,' he adds.

'They'd usually be around, brother. They must have gone into Nimbin,' says the woman. 'You'll probably find them there.'

'Thanks,' says Flinch. 'Thanks very much.' Then, because he feels they are waiting for him to leave, 'Carry on.'

He moves away as quickly as he can manage.

The town centre isn't far from the site of the commune. Though Nimbin itself is more of a village than a town. It consists of even fewer amenities than the bay. As early as the 1880s, there were facilities in Byron Bay for tourists and travellers. But the days of ladies with parasols promenading along the pier and big ships coming into port to impress the bystanders are long over. The Pier Hotel has since burnt to the ground, the Great Northern Hotel reduced to ash and rubble twice. Pubs have a way of catching fire in the bay. The area had still been popular with visitors before the pier washed away during a cyclonic storm that Flinch remembers from his childhood. (He and Audrey had hidden under the kitchen table as it raged outside the pastel house and threatened to tear the roof off. He had sung 'Amazing Grace' while Audrey drank and swore.) The sunbathers only stopped frequenting the local shores when the meatworks opened up, as the beaches reeked and the sharks shadowed the waters like stray dogs waiting to be tossed a bone.

Nimbin was simpler. One road split into two as it headed down the hill. Some sections lined with doorways and shopfronts. A general store that sold groceries and produce. A post office. A police station. A pub. A community hall. All the local farmers might need. Embracing the influx of youth and the business it promised, some Nimbin shopkeepers painted their shopfronts with bright cosmic murals. Slogans preaching peace and joy.

The town is more or less deserted. Flinch parks Milly on the side of the road and turns the engine off. At the end of the main street the town falls off abruptly into muddy paddocks strung up with barbed wire and rotting wooden fence posts. Karma and a few other women are walking out of a grocery store, carrying bags of grain and rice, heading in his direction, laughing and talking.

'Hello!' says Flinch as they approach. A little too loudly.

'Well, hello, Flinch,' says Karma. He is pleased she recognised him, remembered his name. But figures, too, that she probably doesn't meet a lot of cripples. 'I've been wondering if you'd come to visit us.'

'I went to Nim Eden,' says Flinch. 'But you weren't there. Well, of course.' He shrugs his shoulders. 'You were here.'

Karma smiles at him. It's a kind smile, Flinch thinks, though he can sense something like suspicion behind her eyes. He realises it was probably there when he met her last time, despite the carefree façade, the singing and stories. It remains even as her expression changes, as if she's always weighing and measuring in her mind, gauging the worth of people or situations. Today she is wearing a loose sleeveless white top and a long orange skirt. Small tufts of auburn hair sprout from her armpits. Like last time, the scent of frangipani.

'How did you get here?'

'I drove,' says Flinch.

'Cool. Would you mind giving us a ride back to the commune?'

'Sure,' says Flinch.

'I hope you will hang around for a while this time.'

'Yeah, thought I might.'

'Okay, then. So where's the car?'

'Over there.' He points at Milly.

'Cool.' She takes his hand so that she can walk at exactly his pace. For once, Flinch realises with a buoyancy, he doesn't feel annoyed or embarrassed that he's inconveniencing someone. He allows himself to lean on her when the road gets a little too steep for him to move freely.

Flinch opens the passenger door for her. The other women hitch their skirts and clamber onto the tray. Flinch winces as he hears them throw a fishing line aside.

'Hey,' says Karma. 'What's in here?' She pulls the lid off the esky and the stench of the fish and a burst of cold air fill the cabin. Even from where he's standing, Flinch can see the frozen expressions of the fish, the clear glazed eyes and the mouths agape.

'Oh,' says Karma, and puts the lid back on quickly. 'Dead animals.'

'For dinner,' says Flinch. Feeling as if he's confessing. They stand on the footpath. A shy sun slips behind a cloud.

Karma sniffs and looks into the distance. 'I don't eat meat.'

'I'm sorry,' Flinch says. 'I didn't know.'

She sighs and shrugs her shoulders. 'It's alright. I don't but some of the others do. They won't go to waste.' She opens the lid of the esky again. 'Thank you for giving your lives, little fish. Your deaths will provide us with nutrients and will not be in vain.'

Flinch covers a smile with his hand. He decides not to tell her that they didn't exactly swim up to the shore and throw themselves on the beach at his feet.

'Right then,' he says.

Karma lives in an orange tepee.

'It's the colour of energy, a celebration of all things living,' she says. 'Buddhist monks wear this colour, you know.'

Flinch doesn't know but nods. They sit down on some brightly coloured cushions on the floor. Karma lights a little gas cylinder and boils some tea, and hands Flinch a cup that is really an old jam jar with a tea towel around it. It's unlike any tea that Flinch has ever tasted. A little like apple. A lot more like cut lawn. No milk or sugar either. They've emptied the esky of fish into a metallic icebox in a hay-bale house that is otherwise stacked with hessian bags marked *Rice*, *Pasta*, *Barley*. A crate full of apples. Some sort of communal food stash.

'There, now you've contributed to the good of the community,' Karma had said. 'A gift of sustenance from an anonymous good-doer.'

Flinch had kept an eye on the magpies that were perched in the trees above, knew they'd probably steal whatever they could manage as soon as there was nobody around.

He leans back on the pillows. A woven rug covers the ground. Bull ants have made a nest in one corner, under the rug's tassels.

'Ants,' says Flinch, pointing at the nest. 'Nasty ones.'

'Oh, yeah, I know. But you know, they were here first. I'm intruding on their home really.'

'Don't you get bitten?'

'Yeah, quite often. But what can you do? They deserve a place here as much as I do.'

Flinch makes a mental note to buy some ant-rid powder next time he's in town.

'You know, it's good for healing, too,' Karma says, leaning towards him. 'Orange. And I sense you need healing, Flinch. That's why I hoped you would come back.'

Flinch takes a large gulp of his tea.

Karma waits, looking at him, silent.

'There's nothing that can be done,' Flinch says finally. 'When I was young I wore a shoe that was built up so that I walked evenly. Big braces up to my knee. Leather straps and everything. Looked a bit like a monster, I think.'

He smiles to demonstrate to her that he is unconcerned and she smiles back.

'But I couldn't wear that on the boats. So I just got used to it. I can get around. It's not really a big problem.'

'I didn't mean your leg,' she says.

'But there's nothing else,' he replies. He hopes she hears the finality in his tone.

SIX

'It's like a village,' Karma is telling him. They're walking on a path that weaves through the commune, past soggy gardens sprouting stunted green lettuce leaves, picketed with empty stakes, everything planted struggling except a rampant cherry tomato vine. They pass a cluster of tents set up like small domes. To Flinch, they look like the alien pods from his childhood comic books. It is that hazy gloaming period, a mauve twilight that makes the fields and surrounding hills seem mystical, a landscape out of the pages of a children's fairytale book. Flinch is surprised he sees them this way, knowing them for what they are. Frequently flooded, muddy cow paddocks full of weeds and brambles.

'We're a tribe,' she is saying. 'The Aquarians. The Alternatives.'

The commune, sluggish and silent in the after-noon, is now gently humming and seems to have a pulse of its own. As people drift back from the town, the field, out of their tents, the commune starts to awaken, like some nocturnal creature stretching and scratching as darkness falls. Lamps are lit, small bonfires struck alight, someone thumps out a soft-sounding rhythm on some drums and, as if in answer from across the field, someone else strums a guitar. Flinch feels inexplicably light-headed. When he breathes, feels a little like he is gasping for oxygen but instead inhales the exotic smell of the commune, a rich, smoky scent, a combination of incense, spices, grilled meat, burnt rice, the odd whiff of tobacco and marijuana.

'Do you need a shower before we eat?' Karma asks him.

Flinch realises that he must still stink of fish and sweat and ocean.

'Yeah,' he says. 'I have a towel in the ute.'

'Cool. Okay, well if you want to go and get that, you can shower over there.' She points to a square, open-roofed bamboo room at the bottom of the sloping paddock. 'You just use a bucket and a sponge. The buckets are over there already.'

Flinch has had to bathe like this before, once when he worked on the fishing boats and the crew were forced to camp overnight on a remote point due to inclement weather, but he hasn't heard of anyone washing like this unless there was no alternative.

'When you're done, head over to that big tent there. I'm on cooking duty tonight. I'll save you a meal.'

'Fish?' he asks as she walks off. Though not far from him, she doesn't turn to answer.

In the shower room, there are a couple of bush showers — waterproof canvas bags that can be filled with warm water, which then filters out through a nozzle. Flinch decides to try one. Nearby is a fire, over which buckets of water are boiling. He uses his towel to grab hold of a bucket's handle, and pours some hot water into a cold water bucket until the temperature is suitable. Spills almost half of it before he's even reached the shower room, sloshes it up and over the edge, wets his trousers at his crotch and thinks, *That'd be right.*

The showers have no partitions. It is fairly dark, though, and Flinch, aware of the laughable sight of a man whose willy hangs longer down one thigh than the other, is grateful that there is only the dim light of a nearby lantern by which to bathe. In the corner, under the lantern, another man is bathing with water from a bucket, using what looks like a sea sponge as a loofah. He notices Flinch staring, and smiles at him.

'Beware the ulcers,' he says, and points to some open wounds on his ankle. 'Bloody tropics. Everybody has them. Spread like bloody wildfire.'

Flinch dries off and dresses quickly, then heads back into the thick of the commune. The damp crotch of his pants clinging to his thigh, the seam sticking to his bare skin promising a rash.

When he gets to the food tent, Karma is nowhere in sight. A young woman with fair hair in a plait to her waist is scrubbing a pot. She seems fixated on it, moving the cloth in a slow circular movement over the same spot.

'Excuse me,' says Flinch, 'where did Karma go?'

The woman looks up at him and wipes her brow with her wrist. Her eyes are a very pale green and have a glaze over them that reminds Flinch of a fish.

'Karma?'

'Yes,' says Flinch. 'She has wavy brown hair and it's long, not as long as yours but long, and she's kind of tanned but a bit freckly, and she's on the thin side and—'

'I know Karma,' says the woman.

Flinch waits but she says nothing more.

'Do you know then?' he asks eventually.

'Know?'

'Where she is?'

'Karma?'

'Yes,' says Flinch, trying not to sound frustrated.

'Oh,' says the woman. 'Karma. Yes. She's probably at the concert. Follow the music, man.'

The woman goes back to scrubbing the pot.

When he steps out into the field again, he hears it clearly. A cacophony of drums, strings, horns and what he suspects might be bagpipes. The sound billowing out like hot air from one of the larger yurts. When he gets nearer he is relieved to see that Karma is standing outside it, her back to the darkness, her face lit up with the glow of the lanterns inside.

He sidles up to her. He wants to touch her. Instead he leans forward, so that he is close to her ear.

'Hello again,' he says.

She inhales sharply through parted lips. He notices her hand skip to her breast.

'You startled me! Here.' She hands him a few hot pieces of pastry wrapped in a scarf. 'They're veggie pakoras. Delish.'

Flinch, suddenly realising how hungry he is, doesn't bother asking what a pakora is, even though he's never heard of one before. He's had a steak and three veg, fish and chips, meat pie kind of upbringing. But in this atmosphere, he feels braver than usual, and he bites into one and finds its spicy, buttery heat tasty and somehow comforting.

'C'mon,' says Karma. 'Let's go and sit down.'

They squeeze through the crowd, into the heart of the yurt, engulfed by the thick smells of sweat and hash. Karma heads towards the stage, on which a bald black man is singing in a language Flinch has never before heard, a language, it seems to him, born first in music. He recognises the yearning in it. The black man is accompanied by a shirtless man playing animal-hide drums, and a woman blowing into a wind pipe. They reach a space just off to the side, where Jed and Matt are sitting cross-legged on some cushions. Jed is smoking through the pipe of a hookah, his eyes shut, inhaling deeply, one hand resting upturned on his knee. Flinch, reminded of the fat caterpillar on the mushroom in

Alice in Wonderland, smothers a grin by sucking his lips in.

'Hey, man,' says Matt.

Jed opens his eyes and then shuts them again slowly, a reptilian gesture both lazy and cold.

'Hi,' says Flinch. Feels a piece of pastry fall off his chin.

They sit down on the cushions. Matt takes a shrivelled joint from the pocket of his vest and lights it, squeezes his eyes shut as he inhales. He passes it to Karma, who breathes it in, coughs with her lips closed. She passes it to Flinch, and he takes it between his fingers and thumb, as he has seen them doing. He smoked a cigarette, once, on the fishing boats. He was sixteen. He had refused offers of beer, so one of the blokes said that there was no law against smoking at his age, and handed him a lit cigarette. Flinch, wanting to impress, had drawn hard and long, and ended up coughing and spluttering and losing the cigarette over-board, to the great amusement of the crew. It wasn't so much the tobacco as the overwhelming reminder of Audrey, of being like *her*, his mouth puckered, breathing out smoke when he spoke, that made him feel nauseous.

But the joint smells and looks different. He puts it to his lips and draws in tentatively, swallows down hard on the smoke. He coughs a small cough and his eyes water but the others don't seem to notice. He hands it back to Matt.

The black man and the woman with the wind pipe have left the stage. The drummer remains, pounding out a steady rhythm that resonates through Flinch like a heartbeat. Six women in brightly coloured loose skirts and bare midriffs walk onto the stage. Slowly they sway in rhythm to the drumbeat, then start twirling in circles, dancing, arms above their heads, the silver bands around their ankles glittering in the candlelight and the bells around their waists tinkling as they move. The drummer speeds up the pace of the beat, and the women dance faster and more erratically, dipping and swaying and swirling their skirts. Flinch can see the glistening perspiration on their arms and torsos. They appear to him preternaturally luscious, as shiny and desirable as forbidden fruit. Dizzy with the effect of the joint, intoxicated by the movement of the dancing women, Flinch feels that he's stumbled on some kind of oasis. Though squeezed between the others, he feels totally alone, an explorer wandered out of the desert and into a culture he is immediately drawn to but can't understand. In the atmosphere of the yurt, he feels forcibly immersed, as if his head had been pushed underwater and he is meant to emerge baptised.

Next to him, Karma is swaying in rhythm to the drums. Her eyes are shut. Every time she leans in Flinch's direction he can feel the soft brush of her hair against his shoulder.

'Here,' says Matt, and hands him a fresh joint.

'It's amazing,' Flinch says. Before he can stop himself.

Karma opens her eyes and nods, puts an arm around him.

'Told you,' she whispers.

'You should come to the cliffs,' he says, overcome with a need to prolong the experience, to repay in kind. 'Come see the whales.'

Jed moves the hookah to one side. He leans towards Karma and takes her chin in his hand and kisses her hard on the mouth. She pulls away sharply.

'Not now,' she mutters.

'Have it your way, baby,' says Jed, and laughs.

Flinch is quiet.

Later, he wakes in the same place he has been sitting. It is dark and, except for the croaking of frogs and the sound of someone nearby snoring, it is quiet. The stage, now black and bare, makes him question for a moment if he had imagined the entire show. He can't remember falling asleep. Someone has covered him with a light woven rug. His head is thick with a woolly fog, his mouth tastes like dirt and he is thirsty beyond anything he has previously experienced. He looks around. Next to him, he can make out the shapes of Karma and Jed, her head resting in the crook of his arm. Matt is asleep behind him, wheezing when he exhales. Flinch had been dreaming that he was standing on the cliff, near the lighthouse. Someone had been walking up behind him but he was unsure whom and he had woken before he had found out. The soft vibrations of a whale song had been reverberating in his ears.

He lies awake, uncomfortable, until the crisp pre-dawn when he decides it is best to leave. He folds the rug, then crawls over the pillows, around other sleeping bodies, and out through the open doorway. In the burgeoning light, Flinch makes his way along the pathways that have been trodden between the tents and hay-bale houses. He stumbles over one small vegetable garden and clutches at a trellis to steady himself, squashing a tomato in his fist. A woman emerges from a tent, brushes her forehead with her arm. A naked toddler clings to her skirt. Outside a tepee, the remnants of a pig on a spit cool over a shallow pit. A little further on, the muffled sounds of people waking slowly, the dawn chorus of magpies and the whip-crack of a storm bird. From one of the bale houses, Flinch can also hear a soft chant, like a bene-diction, some sort of praise for the birth of a new day.

Back at the ute, he drinks all of the water that he usually reserves for the engine, then takes a swift shot of rum. He sits in the cabin watching the sun rise over the paddocks, tinging the grass mauve, then pink. From somewhere on the other side of the commune, he can hear hammering and someone singing, baritone. A couple of cows wander to the edge of their paddock and stare at him with placid curiosity. When his head has cleared a little, he turns the key and the ute chugs to life, sounding a little worse for wear.

'You and me both, Milly,' he says.

On his return to the pastel house, Flinch puts the kettle on and brews himself a strong cup of tea. An easterly rips through the open door of the kitchen, sweeping sand and dirt from the bare patches of yard into the house. Flinch gets up to shut it, as Audrey would have ordered him to do had she been there. She hated the wind, said it got up her nose, so she kept all the doors and windows shut, even through the stifling wet summers. She was erratic when it came to cleanliness, polishing the silverware and turning the tins in the pantry label-out one week, leaving plates to grow mouldy in the sink and lying in bed unwashed for days on end the next.

Flinch had learnt to watch her carefully, trying to gauge a pattern. But she was always a step ahead of him, and began shaking him awake in the middle of the night, asking him questions that he could never answer correctly. Once, when he was about nine years old, he had yelled back at her and she had slapped him so hard across the cheek it had sent him reeling. But it was she who collapsed on the floor, sobbing, and he spent the rest of the evening with his arm around her, trying to piece her back together. She was just better at the game.

The anger always brewing in her had surfaced in fits, sudden and violent. It made her hands shake. Dark moments of insecurity slid rapidly into a black hole of emotion and she yelled at him the same words, over and over. *Bastard Idiot Bastard Bastard Bastard*. Until he felt the words were tattooed all over him and that people on the street could read them on him as well. He wore her love and hate of him like a mismatched pair of socks, never knowing which would be exposed at any one time, knowing the other was always there even if it was not apparent. Understanding that either way, something about him just wasn't quite right.

Bitterness had kept her strong for a long time, but in the end she'd just decayed. The year after Nate's death, cancer ripped through her body like a fire in a forest, leaving the singed flesh melted over her bones.

'Typical,' she had croaked, and stopped breathing. They didn't try to resuscitate.

The day after she died, Flinch had scrubbed every square inch of the house and shoved open the windows and doors, shattering the dried-up nests of hornets and dislodging a long-abandoned bird's nest. The scent of the ocean filled the house and Flinch could hear the waves and the cries of gulls when he lay in his bed on the long, languid mornings that followed her death. He had left the house open for an entire week, only relenting and closing the front door after one of the goats wandered in and started chewing at the corner of his newspaper while he was reading it.

In the late afternoon, despite a frowning grey sky, Flinch takes his fishing rod and drives down to Tallow Beach. The threat of an oncoming storm has stirred up the ocean, the surf frothing like a rabid dog.

The easterly has washed thousands of bluebottles onto the shore. They hem the tide line like glistening beads. Flinch decides against casting his rod. He sits on the sandbank, listening to the surf seethe, and sees in the distance a single black hump rise out of the water in an arc, then the creamy underside of a fluke raised vertically out of the water, like a signal for something bigger than himself.

SEVEN

To Flinch, his life is not a seamless continuum as other people's lives seem to be. There is no progression. No evidence of that cycle of birth, schooling, job, marriage, children, retirement. That path of an average life, which ends with long pointless days drinking cold beer from ten in the morning until nightfall, and the odd weekend fending off the grandkids. The job-done-well-enough period to which most of the town's blokes aspire.

In Flinch's life there is the moment that cuts through his existence, separating it into two sections, neat as an axe through a block. The *before* and *after* periods. He sees examples of *before* and *after* photos in the newspaper. Men with fat, sagging bellies. *Before.* The same men grinning like fools, flexing bulging muscles and swivelling lean torsos. *After.* He wonders whether, if someone had taken a photo of him *before* and *after,* it would have showed, if it would have been revealed in his grainy black-and-white visage. Man. *Before.* Murderer. *After.*

When he steps outside the pastel house, he sees whales. At least once a day anyway. It's well into the season. They're hugging the coastline, following that cold Antarctic stream until it meets, with a tidal clash, the warmer Pacific current, creating a whirlpool in which the jetsam and flotsam and marine life from two different spheres intermingle, the water just tepid enough to keep both ecosystems alive.

He figures he can't help but spot them after spending his days in the crow's nest for so many months. During that last season they'd been out on the water for one hundred and forty-four days in a row, hour upon hour, but the number of whales they could sight and kill diminished regardless.

He knows what to look for. First the blast of fine spray from the blowhole, like some watery volcano erupted. Then the black metallic back and jagged fin above the water, the graceful arch of the leviathan. Occasionally the spy hop, the huge pointed head upright above the surface, just to have a look around, gauge what might be hovering in the strange world above their own. Flinch wonders if they remember the shores from which they crawled into the ocean sixty million years ago. They seem almost joyful when they reach the warmer waters, breaching and crashing in an explosion of white water. They rise two storeys out of the sea, propel themselves up and curve backwards, their pectoral fins like sails, exposing their huge white bellies, ribbed like accordions. Almost airborne. On quieter days, just the flukes rising out of the water like the static wings of some great bird. Leaving footprints on the surface as they dive; still, glassy ovals flecked with the creamy slivers of whale skin. Flinch is always surprised to see them at play, see them take themselves so lightly, especially in the waters that would have been their graveyard little more than a decade ago.

For weeks after his visit to the commune, he wanders the pastel house in a fog, losing things like car keys and cutlery only minutes after putting them down. Unwilling and unmotivated to leave, he eats his way through the pantry — baked beans, tinned tomatoes, cocktail onions, asparagus and peaches. He misses the six pm radio news, forgets his nightly routine. A stack of books lies untouched near his bed, the top one marked with the rings of coffee mugs and swollen with the damp. The corners of the photo of his mother turn up at the edges. The dust on every surface remains undisturbed.

He tries to sleep but his back aches, his spine feeling as twisted as wrought metal, his right hip bone grinding against his ribcage. But it is more than just that. He is unsure of what it was about his visit to the commune that has made him feel so disjointed. So dysfunctional. He often finds himself awake for hours in the night, irritated without reason. Some mornings, he wakes terrified and claustrophobic and exhausted, as if he's been buried alive and has spent the night scratching at the inside of a coffin.

When he eventually runs out of tins of food, he realises he will have to venture into town. Milly, unused for weeks, is recalcitrant, but he thuds the accelerator with his good leg until she turns over, and speeds off down the hill, revving the engine in case she has second thoughts.

At the grocery store, he stocks up on all the food he's been through and a whole lot more that he suddenly craves. Tins of tomatoes, rosella jam, hot English mustard, three loaves of fresh white bread, a side of corned beef, lemonade. When he takes his basket to the counter, he realises he hasn't brought enough money for it all.

The lady behind the counter sighs. She's old, about as old as Audrey would have been had she still been alive, sitting on a stool reading a magazine. Her eyes are enlarged by massive glasses that remind Flinch of butterfly wings, sharp points at the outer edges.

'It's alright, love,' she says. 'You fix yourself a good meal. You can make it up next time, eh?'

Flinch nods, grateful, and shoves the goods into a hessian sack and limps from the store, making an effort to appear stoic. Sometimes, he thinks, the leg helps, especially when it comes to people who are moved by pity to perform acts of kindness they wouldn't otherwise be inclined to. He throws the sack into the tray and climbs into the cabin. He is exhausted by even this much of a journey, this interaction. It is as if the experience of the commune overloaded his senses, offered too many challenges, too many differences, all resulting in questions. That's the last thing he needs. More questions. He feels a need to retreat. To clear his head. And he would be able to successfully, if only he could overcome the nagging irritation of his curiosity. To see how other people start over.

He sits unmoving in the ute for some time, just watching the slow, steady rollover of the town. At this time, the middle of the day, it's more or less deserted. A couple of women who look like farmers' wives, in checked dresses and stockings and shoes and hats, chat in front of a dress shop window. A few bronzed teenage boys, all shaggy fringes and lanky limbs, lean against the bonnet of a car, trying to appear nonchalant but obviously keeping an eye out for authorities, or anyone else who might ask why they're not in school. A surfer rests his board against a wall while he eats a dripping corner-store steak and beetroot burger. One of Flinch's old fishing mates, a lot greyer than Flinch remembers him, walks across the street and catches sight of the ute, waves at Flinch. Flinch waves back, hoping they can leave it at that. He's not feeling up to socialising. Especially not with old Macca. After the accident, after Flinch retreated, Macca had made quite a few attempts to bring him into town, have him to dinner, take him fishing. Mrs Mac there too, sometimes, sitting in their car parked in the driveway of the pastel house, beckoning. Tins of shrivelled meatloaf wrapped in a teatowel and left on his front step when he hadn't answered the door. The McTavishes had been the only ones to bother, really, after the whaling days. Everyone else offering a vague nod in Flinch's direction when they passed him in the street, but that was all. Preferring to forget about the whole damn mess. But Flinch, frightened of the everyday conversations that turned inevitably to whaling, Nate, the accident, had always turned down the McTavishes' invitations, excusing himself by nodding towards the leg, grimacing and hobbling as if it were paining him. Something he had never done before, and did only out of a desperate need for isolation. He remembers with shame shutting the door on Macca, the expression on the man's face, like some big old dog locked out in the cold. But even now, despite that, Macca pauses in the street and then comes over to the ute, leans in the passenger window.

'G'day, Flinch.'

'Yeah, g'day, Macca. How's things?'

'Y'know.'

'Yeah.'

'What's brought you to town?'

'Aw, the usual.'

'Yeah.'

Macca sniffs, hawks and spits. 'So, you seen any of those commies around here? Bloody joke, I reckon.'

'Commies?'

'Y'know. Based up round Nimbin. Bunch of bloody pinko lefty bastards. Wouldn't know a real day's work if it bit them on the arse.'

'You mean the hippies?' says Flinch.

'Yeah, whatever.'

Flinch coughs. 'I think they're just students,' he says eventually.

'Exactly,' says Macca. 'Too much time to think, too little time actually earnin' their bread. What would they know?' He laughs. 'World's become a funny place, hasn't it?'

'Yeah,' says Flinch, not sure what prompted the observation.

'Well, better get on me way. The missus is expectin' me to fix the gutter this arvo. Nice catchin' up with you, mate.'

'Yeah.'

'Take care, son.'

'See ya later,' says Flinch, and hopes he doesn't.

When he arrives back at the pastel house, it is drizzling. The point is concealed behind a sheet of mist made up of rain and sea spray, the beam of the lighthouse flashing its warning through the grey. The goats are clustered together nose to tail against the wall of the house, looking damp and miserable.

He has left the front door unlocked but closed,

and is curious to see it ajar as he nears the house. Expects a wily, slit-eyed goat has eaten the toilet roll off its holder and shat hard green pebbles in the kitchen. His hands full with the sack of groceries, he pushes the door open with his hip. In the kitchen a newspaper is laid out on the table, next to a cup of steaming tea. He recognises the grassy scent.

'Oh!' she says, coming out of the bathroom, plaiting her hair. 'There you are! I was hoping you might be home soon.'

Flinch stalls in the doorway, too surprised to move.

'Well, come in!' she says. 'Don't get a cold!'

He shakes the wet from his hair, wipes his feet and enters the kitchen.

She's cleaned it. The dishes are drying in the drainer. There are fresh tea towels folded over the oven door. The benches have been wiped, revealing the speckled grey laminex.

'How did you know where I lived?'

'Oh, easy,' she says. 'People in town seem to know you. Well, when I described you anyway.'

'How did you get here?'

'Walked.'

Flinch puts his groceries on the kitchen table.

'You left without saying goodbye,' she says. 'We were worried.'

'We?'

'Yeah.' Karma takes a sip of her tea.

Flinch, awkward and unsure, looks for something to do, starts putting away the tins. Takes extra care to turn the labels out.

'Anyway. We're having a healing ceremony tomorrow night. We're, you know, channelling the positive energy of each other. It's going to be really cool. It's a full moon as well, which means really amazing things might happen. I thought you might like to come.'

'Oh. Right,' says Flinch. 'I might be too busy.'

'Too busy doing what?'

'Um. Stuff. And fishing. I'm thinking of getting another job. Bit low on cash at the moment.'

'You could still come! You seemed to enjoy yourself last time.'

'Oh yeah, I did. It was good.'

'Good? Is that all? I thought you were getting into it. Letting go.'

Flinch stiffens. Was he? Over the years, he has fixed himself to so many things, nailed himself to one place with Audrey's criticisms, Nate's death, a life of getting by in the pastel house. He knows the way around his thoughts and memories, around his guilt, because he knows where those fixtures lie; they are the landmarks by which he maps himself. Letting go of them feels as reckless as setting himself adrift in his leaky dinghy without a rudder.

'It will be fun,' she says, after a moment.

'Why are you here?' he asks.

'I wanted to see you.'

'But why?'

'Because you're my friend.'

'I hardly know you.'

'But you were friendly to me. And you looked like you could do with some company.'

'I have company.'

Karma looks around the room, raises an eyebrow. 'Goats in the garden don't count,' she says.

He sighs. 'I don't know what you want.'

'Do I have to want something?'

Flinch doesn't say anything.

'It's part of my belief, Flinch. You could almost call it my duty. I sense that you're tending a wound somewhere inside you, and I want to help. It's part of a lifestyle I chose a long time ago. To heal the world in the ways I could.'

'You sensed that about me?' Flinch is sceptical.

'Well, I guess recognised is closer to the truth.'

'So I'm your cause of the week?'

'Don't be like that.'

Karma sighs and sips her tea. She flicks over the page of the newspaper. Flinch notices bruises around her wrist.

'Is Jed going?' he asks.

'Probably,' she says. 'I don't know. I don't have much to do with him anymore. He kinda drops in and out of the commune these days but he doesn't stay around. Busy saving the world, is Jed.'

'Oh,' says Flinch.

Karma folds up her newspaper, brushes her hair out of her eyes and, with a gulp, downs the rest of her tea.

'Well, have it your way. I'd better be getting back.'

'No,' Flinch says. 'Um, I mean, I'll come. Why don't you stay around here, go to the beach in the morning or something, and then I'll drive both of us out there tomorrow.'

She smiles. 'Cool,' she says.

When he stands at the entrance to Audrey's room, sheets under his arm to make up the bed, he notices Karma has already unpacked a few of her things onto the dresser. The room has been cleaned but otherwise left untouched since his mother died. He sleeps in the room of his childhood, on the lumpy single bed under a quilt of faded cartoon characters, despite the more comfortable double bed of Audrey's, unused in the next room. He has never been able to claim that space, it's still as much hers as if she had been standing in the doorway, scowling, a lit cigarette in one hand.

But Karma breezes past him and Audrey dissipates like smoke in the wind. 'This room has an amazing view. How could you ever be unhappy, waking up to this every morning?'

Flinch doesn't even try to explain.

Karma cooks dinner for them. She soaks beans, rinses rice until the water runs clear, chops up more types of vegetables than Flinch has ever eaten at once and throws them all into a pot with a tin of tomatoes. She adds one fresh red chilli, a clove of garlic and some sweet-smelling powdery spice that Flinch doesn't recognise. He is engrossed by the care she is taking to prepare the meal, her involvement with it. Audrey used to bang a frypan on the stove, throw whatever meat she could find in the fridge into it and remove it only when she smelt it burning.

'It smells good,' he says.

'It's nothing really,' she says, but he can tell she is pleased.

After dinner, they play backgammon under the exposed fluorescent kitchen light, on a dusty board that Karma has found under the bed in Audrey's room. Flinch had discovered it only when Audrey died, along with an old photo album, from which he'd retrieved the photo of her that he uses as a bookmark, and a stack of empty wine bottles that rolled and clinked when he shoved the broom under. He had forgotten it was there. A few of the white pieces are missing, so they use dried broad beans as replacements. She beats him. Twice. But he's a good-natured loser. He's always taken pride in that fact. Had a lot of practice.

During the night, he has underwater dreams of being tangled — in fishing nets, in the tentacles of octopuses and jellyfish — and he hears whale song, like a dirge, growing steadily louder. He wakes near dawn and gets out of bed, heads to the kitchen to pour himself a glass of milk. He hears her snoring lightly from the other room, and leans around the corner of the doorway to look in on her. She is sleeping face-up, her hair matted around her neck, one arm flopped over the side of the bed. He wonders if she sleeps so soundly in her orange tepee, on the hard floor of the earth, being bitten by angry bull ants.

He doubts it.

When he wakes again later in the morning, she is gone. There's a note stuck to the fridge with a magnet advertising the local bait and tackle. Scrawled on the back of a used envelope in what looks like ruby-red lip liner. Maybe one of Audrey's, Flinch thinks, because he's never seen Karma wear makeup. *Gone to beach for swim. If not back by dark, get worried. But still go to healing ceremony! Doctor's orders. Ha ha. See you soon. K.*

Flinch cooks himself a massive breakfast — three fried eggs, a T-bone steak, a piece of bacon, a tomato, a tin of baked beans and two pieces of toast. He eats quickly, making sure to wash the frying pan and air out the kitchen before she returns. Covers the evidence of his carnivorous feast by burying the T-bone in the backyard, like some dodgy cop-show killer. When he comes out later, it has been scratched up but neither it nor the goats are anywhere to be seen.

Karma is gone for almost the whole day. Flinch makes her a lunch of tomato sandwiches on white bread that grows soggy over the course of the after-noon. He eventually throws them out the window for the goats. She comes back at dusk. Flinch, bored with waiting, is napping on the couch when she returns.

'Hey,' she says softly, grabs his foot and shakes it. It's his short leg. He always sleeps curled up on his good side. Flinch awakes with a start at the shock of being touched on his malformed leg, and recoils to the edge of the couch.

'Not there,' he says.

'What?'

'Nothing.'

'Oh, okay,' she says. 'Sorry.'

'It's alright,' Flinch says. 'I just got a fright.'

They sit quietly. Flinch rubs his eyes.

'I was dreaming,' he says. 'Must have been kind of a nightmare.'

'It's okay,' she says.

'Did you have a good day?' Flinch asks after a moment, still blinking.

'Yeah, I did! I went for a swim, then some of the others were in town so I grabbed lunch with them, then I walked all the way up to the lighthouse by myself and just sat there, you know, taking in the vibe. And then, just as I was feeling really, like, peaceful, these whales appeared right out in front of me. They rose up way out of the water. It was awesome!' Her eyes are shining. She is flushed.

'That's nice,' says Flinch. 'The whales are everywhere at the moment.'

She brushes her hair back from her face and sniffs.

'Well, they might be, but this was different. It was, like, cosmic. Like a message for the moment. You know.'

Flinch nods and thinks he might understand what she is talking about, but isn't sure.

'So, anyway. This ceremony. I checked with the others and it's definitely on. It's in a field near the commune. It will go all night. But we should probably get there soon.'

'Alright,' says Flinch. 'I think I'll shower here first, though.'

Only one of Milly's headlights is working. The climb up the dimly lit road to the hinterland slow and tedious. Possums that would have become roadkill in front of any other vehicle have plenty of time to cross the road in front of them and scurry up trees on the other side. Karma, in the front seat, alternates between impatient sighing and humming. Flinch can't decide which is more irritating. He turns on the radio, but the signal is lost in a sea of static as they descend into the valley.

They pull up under the fig tree near the commune. A procession of people carrying lanterns and candles streams from the tents into the paddocks beyond. In the darkness, the lights look like they are floating and to Flinch the whole scene looks religious, somehow otherworldly.

'Oh, it's beautiful,' says Karma, breathless.

She grabs Flinch by the hand and they half stumble, half jog until they reach the end of the procession. Karma's laughter like bubbles rising to a surface and Flinch, suddenly elated after the short, wobbly sprint, feels himself rise as if upon them.

Up and down the procession, people sing. All sorts of songs. Mutating tunes, verses snatched out of the air as they float by and turn into something else. Someone behind Flinch beats a shallow drum, pauses every now and again when the track gets narrow. Thick, exposed roots of fig trees that snake out of the earth have to be negotiated.

'Hey, Karma!' someone yells.

Flinch turns around to see Matt jogging towards them.

'Hey, darlin',' she says. Gives him a hug. As if they hadn't seen each other for a year, Flinch thinks. Snorts softly to himself.

'Hi,' he says.

'Man, you should come up the front! It's great up there, the energy is amazing.'

'Oh, cool,' says Karma. 'Come on, Flinch.'

Flinch is already having difficulty keeping up with the procession. He feels he is in the middle of a current, anchored to something that is slowing him down while debris streams around him. Feels his back up against it, the cool, steady pressure of it making him sway slightly as he limps forward.

'Aw, no, I don't mind it back here. I like the sound of that drum, and everything.'

Matt shrugs his shoulders. 'Whatever turns you on, man.'

'You sure?' says Karma.

'Yeah, sure.'

'Okay, well I'll catch up with you later.'

Matt takes her by the hand and they rush off, carried away with the flow of the crowd. Flinch, suddenly exhausted, slows down until he is one of the last few in the procession. Reminded with a tiny, bitter pang of school days, being last in line, last on the team, the pressure of keeping up more painful than his aching back and hip, trying to block out the glances of frustrated teachers and the whispered taunts of his classmates.

Just as he is about to give up walking and return to the commune and then to the familiar vinyl safety of Milly's cabin, the head of the procession turns tightly and rounds back on itself, meeting up with the stragglers at the end so that a circle is formed. Flinch looks for Karma, but cannot see her among the throngs of people who have grouped around him. A few move into the centre of the circle. The man with the drum. A woman with a harp. Others, too, all clad in flowing robes. A large bonfire that Flinch hadn't noticed in the darkness of the night is set alight with a sudden roar.

From somewhere in front of him, a man shouts

something Flinch can't quite make out. Something about spirits, he thinks. The moon maybe.

Some people near Flinch stomp the ground and holler.

'Like Indians,' Flinch says out loud, accidentally.

'That's *Native Americans*, man,' says a girl next to him. Rolls her eyes. The emphasis on the words like a rap over the knuckles.

From the middle of the circle, a chant begins and spreads through the crowd like a virus, getting louder and louder. Flinch can't decipher what is being said but hums along until he becomes confused and loses the pitch. When people around him start clapping, he watches carefully and tries to join in, but finds he keeps losing the rhythm and his claps are like an echo when everyone else falls silent. Every now and then, a voice from the circle hollers to the heavens, sometimes a loud sigh, sometimes laughter. The girl next to him starts to weep.

A joint is passed to him and he closes his eyes and inhales, sucks small grassy seeds into his mouth. They stick to his teeth. When he swallows they make his throat itch. He knows he is meant to pass the joint on, but instead he holds it low by his side and steps back out of the circle, moves away one careful step at a time. When he is free of the crowd, he sits down in the darkness, watches the shapes move around the glow of the bonfire. Takes a few long drags on the joint. The silhouettes of bodies blur in front of a haze of red and orange. The chanting sounds as if it is coming from somewhere in the distance, softer and more musical than it was earlier. Eventually he feels he should get up, and he levers himself to his feet, surprised at the effort this takes, and staggers a few metres before he feels the drug lift his head off his neck. He takes large steps, as if he is walking on the moon, though he has to drag the long leg a little at first to manage it. He stumbles over something — he thinks for a second it was something moving — and sprawls on the dew-wet grass. He concentrates on lying very still, but can't help chuckling quietly to himself.

He is shivering when she bends over him but he doesn't feel cold.

'God. Flinch, are you okay?'

He squeezes his eyes shut and when he opens them again, a second later, he guesses, he is lying in her tent on a mound of pillows, wrapped up in a number of glittering, brightly coloured saris. Candles flicker, splattering strange dark shapes against the orange canvas.

She is leaning over him, staring at him with wide eyes. 'What happened, Flinch? Were you overcome?'

'Huh?'

'By the energy.' She sighs. 'Do you feel different?' With the hope and fervour of the born-again.

'Yes.' He lies. 'A bit.' He doesn't want to disappoint.

She leans back and smiles. 'Wow. That's so cool. It's like … it's like something divine.'

'Yes,' he says. And wonders if she really believes it happens, just like that.

EIGHT

Like a grumbling schoolmaster, the sea insisted that
Flinch learn certain things over.

That depth and colour are matters of perception.
That if you stare only at the surface, you will miss the
wonders below and may also become snagged on
what lies there. That even wrecks become fixtures,
develop a jagged loveliness of their own.

During his time on the fishing boats, he was
washed overboard twice while contemplating the
ocean during rough seas. One of those times, almost
drowned. He had to be wrenched out of the ocean by
his collar and the waistband of his shorts. An hour later
he was still vomiting up sea water. Flinch considered
himself a good student.

Knowing that Audrey would be lying in wait for
him like a cat for a mouse, twitching with anticipation,
Flinch prolonged his shift on the boats any way he

could. After a night out at sea, he would settle into the cool white sand at Tallow Beach with a thermos of sweet milky tea and sip it slowly while the sun rose over the ocean. Sitting on that beach, he knew himself to be the first person in the country to see the sun rise and he always thought of that as a little reward, some sort of shining acknowledgement, much like the sticky gold stars that his primary school teacher used to hand out for a good maths test result. After a day shift, the blokes would retreat to the pub like soldiers back to the barracks, covered in scales and oil, reeking of sweat and salt water and fish gut, and Flinch would go with them. Usually ordered a tall glass of soft drink in those days. When the bartender was in a good mood, he could get away with a shandy. A sweet one, more lemonade than beer.

Night or day, she'd be sitting in the kitchen for his return. Straight-backed as if she had a cold steel rod for a spine. Stockings on under slippers. False nails clicking on the laminex. Wisps of cigarette smoke still visible, the curtains reeking of it. Flinch's eyes stung when he walked through the door.

'Good catch?' Her voice a rasp.

'Yeah, Mum.'

If he was lucky, she'd sigh and leave it at that.

On the unlucky days, there'd be the stories. The miserable accounts of her life, anecdotes that spread out like spider's web, entangling all sorts of incidents, stringing one to the next with a leap of memory or

regret. The men who had betrayed her, the hairdress-
ing apprenticeship she had given up pursuing when she
found out she was pregnant with Flinch, her father's
callous refusal to allow her into the house even after
Flinch was born, and then the time she was a child and
her mother had forgotten to fetch her after school.
Inevitably all stories led her to recount her dismay that
Flinch didn't Continue to Senior, didn't Make Something of Himself. The regret that comes when you
know you were meant for better than this, all this. For
the brief time she could muster the energy after Nate's
death, there were the sly insinuations, acid-laced and
concealed in conversational tones, that if Flinch had
been a better man he could have saved Nate, maybe
wouldn't even have ended up a whaler in the first place.

Audrey was a persistent storyteller, following him
into the bathroom and sitting on the toilet seat while
he showered so that she could continue uninterrupted.

'You know, when I was young they said I had the
legs of Ginger Rogers. Lot of good it did me, eh? All
I managed to attract was the scum of the pond — that
bastard who fathered you, for instance.'

The cigarette stubbed out on the nylon bath
mat. Audrey frowning and stomping it under the heel
of her slipper until it smouldered. Brief foul smell of
burning toxins.

'And Lorelei, you know Lorelei, she'd always said
to me to watch out for sailors and the like. Though
she can hardly talk, look who she ended up marrying,

and that daughter of hers is a mess now, ran away to Sydney and why wouldn't you when you consider the way Lorelei runs that house.'

The exhaled smoke was always trapped on Flinch's side of the shower curtain and he rarely bathed without coughing.

'That reminds me, meant to drop into her place for coffee tomorrow. But my arthritis is playing up again, wouldn't you know it. Can hardly hold a teacup, that's what comes of working your life away in some factory just to get by and feed your child.'

A jumble of regrets and broken lives, over and over. Her voice grating up against his bare skin, the words a dull buzz in his head. He'd heard it all before. Occasionally she added something, rewrote the past a little to shift the spotlight, depending on her mood. Like an actress working out whether today she would be playing the role of the betrayed lover, the neglected daughter, the stoic mother, the glamorous youth, the child prodigy, the forsaken woman, harlot, heroine.

She required no feedback, no comment. Flinch was a receptacle for her acrid disappointments and that was all. She didn't ask for his opinion on any of it. Or on anything. When he tried to console her — he did right up until the end, he couldn't help himself, pleading with her over tight, greying hospital sheets — she would look at him blankly, pause, and continue as if he had not spoken. She never asked him a question unless she intended his answer to provide a launch for her own stories. Flinch grew to believe he had nothing to offer her. At first, on the boats, unused to being asked questions and unprepared to answer, he was also regarded as 'a little bit slow'.

A little bit slow, the bloke with the short leg. But a good little fella.

The ocean taught Flinch that beautiful creatures can have painful stings. And sure enough, between the fishing and his near drowning, the sea seeped into Flinch's blood. A combination, perhaps, of his willingness to open his veins to it and some sort of genetic code in his makeup, courtesy of his father. He convinced himself that he felt it as it happened. The fluid thinning in his arteries.

'How did you meet him?' he used to ask Audrey when she started on the topic of his father. She was not shy about the details. More than anything else, Audrey loved a rapt audience. Flinch knew the story almost by heart, though every now and then Audrey spiked it with more detail, which Flinch found irresistible and intoxicating.

'Well, there I was in my red dress, just sitting with Lorelei at the Great Northern minding my own business. I had just ordered a glass of shandy. The sun was shining right in on me through the window and Lorelei says even to this day that I did look like an angel, just as he said I did when he came up to me.'

Flinch pictured his mother perched on a stool, auburn hair glinting in sunlight. He imagined his father as tall and muscular, dressed in a proper sailor's white uniform, clean-shaven, crease-free, though Audrey had told him otherwise. She described him fairly consistently as short and squat, dressed in a faded blue singlet and stained trousers, with a ginger moustache that had grown down below his jawline, a recent tattoo on his shoulder still scab and pus. But if she could describe herself as an angel, Flinch reasons, he could alter the image of his father, too.

'Of course, he was a sweet talker.' She always said it.

'He said I was the most sophisticated lady he'd ever come across.' This too.

'Mongrel seaman.' The inevitable ending.

Flinch knew the script and had learnt from experience at which point she was going to need a few tissues into which to snivel. Poured more whisky into her coffee at the end of her monologue and watched her slip into her own world, slack and dull-eyed, sinking into the worn velour of the couch. Flinch turned the radio on and left her there. She was always in her own bed by morning.

Flinch figures that if she could slip away with such ease, maybe he can as well, so sometimes at night, in the dreamy half-world before sleep, he squeezes his eyes tight and forces himself back to some other place. Onto the boats, over the breakers, through to the sighting of the whale, the shining black mound rising above the surface of the water. The flensing floor and the stench of the vats. Hacking his way through sheets of blubber as thick as his torso. Finally to the pub, perching up on a stool, his bad leg dangling. Nate next to him, always.

After a day in the sun they were cooked through. Their noses uniformly bright pink, despite their hats, skin flaking on brown forearms. Eyeballs streaked red.

'We're actually baking out there. Roasting, like chooks,' Nate had said.

They were light-headed. Flinch found it difficult to concentrate. Felt drunk on the first three sips of his stubbie.

'Too much sun affects the brain. Too little of it and you fall into depression. When Cook explored the Arctic during its months of darkness, he said his men fell into dreams of melancholy,' Nate continued. Paused and sucked his lips at the end of each sentence.

'Ah, bullshit. Cook never explored the Arctic,' growled Macca.

'Well, actually, he did to some extent, but I'm not talking about Captain James Cook anyway. Frederick A. Cook. Different explorer.'

Macca had snorted into his beer and shot Flinch a sideways glance. Meaning, *here we go*.

'The light affects the chemistry of the brain. The further you are from the equator, the more likely you are to be depressed during winter. Whereas with us, out in the sun all day, it's giving us a high and altering our sensations to regular stimuli.'

'Sun–fucked,' said Macca. 'That's what we are.' And laughed.

Nate had glared at him.

Macca coughed and slid another stubbie of beer in his direction. 'Jeez, mate, where do you find out all this crap?'

'Unlike some, I read,' said Nate.

'You shut up long enough?' Macca chuckled. 'Nothing you can't learn about life that isn't in a racing guide, if you ask me, mate. Or in the tide books even. The highs and the lows.'

Nate had taken a swig of his beer.

'It's very interesting, Nate,' said Flinch. Like a pat on the back.

Flinch would wake at four am after fitful dreams to turn off his bedside lamp.

A week before he died, Nate had given Flinch his copy of *Moby-Dick*. Dog–eared and yellowing. A few pages in the middle swollen where they had once met dampness.

'One of my most prized possessions,' he said as he handed it over.

'Is it about whaling?' asked Flinch, looking at the picture of a white sperm whale on the front cover.

'Sort of,' said Nate. 'It's about a lot of things. Madness. Obsession. The political and moral state of the US at the time it was written.'

Flinch read the blurb on the back cover. 'Hey, this captain has a bung leg too,' he said. 'It's about a whaler with a bung leg. Just like me.'

Nate smiled and slapped him on the shoulder. 'Yeah, well, he's not really like you, but you do have that in common. I thought you'd like it.'

Flinch only noticed later the inscription on the inside cover, revealing Nate's intention of leaving the bay.

Dear Flinch,
The world finds ways to reunite old friends. Keep this for me until we cross each other's paths once more. I'll miss you, captain.
Nathan West

Now Flinch thinks of the exchange as fortuitous, like a special parting gift from his friend. He reads it often. It's unlike anything he has ever come across, and he finds the language like the sea itself, tossing him to and fro, sometimes at a quiet flow and sometimes wild and incomprehensible. But each time he reads about the fraternal bond that forms between Ishmael and Queequeg, he understands precisely and he cries.

'Call me Flinch,' he says to the goats in the

morning when he steps out to face each long day. He knows that if Nate were around, they'd both have a laugh.

Flinch has spent a lot of the past decade thinking about obsession and madness. Recently he has decided that he is depressed.

It's not depression of the dark or suicidal kind. More like a sleepy malaise. A discontent with which Flinch has grown so familiar he might feel uncomfortable or underdressed if it were lifted. It's a feeling that he's meant to be elsewhere. That he's missed a bus or an important appointment. Just a small, cold, consistent panic. He has stopped wearing watches because he had found himself checking the time with such frequency that he developed a tic in his wrist. It did occur to him that he might fill the day just by watching the time tick away. But it only seemed to slow it down.

Hardest of all, perhaps, is just the plain old emptiness of his life. The something missing. On windy days he would swear he feels the cold breeze pass through him and whirl around the spaces inside him. He feels himself filling up with dust and debris. At nights, there are the hot pangs that wake him in the early hours. That have him stand still as stone under a hot shower, hard pellets of water scorching his skin while he sobs against a mouldy tiled wall. Walking outside too many mornings with that sliver of hope that he may find Nate asleep in the dinghy in the yard.

The sliver like a slender blade, his disappointment as sure and sharp as a piercing.

And still there is the question of the sea and its lessons and his destiny. He sleeps with the sound of it in his ears, the waves smashing against the cliffs. The screech of gulls like alarm bells every morning. Some days he feels its siren voice calling his name and he longs to set himself adrift, just to feel the force of the currents rocking beneath him, to have that space above, below and around.

Even though he hasn't set foot on so much as a raft for the past decade, Flinch can see the stain of the sea on other men and he knows that those men can see it on him. When he bumps into them in the pub, or on the beach, they watch each other, looking for an indication of that urge to head to the water, to find a vessel, and when one moves towards the docks the others gravitate towards them also. Like the dogs of Flinch's childhood — a series of dirt-yellow mongrels — who would growl when they heard other dogs bark, even in their sleep, the men react instinctively to the water that they sense in each other's blood. It is an understanding that they don't share with others, though the disdain in the term 'landlubber' is obvious to the tourists who stroll past the fishermen on the docks, even when said with laughter.

NINE

The day after the healing ceremony, Flinch sleeps for hours longer than usual in Karma's orange tent. In the afternoon, the sun blazes across one side of it and the heat through the canvas causes him to wake sweating, feeling drowsy. Karma is not there. Through a gap where the tent flaps hang partially open, he watches the activity of the commune. There seems to be a kind of haphazard sense of duty. A woman is planting seeds in the vegetable garden and two small children guard its perimeter, chasing away the persistent chickens that are scratching at its edges. A few men are stringing up a tarpaulin between the branches of a fig tree. From somewhere nearby, the sound of an axe splintering wood. Fires have been lit, the smell of wood burning thick and blurred against the damp odour of the hinterland.

The inside of the tent feels like some sort of

cocoon. Flinch is reluctant to emerge. He's more comfortable with caterpillars than butterflies.

He leans back on the pillows. One of the bull ants bites him on the base of his palm and he recoils. He is scratching at the bite and swearing when Karma pokes her head through the tent flap.

'Itchy palms, eh?' She smirks.

'Bloody ants.' It's the best he can come up with.

She flicks on the single gas cylinder and waits a second before striking a match. She holds the match over the gas and a blue flame bursts to light with a small pop.

'Not really very safe, you know,' says Flinch.

'Safe enough. Do you want some tea? Peppermint? Chamomile and honey?' An old tin kettle balanced precariously over the flame.

'No. Thanks.'

She shrugs. 'Have it your way. But you'd feel better, you know.'

'I do, though,' he says. Like a reminder. Hoping she won't start again on the business of healing him.

'Now, darl, since you're staying, we'll have to work out what you can do around here to contribute.'

'What?' says Flinch.

The kettle whistles and she removes it. From a small jar she scoops some dried leaves, and filters the water through them into a mug.

'Smell,' she says, puts the mug underneath Flinch's nose.

'Nice,' he says.

'Bliss in a cup,' she replies. 'Sure you don't want some?'

'Sure.'

'I was thinking maybe you could catch fish once a week or so, that seemed to go down well with the meat-eaters, though I have to admit I don't entirely approve. But it's against my nature to force my beliefs on others. We're not evangelists here, that's not the point. Live and let live. At some stage you have to decide whether you'll save your own soul or run about saving the world. That's the dilemma, isn't it? I know they're not mutually exclusive goals but very few human beings have the spiritual energy and wisdom for both. The Dalai Lama maybe. Or some of the Indian swamis, but I don't think many of them are all they're cracked up to be. Each to their own guru, I guess.'

Her voice washes over him, Flinch swept back by the flow. He waits to snag on an understanding of something that she is saying but she may as well be speaking another language. She takes a sip of her tea and looks at him, as if for a response.

'I'm not staying,' he says.

She furrows her brow and takes another sip of her tea. 'What do you mean?' she says, swallowing. 'I thought we'd been through all of this.'

'I had fun, like you said, and it was good. Very … um…' Scrambles for something that will impress her enough to release him. 'Rejuvenating.'

'I see,' she says.

'Thanks for, you know. And everything.'

She nods and turns her back on him.

The air in the tent stales.

Flinch crawls out through the tent's opening on his hands and knees.

Milly refuses to cooperate, as if she is holding a grudge.

'Aw, c'mon, you rusted piece of shit.' Flinch slams his foot on every pedal, to no avail. 'Please, Milly.'

A man Flinch hasn't seen before walks slowly towards the ute. 'Now, Milly, now,' he begs from between clenched teeth.

'Hey dude, what's the problem?' The man is American. He leans in through the window and grins at Flinch, a little slack-jawed. Some of his teeth are missing. One of the remaining teeth in the front is gold. He is burnt brown, the skin on his forearms and the back of his neck the colour of cut redwood. Baggy clothing hangs over a lean, wiry frame as if over a coat-hanger, takes no form.

'Aw, yeah. It's nothing, mate, she's just a bit run-down,' says Flinch.

The American laughs out loud, snorts. A few people look over in their direction. Flinch slides a fraction down the seat and pulls his collar up closer to his ears. He wonders what he said that is so funny.

'Jesus, you Aussies.' The American wipes tears from his eyes. 'How do you say it? Goo-day.' He offers his hand. 'I'm Drew Daniels, Grover Beach, California.'

Flinch notices the man's hand is shaking. When he takes it in his own, it's as clammy as damp cloth.

'Flinch,' says Flinch. 'I'm from around here. Kind of.'

'Cool, man,' says the American. He looks around the paddocks, then up into the trees, as if expecting to see Flinch's house perched there.

Flinch sits quietly for a while, pretends to fiddle with knobs on the dashboard, hoping Drew will go away. But when he looks up again, he is still standing there outside the ute, nodding and grinning.

'Well? Dude? You staying around or what?' he asks. Louder than necessary.

'I was on my way back to the bay, actually. Sorry.'

'Man, you ain't going *nowhere* right now in that pile of junk.'

'Yeah, guess not,' Flinch sighs.

Drew smiles broadly.

Flinch opens the door of the ute and swings his legs through it.

'Hey man, one of your legs is shorter than the other.' Loud enough to cause Flinch to wince. Exclaimed, as if Flinch may not have noticed.

'Yeah,' says Flinch. Thinking, *Well there's the bleeding obvious.* Wondering what is coming next.

'Lucky bastard,' says Drew.

Flinch walks slower than usual back towards the commune. He hopes Drew will go on ahead, so that he might sneak back to the ute unnoticed, hide in the back while he decides what to do. But Drew just circles him, talks loudly and constantly, walking backwards occasionally so he can address him face to face. When Flinch pauses, Drew takes the opportunity to act out the scenario he is describing. Wild hand gestures, rubbery facial expressions. Flinch finds him amusing and laughs despite himself.

'Enjoying yourself?' she asks without smiling.

'Hey Karma, this dude is, like, stuck here.' Drew nods when he talks, as if everything he says has to be reaffirmed.

'He must be,' she says.

'Hi again,' says Flinch. Tries on a sheepish grin.

'We're having a singing circle tonight.' She looks at Drew when she speaks. 'Starts at sunset.'

'Cool, man,' says Drew. 'Dude, can you sing?'

'Um. No. Not really,' says Flinch.

'Hey, cool, neither can I.' Drew bursts into raucous laughter, more snorting.

Karma walks away.

Flinch knows he can't sing. Even when he's drunk. Even when Nate insisted that together they were melodious. Lying under blankets in the dinghy while it drizzled down upon them. Drunk as vicars, Nate had declared. Ten straight minutes pounding on the door of the pastel house before Flinch had awoken, a couch cushion over his ear. Nate strangling a bottle of rum in each hand and two long-necked bottles of beer under his armpits.

'We're on early shift tomorrow,' Flinch had said.

'We'll manage.'

'Mate, I dunno.'

That sly grin, the raised eyebrow. Nate had already had a few.

'Come on, captain. Live a little.'

And later, both of them singing an unstructured melody that consisted of the choruses from a jumble of songs.

Oh Danny Boy
The pipes, the pipes are calling.
O whim o whey o whim o whey
The lion sleeps tonight.
In the jungle, the mighty jungle
The lion sleeps tonight.
Oh Danny Boy, oh Danny Boy
I love you so ...

The goats roused from where they napped near the house, moving off down the hillside and into the thick silence of the scrub.

Flinch remembers waking in the morning with dawn. Wincing into light stark as ice. A pain between his brows that he felt would crack him right open. Nate sprawled across the plank seat in the dinghy snoring and immovable. And he remembers the singing. Joyful, ardent and painful even to his own ears.

Flinch spends the remainder of the afternoon in Drew's tent. It is one of the tents shaped like a pod. Drew has sewn camouflage army fatigues on the inside, over the entire sheeting.

'Welcome to the jungle,' he says as they crawl inside, and laughs.

The sleeve of a jacket that has been sewn to the roof has come loose and hangs like a limp arm, brushes the nape of Flinch's neck as he crawls underneath it and sends shivers up his spine.

Drew flicks on a torch that hangs by string from the wall of the tent. The inside of the dome is cluttered. Blankets, mismatched clothing, tins and tins of Spam, jars full of odds and ends, thread and needles. A woman's tiny beaded slippers. Drew takes a safety pin from a jar and pins the loose sleeve back onto its jacket. Over the place the wearer's heart would be. Flinch notices the other sleeve is pinned out from the jacket, bent at the elbow as if saluting.

'Insulation,' Drew says. 'Courtesy of the United States Armed Forces.'

Drew sleeps on a bundle of clothes.

'This is comfort, dude,' he says, taking a sock from the bundle and stroking it like it was a pet. 'You should have seen how we slept in 'Nam. If we got to sleep, that is.'

He laughs again, and Flinch laughs along to be polite, but still doesn't understand the joke.

Drew swings the torch as he talks, absent-minded, like a habit, lighting up different objects at random. One jar full of bullet cases. Another full of what looks like blonde human hair. Pinned along one side of the dome, hanging evenly and reflecting the light when it catches them, seven army dog tags.

From one of the containers, Drew takes a pinch of weed, deftly rolls a joint and hands it to Flinch, then lights one for himself. Flinch lies back on a clump of clothes that smells like a mixture of other people's sweat and smoke.

'It's a funny place, this corner of the world,' says Drew, and sighs.

'Yeah,' says Flinch. Coughs. The drug is strong. It goes straight to his head and he feels the tent start to spin slowly, taking his body with it.

'Hey man, what's the worst thing you've ever done?' Drew says it as casually as he might if he were asking Flinch his favourite colour.

'What?'

'C'mon dude.'

Flinch registers panic, subdued by the drug but rising steadily. He feels like prey lured unaware into a trap. Drew holds the torch under his chin, lighting up his face, demonising his features. The drug is making Flinch feel untouchable, as if he is floating in a bubble. Safe and far enough away from the world to confess.

'I killed my friend.' He's never said it like that. Out loud. Not since the police reports. Though the local constable, first on the scene, had quickly convinced him not to say 'killed' or 'murdered', and had even crossed out 'manslaughter' as a cause of death. The report was filed under 'Accidental deaths'. Everyone had agreed in whispers loud enough for Flinch to overhear that he had a tough enough life already.

'Whoa! Really? Like in a murder? Was it over money?'

'No,' says Flinch. 'It was an accident.'

'Heavy.'

'Yeah.'

'What did you say to his mom?'

'I never knew his parents. He never mentioned them.'

'I have to say a few things to various moms when I get back to the States one day. Guys I had hardly known before they were shot to pieces begged me. Here,' he says, emptying another container full of shredded bits of paper. 'Here's where everyone's moms live, and what they wanted me to say to them.'

Flinch picks up a scrap of paper.

The writing on it is scrawled, almost inde-cipherable.

Jerry Simons, it says. *Mayville, Chautauqua, NY.*

Love you mom and just want you to be proud and don't be sad for me because no more pain where I am now.

He picks up another one.

Another name and address. But an almost identical message.

A third (*David Dougherty, Fort McPherson, GA*) reads: *It's in the back of my closet, tap for the loose board and you'll find it.*

But when he unfolds a fourth it reveals the same sentiment as the first two. A message to a mother.

He wonders if Nate wanted to say these things to his mother as he lay dying. Things that appear to be universally what young men say on their deathbeds when their lives are cut short. Flinch has always worried that Nate's family never received the priest's letter. He thinks perhaps that he should find the family, to tell them what became of their son. Makes up his mind then to do that. He will return to the pastel house tomorrow and prepare for a journey. He'll endeavour to make things right, in some small way.

Drew takes a long drag on his joint, breathes out very slowly. His eyes watering.

'Well then, what does yours look like?' he asks, between exhalations.

He sidles closer to Flinch and leans near enough to hear a secret. His breath rich and rank with stale smoke. Strings of pasty white spittle form when he opens his mouth to speak. Up close, the thing behind his eyes that Flinch thought might be the drugs looks more like a long-standing panic, something that may have fused there permanently.

'I don't know what you mean,' says Flinch. He

looks around the tent, tries to shuffle away, but the dome is small and doesn't allow for much movement.

'Yes, you know what I mean.' Drew raises his voice.

Flinch clears his throat. 'Are you okay?' he asks.

Drew snorts loudly and starts chuckling. Tears leaking down his face leave glistening streaks.

'I'll tell you,' he says, in the tone of a conspirator. Suddenly serious. 'I'll tell you what mine looks like. It has horns. Big as a bull. It's black, but it has red eyes. And — get this. It hunts me, man. I can feel it all the time. Stalking me.'

'Do you want some water or something?' says Flinch.

Drew appears not to hear him. 'I think it's like a jungle spirit, or something. At least that's where it started hunting me. The fucker followed me right down to the swamps, all the way to the Mekong Delta. I saw it once right behind our boat, just its horns, poking out of the water. And the water, dude, it was *boiling*. All around it. That's how I knew where it was.'

Flinch nods but doesn't look at him. The stench of his breath when he exhales his words almost overwhelming.

'Everyone who killed someone got something like that following them around. Not everyone admits it but I can see they do. That's just what mine looks like. Nasty fucker.'

He seems almost nostalgic now. Shuts his eyes. Almost in slow motion, he tips sideways and collapses onto Flinch's shoulder. Flinch leans over and pushes him gently away and he falls backwards onto his pile of clothes and lies still.

'War,' he says. It comes out as a small sigh, like a whimper. His eyes stay shut.

He falls into a sleep that seems to Flinch like a coma. Flinch curls up in a corner too, wraps a mottled sweater that reeks of Old Spice and mothballs around his head to block out the sound of Drew's snoring.

Just before sunset, they wake. Drew stretches, yawns, takes a container from the pocket of one of the jackets that is sewn to the canvas. He removes a small capsule and puts it in his mouth.

'And here's one I prepared earlier.' Grins as he swallows.

When they crawl out of the tent, Flinch is surprised to find it is still light on the outside, even though it is dusk.

Flinch can't sit cross-legged. It's his knees. They ache. Too many times folded into the crow's nest on winter days. Snap-frozen and salted like a fillet of cod. He ends up leaning forward and clinging to his knees like a monkey in a barrel. They come up to his armpits and he can't get them to the ground.

'You know, if you practised a bit of yoga, you'd manage it,' says Karma, standing over him.

He winces. Says nothing.

'I'm glad you stayed,' she says, sitting next to him. 'See. It was meant to be.'

Flinch starts to tell her a thing or two about Milly but she shrugs her shoulders.

'Either way,' she says, and looks away.

The singing ceremony turns out to be not so much singing as chanting. After a while Flinch's buttocks start to numb. His right foot buzzes with pins and needles. He is hungry, too. Darkness outside and he figures it is well past six pm. He fidgets and bumps Drew, who is sitting next to him, but Drew doesn't seem to notice. His eyes are glazed and his pupils have expanded almost to the size of his irises, like a cat meditating on prey. On the other side of him, Karma hums under her breath, sounding like a bee trapped in a jar. Flinch tries to rub his aching foot without being conspicuous. Just as he leans back to rearrange himself, he notices someone else stand up on the opposite side of the tent. Recognises the shadow that falls long and dark in front of the lantern. Jed.

'What's he doing here?' Flinch says out loud.

Karma opens her eyes and stops humming.

'I thought he'd left.' Flinch says it in a whisper but it comes out like a hiss.

Karma shrugs. 'It's a free world, Flinch,' she says. But Flinch watches and sees that she doesn't shut her eyes until Jed walks out of the tent.

'What happened with Jed?' Flinch asks her later.

'You mean between us?'

'Yes.'

She is brushing her hair from her eyes with both her hands, over and over, as if her fingers were a comb. A gesture that Flinch finds distracting, and suspects that this is the reason she is doing it. The ceremony over finally when incense burnt to ash. They have moved with the rest of the group to the hay-bale house that serves as a food hall of sorts. Drew calls it 'the mess', which earns him the frowns of some of the others.

'We were together for a while, but in the end we wanted different things,' she says eventually.

'I saw bruises,' he replies.

She stops brushing and looks at him. Straight at him. She is, for a second, transparent and they both know this.

'Nothing is ever as simple as what you think you see, Flinch.'

She ties her hair in a knot to keep it off her neck and Flinch realises that the screen usually around her is in place again. She's fixed it there with the same quick efficiency with which she tied up her hair. Almost with the same gesture.

'Why do they let him stay?' he asks anyway.

'I thought this was paradise. I wouldn't think he'd be allowed back.'

'Paradise doesn't suit everybody,' she says in a quiet voice. 'But who are we to judge, hey?' She doesn't look at him.

'You should move to the bay,' he says. Suddenly, like an urge.

'Why?'

'I, um, there are whales. It's, you know, spiritual.'

She smiles at him. 'Good for you, Flinch,' she says.

He doesn't know what she means. He hopes it means she will come and stay there one day, maybe when he gets back from his journey to find Nate's parents.

They are at one end of a long wooden table. Left over hay bales serve as bench seats. They had managed to secure a corner, but the table is filling up as people return from the cooking area to sit down with their food.

Jed and Matt are at a nearby table. Drew sits next to them, shovelling spoonfuls of lentil stew and home-baked sourdough into his mouth.

Flinch tucks his legs against the bale and leans back slightly so that he can listen in.

'What I mean,' Jed is saying, 'is that Drew is an example of someone who threw themselves against the system by refusing to participate in it. He was a cog in the wheel and he removed himself, so the whole machinery, the machinery of conscription, and therefore of an unjust war, will not run as well. If every conscripted American — or Australian — did that, the government would be forced to listen to the people. We have to encourage that kind of movement.'

'Hey man, I was just shit-scared of going back,' Drew says, bread stuck between his teeth. 'So, like, I decided to interpret R and R as "Run and Retire from duty".' Laughs at his own joke. A lentil shoots out of one nostril.

Jed ignores him. 'We need to set up proper channels so that we can let conscientious objectors know that we can provide safe harbour,' he says.

'The only thing evil men need to succeed is for good men to do nothing,' says Matt, nodding, rattling dreadlocks.

'Or women,' says a woman nearby.

'People,' says Matt. 'I meant people.'

'You guys got any skunk?' asks Drew.

In the bay a storm rides in on the east winds, swallowing the moon. During the day, as he had wandered over to Drew's tent, Flinch had seen the clouds gathering over Mt Warning as if they had agreed to meet there, to wait, bide their time. The rest of the sky was clear. It seemed to him conspiratorial, at the time. When he steps outside the dining hall, the smell of the storm, like some rank animal. He breathes it deep into his lungs.

'Looks like it's coming this way.' She has followed

him out. She stands close behind him; almost touching, not quite. The heat of her body makes his skin prickle.

'It is.'

'Rain? Or just all noise and lights?'

'Everything,' says Flinch. 'I reckon it's going to be the whole shebang.'

Sheet lightning flickers over them, the jagged heads of the Nightcap Range silhouetted against it, their imposing outlines like slender giants. From inside the food hall, they hear Drew shouting something indistinguishable and Jed raising his voice.

'I'll come back with you, if you want to go tomorrow,' she says.

'What for?'

'You asked me, didn't you?' Her irritation sudden and palpable. Flinch wonders if he has done something to make her that way. The rain starts; tight, hard drops that sting the skin when they land.

'I have something I need to do first,' he says. She is so quiet behind him he thinks for a second that she has walked away.

'Next week, then,' she says eventually.

'I'm going away,' he says. 'I don't know for how long.'

'Where to?'

He doesn't answer her. The rain starts to pelt down and thunder crashes overhead, a streak of lightning blazes in front of them and strikes a nearby tree, splitting it in two and setting it alight. The noise and explosion send Flinch and Karma reeling backwards and Flinch falls, hitting the ground with a thud, twisting an ankle. The noise of the strike brings people rushing out from the food hall.

'Wow,' says Drew. 'Hey, check it out! A burning bush! Do you think God is in there?' He is laughing again, out of breath. 'Deliver your people to peace and safety!' he yells in the direction of the tree.

Others are looking at him, expressions laced with sting and disapproval, but Drew doesn't notice or, Flinch suspects, doesn't care.

Flinch is soaked through. People mill around him but, distracted by the storm, nobody offers to help him up. With some effort he levers himself to his feet. The fire dies off in the rainfall. The crowd retreats to the food hall.

'I think we'd better stay in here tonight,' says Karma. 'Don't know that my tent is up to this kind of weather.'

During the night the number of people sleeping in the hall grows larger as tent pegs are ripped from the earth and lean-tos are blown away by the wind. The food hall leaks in places. As Flinch sleeps, the monotonous drip of water hitting the table nearby soaks through into his subconscious and he drifts off towards the whaling station, the thick drops of blood from a dead whale staining his dreams red.

The morning is dank with a drizzle that casts a

silver sheen over the commune. Reflections are everywhere, in puddles that have formed on the uneven
ground, in the ridges of aluminium sheeting. The
whole commune covered with mirrors, begging a
second look at what remains. Many tents are no more
than bundles of canvas on the ground, water collected
between their creases. All of the lean-tos are gone.
Chickens pick through what remains of the vegetable
gardens, where stakes lie prone on the ground and
lettuce leaves are flattened under the mud. Children
dance around the edges of the largest puddle, splashing
each other.

People wander with grim faces, kick the ground,
scratch scalps and rub their chins into points. Someone
organises a search party of sorts for the pieces of wood
and rope and canvas that the storm has redistributed
across the commune. From inside one of the tents, a
woman and a baby cry in pitiful unison. More than
ever, thinks Flinch, they look like they have been
washed up here, as if they are clinging to the smashed
remains of some wreck. Searching for something of
value among the débris that the tide brings to shore.
There's that ragged look to some of them this morning
that Flinch guesses is caused by a long-worn hope of
rescue. Others are laughing. Stacking wood. They're a
motley bunch, thinks Flinch. Everybody seems to
expect something different from commune life.

Drew's tent has remained intact. He emerges
from it and whistles.

'Bastard of a storm! Reminds me of this one we had in 'Nam.'

He pauses, waits for a reaction from the few people searching the ground around his tent for their washed-away belongings. They ignore him. He retreats to his tent. Flinch hears him talking loudly to himself.

'You couldn't have seen it coming,' he is saying.

Karma is wringing her clothes out. The dye trickles dirty purple over her hands and down her arms. Her feet are stained with it.

'Everything got wet,' she says. Offers a small, sour smile.

'At least your tent is standing.'

'Yes, I guess.'

She still looks drenched. Her hair is hanging in heavy clumps down her back. Her beads have left a brownish stain around the sides of her neck.

'I'm going away,' says Flinch. 'But you can stay at the house, if you want. Until you, um, dry out. Maybe. If you want.'

'Can't now, really. I had better stay around and try to fix up this place.'

She cocks her head to one side and breathes in deeply, stares at him with an intensity that disquietens him. 'It's funny, isn't it? It's like the elements set out to destroy the place. I mean, look at the other paddocks around here. They didn't get hit in the same way. Maybe we're being sacrilegious in some way, or some-thing, trying to create our little haven. Just about everything has to be built again.' She sighs. 'It seems almost intentional.'

Flinch sees a heaviness settle upon her. The weight of some unwelcome epiphany.

'Nah,' he says quickly.

She shrugs and returns to wringing out her clothes.

'Nah,' he says again, clearing his throat. 'It was just a storm.'

TEN

After even this brief time away, the pastel house smells stale and damp when Flinch opens the door. He shoves open the windows. A sea breeze lifts the curtains and they flutter like wings.

In the fridge a green fur has grown over the top of some half-eaten dish he had left in there on a plate. The milk has soured. He pours it down the sink and runs the tap, the faucet coughing up fluid like an old man.

He knows Audrey had a suitcase. She'd packed it once in front of him when he was ten or so. He had asked where she was going and she hadn't answered him. She was in a blind rage. A perfume bottle hit the edge of the case when she threw it, bounced and smashed on the floor, but she hadn't even noticed. The room reeked with the musky scent of her emotion. The perfume sweet and sickly, Flinch faint with nausea. She hadn't packed any of his things. He left a pair of undies and a fresh shirt and a pair of shorts near the doorway to her room. She stepped on them, not noticing, the imprint of her stiletto in the soft material.

She had put the case near the front door. She only made it as far as the couch. She left for the night via a bottle of whisky, but the case stayed and so did she, and Flinch put himself to bed in the knowledge that she'd be there in the morning. There was comfort in that.

He finds the suitcase on top of the wardrobe in Audrey's room. The buckles are rusted but they snap open with a loud clunk when he presses them. He packs a few singlets, a couple of long-sleeved checked flannel shirts. Also the only pair of jeans he has that fit him, ones that a shop assistant had altered just for him, so that the left cuff didn't drag on the ground getting filthy and worn like his other pairs.

He takes his copy of *Moby-Dick*, the photo of Audrey, and the piece of paper that they'd found in Nate's belongings. Yellowed and as thin as a single layer of skin, now. But he can still read the writing. *Eleanor. Duchess, QLD, 4825.*

'Duchess,' Flinch had repeated, when Nate had said where he was from. 'Sounds posh.'

Nate had snorted into his beer, sent specks of foam flying. 'Posh isn't a word that springs to mind, mate.'

'Where is it?'

'Back of Bourke. Really. Old Burke and Wills went through there on their godforsaken journey. It's near Mt Isa.'

'Is it nice?'

'It's a shithole.'

'Some people just don't suit their hometowns,' Macca had added.

'I never had what you'd call a home there,' said Nate, and downed his glass.

Flinch knows he can't take Milly. He isn't exactly sure where Mt Isa is, but he's sure it's too far for her. On his way home from the commune, he stopped in town and bought a bus ticket that will get him to Brisbane, and from there he'll take a train to Townsville, then a connection to Mt Isa. He'll have to find his way to Duchess from there. He's not sure how, just yet. He figures he'll worry about it when he gets there. Flinch is usually one for planning. Not the type to venture into the unknown. But this time he has a purpose. He's on a mission. He thinks of himself dressed in black. Maybe with a cape. Like a cartoon hero, arriving on the scene to put things right. He slings his suitcase into the ute and drives to Macca's place.

Mrs McTavish is in the backyard when he pulls up outside their house. It's a worker's cottage, one of the old ones that sit only steps from the road, their verandas almost on the footpath, houses that were built before traffic noise and passers-by were considered a nuisance. When all you would want was to get to work and back with as little walking as possible. From the footpath, there's a gap along the side of the house paved with an uneven concrete pathway. Yellowing weeds sprout between the cracks. The path leads to a Hills hoist. Mrs McTavish is hanging clothes. The sea breeze lifts her hem, revealing stockings that end just below dimpled, spongy knees.

'Flinch, love!' she cries when she sees him. The basket at her feet full of Macca's sopping wet underwear, singlets with yellow stains under the arms. 'Pet, how are you?'

'Yeah, good, Mrs Mac,' he says.

'And how's the leg?' She says *leg* in a whisper, screwing up her nose a little.

'It's fine, no trouble.'

'Oh, that's good to hear. We haven't seen you over here for so long. Are you going to stay for lunch? I've got sausages. Plenty of them.'

It is a hot morning and she is sweating. Flinch imagines her perspiration dripping into the frying pan, sizzling in the oil with the sausages.

'Thanks, Mrs Mac, but I can't. I've got to get on my way. I'm going on a trip.'

'Oh, how lovely! Where are you off to?'

'Queensland.'

'Now won't that be nice. I've heard there are some nice hotels up there.' She is sounding old, Flinch thinks. It has been a long time. Her hair is rinsed a purple-blue. Flinch can see grey roots and glimpses of her pink scalp underneath.

'Er, yeah,' says Flinch. 'Anyway, I was wondering if I could leave my ute here until I get back. I'm catching the bus and it's easier for me to walk from your place.'

'Of course, of course!' says Mrs McTavish. 'Anything we can do for you, love. You know, your mother was like a sister to me.' She pauses. 'Or maybe a cousin. We always said we'd look out for you.' Her smile contains the small trace of a grimace. She busies herself with hanging a singlet. Flinch knows Mrs Mac couldn't stand his mother. Audrey didn't make a lot of friends. But they kept up appearances, these women, clucked and cooed at each other like aviary birds when they walked past each other in the street, then hissed judgments to each other over weak cups of tea or after-noon nips of sherry. When Flinch came on the scene, though, Audrey discovered that the other women softened a little and so she brought him along to town fairs and picnics, propelling him in front of her as if he were her pass, her free ticket.

'Poor little angel,' the women would say. Stroke his hair.

'It's a handful, really, but you love them all the same, don't you? In fact, these ones need it even more,' Audrey would say, voice thick and syrupy with the tone of the martyr.

The women would nod. Invite her for tea and

cake. But eventually her bitter streak got the better of her and the invitations ceased, and not even Flinch looking pitiful in his leather and metal brace could convince the ladies to start offering them again.

The bus stop is near the train station. The trains from Sydney grind to a stop here. None continue into Queensland. Different states, different systems. Flinch has heard the width of the tracks isn't even the same size. Brisbane is closer to the bay than Sydney, but it's a disjointed bloody country, the roads out from the capital cities in every state look like rays from a sun. Nothing connects. The colonisers never imagined the roads ever would over such a vast dry land.

He sits on his suitcase in the shade of a fig tree. The dust around him rises when a car rattles past, but otherwise it is still. Across the road and down at the Great Northern, the television blares out racing commentary. Through the open veranda doors, as he walked past, Flinch had seen a couple of blokes perched on stools near the bar, beers and elbows resting on soggy towelling mats. They're in navy singlets and faded shorts that sag around their hips, revealing their bum cracks when they lean forward to put out their cigarettes in the ashtray. It's almost a uniform, in summer, for the working men around here. Flannelette shirts are about the only variation for winter. It's an hour until his bus departs, and Flinch is tempted to cross the road and down a schooner or two himself, but he is nervous about missing his ride; the bus might turn up early and leave without him, and he can't afford another ticket.

But the bus is late. When it finally shudders to a dusty halt at the side of the road, Flinch's buttocks are numb from sitting on his suitcase. He stands as the bus stops, and the driver snatches the case from him and throws it into the storage compartment with a thud. Flinch is grateful he didn't pack anything breakable.

'You need a hand getting on, mate?' the driver says when he notices Flinch hobbling towards the door.

'No, I'm right thanks, mate,' says Flinch. He takes extra care to lift his short leg high onto the bus steps, clings to the handrail.

The driver watches him in the rear-vision mirror. Waits until he's seated before taking off, the bus exhaling as the brake releases.

There are other passengers already on the bus. Must have come up from Sydney, Flinch decides. They've probably been crammed into their seats for over twelve hours. They don't pay any attention to him. Most of them have taken off their shoes, spread jackets over the seats next to them. Empty chip packets trapped against windows flutter and a soft drink bottle rolls around on the aisle floor. Some of the travellers are asleep. Most look dishevelled. Flinch tries to settle in.

At times like this, he's glad he's a small man. Nate, lanky and lean, would have had to fold himself twice over in a seat this size. Flinch wonders if he came to the bay this way, his knees jutting into the seat in front of him, his hair tangling in his sleep, waking whenever the bus braked.

The trip to Brisbane takes a few hours. The bus labours up over the hills, through the rainforest and farming communities, places with names like Mooball and Murwillumbah. They have a rest stop at the Gold Coast, at a terminal in Surfers Paradise. Flinch stretches his legs, instinctively walks towards the ocean. A cluster of shiny high-rises shadow the beach. It is late afternoon, but the sunbakers are still out, stretched bronze and oily on pastel towels. They look like plastic figurines. The whole place looks plastic, lurid aqua and pink painted buildings, lights and advertisements. Like a movie set, Flinch thinks. Somewhere designed to look bigger and brighter than itself, so that visitors can act however they want when they get here, because it's all fake, there's no connection to their real lives. He hurries back to the bus.

When they arrive in Brisbane, it is dark. Flinch hasn't been to the city. Any city. He asks the bus driver if he knows of a cheap hotel nearby. The bus driver snorts.

'They're all cheap around this part of town, son. The nicer ones are in the centre. Cost you a few bucks in a cab if you want to head in there.'

'No,' says Flinch. 'Something round here is fine. I have to be on a train tomorrow.'

'Righto, then. Try the Grandview across the road. They usually have a good rate going for travellers.'

Flinch takes his case from the bus and drags it down the stairs. The hotel is directly across the road from the bus centre so it's easy for him to get to, though as he stands at its entrance he wonders why they named it the Grandview. It's not grand, would never have been, and the only view is of the road and the grey stucco side of another building. The lobby smells of old cigarettes and mouldy carpet. Behind the reception desk, a large copper clock ticks loudly, the time on it wrong.

The room is much the same. There had been only smoking rooms left, and Flinch can smell the years of accumulated exhalations on the blankets and the upholstered headboard. The stale ghosts of other travellers.

He doesn't venture into the city. For dinner he orders a cheese and tomato toasted sandwich, which costs him four times as much as it usually does and arrives cool and soggy with a wilted piece of parsley on the side. He unlocks his case and takes out his pyjamas. Crawls into the bed exhausted, but can't get to sleep. He takes out the crumpled piece of paper with Nate's address on it, and flattens it between his palms, fingering it for clues as to how he will find Nate's mother. If she is still there, in Duchess. If she's still alive.

Eventually he falls asleep with the bedside lamp on, the piece of paper crunched in his fist.

He arrives two hours early for his train, the wait before him on the empty platform stretching out interminably like a blank page, but he had been forced to check out of his room at the Grandview and he didn't trust the desk clerk enough to leave his suitcase at the reception and venture into town for what the clerk described as 'a little look around'. Even from a distance, Flinch is overwhelmed by the gleaming high-rise office buildings, the cars jammed nose to tail at red lights, the commuters that stream out of the train station with dark, shiny suits and hard eyes.

The train slides into the station with a metallic hiss. Flinch, aboard, is relieved to find the seats more spacious than on the bus. He settles himself into one. Exhausted, with nowhere that he has to be for the next twelve or so hours, he sleeps.

When he wakes, it is dusk. The train rockets through fields of sugar cane, the setting sun turning the tips of the stalks pink. A food trolley is on its way up the carriage, and he buys himself a cup of milky tea and ham sandwiches that taste bland and stale. He feels suddenly homesick for the bay, and wonders what is happening at the little pastel house now. He left a bowl of water out for the goats. A little unnecessary, he knows, they're hardy and resourceful and would survive regardless, but he wanted to connect himself to something there. To something living, something that would remember him. Barrelling along through this foreign landscape, he feels as if his ties to the bay are being stretched too far. He anticipates the snap, the flick and the sharp recoil of them breaking and he huddles in his seat.

There is a dinner service on the train. Meals served in rectangular aluminium containers. He peels the cardboard lid off to reveal stringy grey meat swimming in watery gravy. A few hard whitish peas and a potato. He isn't hungry but he eats it all anyway. It's something to do. He stays awake until late. If he presses his forehead against the window he can see the outline of mountains, the silhouettes of trees like dark figures lurking. If he sits back he sees only his reflection, distorted, pale and worried, a face he doesn't recognise as his own. When he falls asleep, the rocking movement of the train results in dreams of being on a boat, of washing up on a shore lined with broken bottles, all of which contain notes with the names of men lost at sea and their last words, the things they wanted to say to lovers, mothers, brothers. He finds himself again at the lighthouse, and again he is not alone. He turns this time to see the lighthouse keeper filling his pipe. He smells the rich scent of tobacco. The lighthouse keeper points at the lighthouse and it flashes a brilliant white light.

Flinch wakes with a jolt.

The train has stopped.

'Nothing to be concerned about,' the conductor

is saying, walking up and down the carriage like an army major. 'Just a routine stop. You're not going anywhere yet.'

Flinch covers himself with a blanket and goes back to sleep.

At Townsville, there is more waiting. Six hours in the middle of the day. The air is heavy with humidity. Tastes salty. Flinch imagines that if he stretched his hands out in front of him and wrung them, water would fall at his feet. He sweats constantly. He can smell his own body odour. He fumbles around in his suitcase for a while before he finds his deodorant, spends half an hour in the men's toilets with his shirt off, trying to freshen up, but even the cold tap runs hot.

He buys a magazine on boating and fishing at the station kiosk. It's out of date by a month. He reads an article on man-made lures. Makes a note to try to make one when he returns to the bay, maybe ask Macca to try it out when he goes deep-sea fishing. There are advertisements for speedboats and yachts, women in bikinis sprawled across the bows, sipping champagne. Flinch wonders if such a world exists anywhere. Or if people are so easily sold on the concept of paradise. He thinks of the commune and wonders how they are managing, whether they have recreated their Eden. He remembers Karma saying it was paradise, but he didn't see it himself. And he was glad. If he discovered a paradise, he'd distrust it, something so one-dimensional, just as he distrusted Surfers Paradise with its lurid

colours and flashy neon promises. He wonders why she
wants it to be that way so desperately. There are people
at the commune who are palpably happy. Joyous, even.
They look relaxed and fulfilled, brimming with their
convictions. They see the commune as an alternative to
a life crammed behind a picket fence in the suburbs,
only talking to their neighbours when there's been a
crime in the street. They're the ones who have already
spent a bit of time hanging around on the beaches in
Goa, smoking dope and dressing in saris. The commune is just the way they have decided to live. They
accept that it has its limitations and its triumphs.

But Karma, Flinch has noticed, isn't one of
them. She looks like she's arrived there to get away
from something else, not drawn to the commune but
chased in. Hiding in the orange glow of her tent,
feverish to heal. Or to be healed. He wants to believe
she is interested in his company but suspects with an
instinct for truth that her insistence on healing him is
just another distraction from whatever is going on
inside her.

Mt Isa, burning metal and dust. Flinch stands at the exit
from the train station and sees the towers from the
mines rising up out of the city like smoking sentinels.
Mining cranes hover over the gashes in the distant
landscape like long-necked vultures. He doesn't want

to spend much time here. Nate's father had worked here, Nate had said, but they didn't live in Mt Isa, his old man preferring a dirt-cheap mortgage and an excuse to spend the working week away from his family, the evenings drinking and whoring in town. Not that Nate had cared anyway, he said; it was a rough place back then. Part oasis, part open wound. Established by a lonely fossicker who had ridden into the place on a horse called Hard Times, the nag's name like some self-fulfilling prophecy for the town for much of its settlement. It's a more prosperous place now that the bigger mines are set up. The miners do well and promise their wives just another year, just another year. During the day, the women sit in front of fans and water the wilting palm trees in their front gardens, work the cafes and pubs and hospitals, serve drinks and sew fingers back onto bloodied fists. Bar brawls in the rougher pubs become legend, something to aspire to on the weekends. There's a bit of spare cash to be had up here, for those willing to stick it out.

Duchess, Nate said, was a scab on the town's behind, in comparison.

Flinch finds a place that will rent him a car just a short walk from the train station. The girl behind the counter sizes him up and asks him to produce his licence twice before she lets him have the keys. He's hired a little Datsun. It was the most he could afford and the girl behind the counter assures him it will make the journey.

'It's not that far,' she says. 'Not much at the end of the road, though.' She sniffs and wipes her nose on her arm.

'How do I get there?' Flinch asks.

'Take the Duchess road.' The girl looks at him like he's got brain damage.

Flinch has brought a block of wood to tie to the clutch, like he does with Milly, and he waits until the girl has left him alone with the car before he digs through his suitcase to find it. He straps it in place with his belt. His pants hang loose around his hips and when he gets into the car the hot vinyl sears his bare lower back.

He winds down the window. There's a map in the glove box and he sweats while he marks the roads of his journey with a red marker he brought especially for the purpose. The Datsun, to his delight, starts straight away when he turns the key in the ignition.

The country out here is dry and red. Spinifex and pale gums shimmer silver above the soil. The nests of termites rise out of the ground in the shapes of witches' hats and stooped men, some of them double the height of Flinch. On the side of the road, and often in the middle, roadkill in various states of decay is splattered, fur and blood and bone one big sizzling mess on the gravel. Crows feast on the hot meat like diners at a banquet, cuss and flap reluctantly to the side of the road when the Datsun passes.

It takes him just over two hours to get to Duchess. The road is hard going on the Datsun and the car is hot and shuddering a little by the time Flinch arrives. Flinch wonders if the girl at the car hire place has ever been out here. There is nothing much of Duchess. Nobody is around. He parks outside the pub. The dust is still rising around him when he gets out of the car.

He is the only person in the pub. He waits quietly propped against the bar for twenty minutes or so before he clears his throat and jangles his keys. A grey-haired woman wanders out from a back room behind the bar. She's in a singlet that is stretched over saggy breasts and a gut like a man's, a tea towel over one shoulder, a startled look on her face.

'How long have you been here?' she says.

'A bit,' says Flinch.

'You need to sing out,' she says. 'We don't get a lot of drop-ins.'

Flinch nods and puts his keys in his pocket.

'Beer?'

'Yeah, ta,' says Flinch.

The woman slams on a tap and the beer frosts the glass as it is poured.

'A buck,' she says. She puts the beer in front of Flinch and he hands over the note, takes a long, hard gulp of his drink, empties it and puts it in front of her. She refills it.

'Passing through?' she asks.

'Kind of. I'm actually looking for someone who lives around here.'

'Well I know most. Who you after?'

'The Wests,' he ventures.

'Wests. Aw yeah.' The woman waits.

Flinch drinks his pot and orders another.

'The Wests live on a little place just a bit further up. Follow the road you're on, turn right at the first dirt road and then take your second left. It's the place with the green roof. White paint, what's left anyway. You from the hospital?'

'No,' says Flinch.

'From palliative care?'

'Er, no. I'm an old friend of the family.'

The woman grunts.

'Yeah, well, don't be expecting to be too long out there. The old man isn't up for much these days, doesn't have much energy for anything.' She lifts her eyebrows. 'Might be a bit different from the way you remember him, eh?'

'Yeah,' says Flinch. 'Thanks.'

'No worries. Good luck.'

'Ta,' says Flinch. He puts a five-dollar note on the bar as he leaves.

ELEVEN

Flinch follows the woman's directions, the dust from the dirt road billowing behind the car, clouding his rear-vision mirror. The trees grow sparse, the ones still out here greying in the leaves. Along the way he passes a few small weatherboard houses on stilts, a rotting wooden and corrugated iron shed. But at the end of the road the woman described, he sees the house and knows it must be the one. Cracked green roof, white paint flaking like sunburn to reveal the pale, worn timber underneath. The rusted bodies of two vehicles are in the front yard. A truck of some sort and an old Hillman. Next to them lie dismantled engines, bolts and wires, bits and pieces of twisted metal, as if they have been gutted and left on display as some sort of warning. Flinch drives past the place slowly and pulls up a few hundred metres further on. He hasn't thought about exactly what he will say to Nate's parents, and realises now he is here that they too may blame him for Nate's death, even if he doesn't confess to it.

The beer has made him light-headed and he needs to pee. He gets out of the car and stumbles over to some nearby shrubs. As the spray lands on them, a scorpion darts out from underneath the shrubs and scuttles away. A crow caws overhead. There is, though, mostly silence, as if layers of dust have settled over everything, weighed down all signs of life. Flinch wonders how Nate spent his time here. Can't picture him in this environment, all his anxiety and energy like a whirlwind in this still dirt corner. The pages of his books browning with the soil on his fingers.

He returns to the car and reverses the entire way back up the dirt road until he is outside the house. The dust rushes into the car's open window, almost choking him, making his eyes water. He pulls the handbrake harder than necessary when he stops. He has to brush himself off when he gets out. Spits into the palms of his hands and rubs them through his hair. He walks up the pathway to the house quickly, taking the biggest steps he can manage, so that he doesn't have time to think about what he's doing and turn around.

The house sits slightly off the ground, but the steps to the veranda have decayed. Off to the side, there is a makeshift ramp, a couple of planks of wood nailed to the veranda. Flinch walks up them sideways to keep his balance. The front door is unlocked and hinged back. The screen door appears shut, but it moves slightly with the wind, clicking in and out of its latch.

Flinch knocks on the wall to the side of the door. Hurts his knuckles, makes little sound.

'Hello there,' he calls in through the screen.

There is no answer.

He tries to make out what lies behind the screen, but all he can see is a dark hallway. An umbrella stand with a woman's dress hat hanging from it, a cardboard box with a white label on the side. In the next doorway, into what he assumes is the living room, streamers of coloured plastic hang fluttering in the breeze. To keep flies out, he gathers. It gives the place the feeling of a deserted carnival. He can't see what is beyond them.

He waits a while at the door before making his way back down the ramp. He stands looking at the house for a minute or two, and then decides to wander around to the back, in case someone is outside. The backyard is barren of any grass, just packed earth and, at one edge, taking advantage of a leaky garden tap, a sprawling lantana bush. There's a twisted clothes line, cords snapped and trailing on the ground. Another engine, tipped on its side, the metal glinting in the sunlight where it hasn't rusted. The sour smell of the lantana plant carried to him on the breeze. This isn't what he wanted for Nate. Not this place for his childhood. He had wished for him afternoon games of cricket, school friends who teased and laughed and swam in watering holes, a kitchen that smelt of roasting chook and apple tarts. A lush green backyard littered with toy trucks and plastic soldiers that sank into the lawn, footballs and a mother who tended scraped knees with the sting of Betadine, a kiss and a band-aid. He doesn't know why he dreamt these things up for Nate.

Behind him, a door clicks and he sees a shadow recede up a hallway. The steps to the back veranda are rickety but still there and he makes his way up them, expecting them to splinter. There is a screen door here, too, the screen torn in one corner, flopped over itself as if drooping in the heat.

'Is anyone home?' Flinch calls into the cool dark inside of the house.

'Coming.' A woman's voice. It makes Flinch catch his breath.

He hears her talking to someone, furniture being scraped across a hard floor, a man's raised voice.

'Yes?'

She hovers in the shadow just inside. She is in a dressing gown. Greying hair in a bun. She is thin, like Nate; he can see her collarbone protruding below a wrinkled neck, and her fingers, all knuckle. In the mother he can see Nate's jittery, bird-like demeanour, the fusion of nerves and expectations. It's harder in her, though, more like sinew, as if she has been whittled down to pure anxiety.

'Hello,' he says.

'What do you want?'

'Could I come inside for a moment? I have some news for you.'

She moves closer to the door.

'We don't need any religion.' She is fiddling with the top button of her dressing gown. It is hanging from a thread, about to snap off.

'Oh ... no, that's not why I'm here.'

'We won't buy anything. And we don't have money or valuables here either.'

'I just have some news to tell you,' says Flinch, desperate. He doesn't want to say what he has to say out here, separated from her by the screen, exposed and dusty and sweating in the heat.

The woman shrugs and steps back.

'Well, alright.' She opens the door and it swings inwards on one hinge.

'Thank you,' says Flinch.

She turns her back on him and wanders down the hall into the living room and he follows. He sits on the couch, sinking into it and feeling a broken spring under his thigh. Yellowing lace doilies cover the headrests. On the wall, three chipped china ducks in decreasing sizes fly east. There are only a few pieces of furniture in the room. A rocking chair stacked with teddy bears. A coffee table with plastic legs and a fake wood veneer. Kewpie dolls in pink mesh tutus, the kind Flinch has seen dangling from sticks at fetes and fairs, line the windowsill. On the mantelpiece, a broken model plane and a candlestick, a few framed photos. The room is airless and congested. It smells to Flinch of urine and musty piles of newspapers. He has a sense of things trapped. The still ducks on the wall. Dust suspended in the air where the sun cuts to the floor with a beam.

'Do you want a cuppa? Was making one anyway.' The woman is hovering near him.

'Yes, that would be very nice.'

'How do you have it?'

'White with one.' The woman wanders back to the kitchen.

'Thank you,' he calls after her.

Flinch gets up to take a closer look at the photos on the mantelpiece. One photo is of the finish of a horse race. The horse coming second has been circled with red pen. Underneath the photo the caption, *1st Mighty High, 2nd Stormin' In, 3rd Janey's Surprise, Mt Isa Country Cup, 10th October 1964*. Next to that, a photo of Nate. He's only about eight years old, but Flinch recognises him straight away, the long legs with pro-truding knees, the chin jutting out and up at a defiant angle. Squinting straight into the sun. There's another one of a younger Nate, nursing a toddler, a small girl, her hair in tiny curled blonde pigtails.

'My children,' says the woman. She takes a seat in a worn, pilled armchair that groans when she leans back. Her dressing gown, faded paisley, slips apart to reveal flaky, mottled calves and white socks under ruby-red slippers. She smells like mothballs and potpourri. He suspects she wears this every day. Even in the heat. She has placed Flinch's tea on the coffee table.

'So what can I do for you?'

Flinch clears his throat. He sits perched on the couch. He wishes he could be closer for this, be in reach of her hand, ready with a handkerchief.

A dull buzz sounds from the bedroom. The woman sighs.

'Wait,' she says. 'Excuse me.'

She walks up the hallway, the hard soles of her slippers making a clacking noise on the floorboards. The buzzing stops. She returns a moment later.

'My husband,' she says. 'Has Alzheimer's. Not long to go, they reckon. But he didn't want to die in the hospital. The nurses wouldn't let him have even a nip of booze in there.' She chuckles.

'I'm sorry,' says Flinch.

'What can you do?' She shrugs. He can read no emotion on her.

'What … what about your children?' He doesn't know how he will tell her now, here in this place where things seem forever stagnant, the dying husband in the bedroom up the hall.

'Oh, they're fine, I guess. Haven't seen either for a long time.'

Flinch swallows but his throat and mouth remain dry. Thinks of the letter the priest said he would write and wonders if he had bothered sending it — or, if he did, who mistakenly received it, who opened it then shrugged it all off as a bad joke.

'Those kids knew how to take care of themselves.'

She's not looking at him. She's gazing out the window, towards the lantana.

She sighs. It seems to come from some place so deep within her that Flinch is worried that exhaling will exhaust her.

'Anyway,' she says. 'The past is the past. Can't do anything about it, can you? There's no point trying to change things now.'

'No,' he says, though he knows it wasn't a question.

'No,' the woman repeats. Nods towards the photograph of the children. 'Nate knew that anyway. Elly had other ideas.'

Elly. Eleanor.

'His sister,' Flinch says out loud, before he can stop himself. His hand starts to shake and his teacup rattles against the saucer so hard that he fears it may chip, but he can't stop himself. He puts it down on the coffee table. Stares at the photo, the children clutching each other. Nate's arm around the girl's waist. The forced grins for the camera. Not happy children, he can see that.

'What do you want?' The mother. She is looking at him with palpable suspicion. Says it almost in anger, turning on him. He realises he has been sitting in silence for one moment too long.

'Oh,' says Flinch. The confession now seems all wrong, the woman as sharp and brittle as dried bone. 'I was just wondering, have you, if you, do you need insurance?'

The woman bursts out laughing, spits her tea into her saucer.

'What would we insure? Look around you, son.'

'Sorry to bother you.' He is desperate to leave now. The atmosphere of the house has settled upon him like an itch that he cannot scratch.

'No problem. Nice to have a visitor for a change.' It's sarcasm, perhaps, but Flinch can't decide.

He hurries down the hallway.

'You didn't bring a briefcase,' the woman yells after him from the living room. 'They usually bring a briefcase. Who are you? What do you want?'

The screen door slams shut behind him. He waits for the sound of her slippers up the hallway, pursuing him, but she does not.

He needs to double over outside the house to catch his breath, leans against a wall. Through the open window nearby he can hear the buzzer sound, then snatches of a conversation.

'Was it him?' An old man's voice, out of breath, the pain sounding like a blade stuck in his throat.

'It wasn't him, you delirious fool,' the woman replies. 'It will never be him. You had your chance. Go to sleep.'

The man whimpers in short wet breaths, as a child might.

On the way back to Mt Isa, Flinch pushes the Datsun as fast as he can make it go. It shudders over the gravel, makes crackling noises, small stones fly up to hit the underside. Just outside of town he takes a bend at speed and, before he can brake, hits a kangaroo that is bounding lazily across the road in front of him. There's a loud dull thud and the Datsun is launched over the body of the animal as if it were as solid as a speed bump. The car spins out of control on the gravel and comes to rest inches from a tree. Flinch sits shaking in the front seat until he notices that half an hour has passed. He turns the key in the ignition and, to his relief, the Datsun starts. He drives slowly back to the site of the accident, stalls the car twice because his legs are still wobbly, his hands sweaty on the wheel.

The animal is lying by the side of the road. Flinch gets out, leaves the car door open, the engine idling in neutral. He stumbles over to the kangaroo. Its body is intact; its back legs, though, are squashed and bloodied. It's still warm, breathing in and out slowly, its eyelids half closed, long dark lashes covering its eyes. Blood trickles from its nostrils. Flinch looks around for a large rock, lifts it above his head and throws it down hard on the kangaroo's skull. The animal jolts and then it is still. The ribcage ceases to rise and fall. Flinch sits down next to it, knees up to save his thighs from burning on the gravel, and sobs into the crook of his elbow.

NATE

Breathing becomes difficult but I know not to panic. Many times, swimming in the surf, I've been held under water by the pressure of a wave. As soon as I overcame the urge to struggle, the wave would inevitably disgorge me nearer to shore. But that's not where I learnt to control myself.

Even now, I can feel the exact pressure of his hands around my neck, smell the foul stench of the whisky as he spat threats into my face.

Breathe.

Breathe.

I was the distraction so I had to stand still and take it. If I fought him off, and God only knows I could by then, such was the strength of the anger he'd nurtured in me, he'd go for someone weaker. He wanted to dominate. Mum knew to crumple in a corner and take the odd kick up her skirt or slap around the head with little more than a whimper.

Eleanor fought back.

The first time he struck her, she was only twelve. He was very sorry, he said. He cried for days after he sobered up. When he begged her, Eleanor sat on his lap and let him dampen the shoulder of her school blouse with his tears and regret. Never again, he said. He realised, he said, that he was out of control. He had a problem.

He was good for about a month afterwards. All of us crept about the house as if it were a minefield, wondering when the next bomb would detonate, what would set him off. When Mum dropped a teacup and it smashed on the kitchen floor, we froze. 'Better clean that up,' my father said, without putting down his paper. This subdued reaction was discussed at length in the lantana.

But things were back to normal again after payday.

He didn't go for Eleanor often, but it was when I thought he was going to that I stepped in, took him on. Let him win.

Our focus became clearer; we plotted our escape with extravagant plans mapped out on pieces of butcher's paper and in the back pages of school exercise books.

Mum couldn't wait that long. One afternoon, before he came home, she told us to get our toothbrushes and ushered us down the street. We slept that night in the church in town, stretched out on mattresses underneath the pews. The church had stained-glass windows and one depicted Adam and Eve in the Garden of Eden. A lamb was asleep next to a lion. Birds flew in a dazzling blue sky. In the background, a green snake was wrapped around an apple tree. When the sun rose the next morning, the window lit up and coloured reflections covered our bare legs like a quilt.

'That's where I want to live,' said Eleanor.

That same morning, my father was waiting outside the church in his Sunday best.

'Best come home, eh, love?' he said.

Mum heard the threat and nodded.

'Are you sure, dear?' said the minister's wife.

'I just needed a little break,' said my mother.

'If you need us again…'

'They won't,' my father answered.

Breathe.

Hang in there, be brave, *someone is telling me. Empty words, hollow words, like wind pipes. Just statements through which to blow noise so that there isn't silence. Be brave.*

I'd like to say that I am, but I know the truth. If I was brave I would've killed him. But instead I left. Mum and Eleanor stood on the steps crying and hugging. My father didn't come outside when my mate's truck pulled up to take me into town. I saw his silhouette in the living-room window as we drove off.

I left Eleanor my pocket knife and some of my savings. I promised to write.

I took jobs wherever I could. Picked fruit. Loaded boxes off trucks and onto boats at the wharf. Chucked bins onto garbage trucks. Cleared empty beer glasses from tables. Shot wild pigs and culled kangaroos. And somehow ended up here. Butchering whales.

There was a girl in one of the towns. I moved on before it got too serious. I was my father's son, after all, and I didn't want to love somebody so much that I would end up hurting them. I wish I could remember her name now.

Blood dribbles into my ear and fills the cavity. I think it's coming from my mouth. I can no longer hear what they're saying to me.

I sent Eleanor almost half of every pay packet I earned during that time. More than anything I wanted her to escape too. I knew I would never be free of our childhood. I can kill a whale with little remorse, but seeing a bruise on a woman still makes my stomach turn. Eleanor has a chance, though. She could start again, make a place for herself. Build herself a whole new world.

Colour has leaked from my world. I am the black and white photograph of myself that my father took when I was seven. Grazed knees, long socks, missing teeth, a rugby ball under one arm. Hair the texture of a toilet brush, spiked thick and straight despite a palmful of Brylcreem and a wet comb. Squinting into the solid afternoon glare.

The whale is dead. Her massive pectoral fin is flipped upright, extended, so that I can see its pure white underside. It looks like the wing of an angel.

Somewhere around me, someone is reciting the Lord's Prayer over and over.

But this is what I know by heart. Words from a letter I kept folded in a shirt pocket and read nightly, like a vigil.

Dear Nate,

Well, darl, hope this letter finds you well. Would like to say things have changed around here but you probably already know they haven't much. I am out of the house more, have a job at the service station, that one on the way out of town. Just work behind the hot food counter serving sausage rolls etc to truckies. The Old Bastard thinks I am there every day after school but really I am there for two afternoons and Saturday morn and the other days I go to the library to study. That was the plan, wasn't it, get the hell out of here and uni looks like the way to go. So far am doing really well at Gr 11 biology and chemistry so think I'll apply for vet science tho' don't know if I could put down someone's dog but guess that's life isn't it and there'd be good things as well like healing wild animals etc.

Well had better go. Mum would say hello I'm sure, she is very distressed that she doesn't know where you are and talks about you quite a bit and I say you are probably alright but don't want to give away that I know about this p.o. box or anything. The Old Bastard isn't well these days, seems to be losing his edge. Either way it makes him easier to ignore when he's too tired to start anything. Probably rotting from the inside out.

My brother I love you and I miss you and I will come and join you one day soon, just be sure to keep letting me know where you are. I haven't heard from you for a while but you are probably out having adventures either way I hope this letter gets to you. All my love, Eleanor. XX

Well, darl
Thy kingdom come
Thy will be done
That was the plan, wasn't it
On earth as it is in heaven
Give us this day our daily bread
Serving sausage rolls etc to truckies
And deliver us from evil
For thine is the kingdom
My brother I love you and I miss you and I will come and
join you
The power and the glory
Either way I hope this letter gets to you
Forever and ever, Amen.
Eleanor.

TWELVE

Flinch drops the car back in Mt Isa and returns the keys. The girl comes out to inspect it.

'Bit of stone damage,' she says. Flinch nods. She doesn't notice the blood splattered along the chassis. She probably thinks it is mud. He doesn't mention it.

'Boss won't mind that, though. Have to break in these cars on the country roads sometime, hey.' She ticks a few boxes on the paper on her clipboard.

'Alright then. Here's your deposit back.'

Flinch crumples the notes into a pocket and heads for the train station.

He's missed the last train back to Townsville, but there's another one early in the morning. He sinks onto a bench. From his suitcase he takes a bundle of clothes and fashions a pillow at the end of the seat. He straps his belt through one of the belt loops on his pants, then through the handle of the case. If someone were to run off with it, they'd have to drag him along as well. Nate said it could be a rough old joint.

The ticket seller has to sweep before he goes off duty.

'Will you be right there, mate?' He talks to Flinch slowly, as if he suspects Flinch won't comprehend what he's saying. As if he's drunk or mad or slow or foreign.

'Yeah, mate, ta.'

'Righto,' says the ticket seller. Shuffles off. He brings Flinch a cup of steaming tea before he leaves. 'Leftovers from the flask.' Almost heartbroken with gratitude, Flinch makes it last an hour.

He sleeps lightly, waking often, but except for a rat rustling around in a plastic bag and the creaking of the tracks as they contract in the cool of night, there are no disturbances, nobody comes around. Dawn expands quickly along the concrete platform like a sheet of light unfolded. Flinch wakes groggy and disoriented in the early morning heat. The grille on the door to the men's bathroom is locked, so he wanders to the edge of the platform and relieves himself there, checking over his shoulder in case the ticket seller returns early. He wipes his hands on his trousers.

The trip home is a blur. He is in and out of trains, moping around under the fluorescent lights of bus centres, picking at hot chips that taste like stale oil. Surrounded, it seems, by entire families carting pillows and suitcases, children with sticky faces overtired and bawling, people napping upright, their heads lolling forward and back.

On the bus back to the bay, he shuts his eyes, but on the verge of sleep he is jolted awake by the image of the kangaroo, its mangled legs, the shock of the impact.

When the bus finally reaches the bay, dusk has settled pink-hued over the town. The streets are empty, the workers knocked off and home, the surfers eking out a ride on the last few waves before it gets too dark. Flinch breathes deeply of the sea air, the wind flecked with sand grit and the briny smell of the ocean. White gulls, fat on chips and fish batter, shriek and wheel overhead towards the lighthouse. He is home. For the first time in his life, it smells to him like a haven.

Macca answers the door when he knocks. Grunts.

'You made it back in one piece then.'

'Yeah, guess so.'

'Who is it?' calls Mrs Mac from inside. Flinch can smell grilled meat.

'Flinch,' Macca yells over his shoulder. 'Made it back in one piece.'

'Hooroo, darl! Hope you had a lovely trip?'

'Yeah,' calls Flinch. 'Yeah, I did thanks, Mrs Mac.'

'Where'd ya go?' Macca has his eyes half-closed, like he is expecting Flinch to lie.

'Duchess.'

'Duchess? That was where Nate was from, wasn't it?'

'Yeah.'

'Shit, eh. So what was it like?'

'Like he described it, pretty much.'

Macca sticks his bottom lip out and nods.

'You know someone else out there?'

'Nah,' says Flinch. 'I just wanted to see what it was like.'

'Why?'

'Change of scene. You know.'

Macca shrugs. 'Good a reason as any, I guess.'

'Yeah.'

'Fixed your ute up a bit. She's getting a bit long in the tooth, isn't she?'

'Thanks, Macca.'

'Yeah, no worries. Anytime.'

'Thanks.'

Macca sighs and scratches the back of his neck, inspects his fingernails afterwards and sniffs his fingers.

'I'd better get going,' says Flinch.

'Yeah, righto. Keys are in the ute. See you later, eh.'

'Yeah,' says Flinch. 'See ya.'

He is grateful to be able to climb into the sun-warmed creaking vinyl room of Milly's cabin. She chugs over reluctantly when he turns the key, but whatever Macca has done seems to have made a difference, because the engine doesn't sound like it is swallowing chunks of itself, clunking and rattling, like it did when he left her here. Macca's a good mate, he decides, in that don't-ask-don't-tell blokey kind of way. He stopped enquiring how Flinch was coping all these years after the repeated attempts at drawing Flinch out and the stoic rejections. So now he just has a go at fixing the obvious things Flinch leaves in his proximity. That's a gesture, though, from a man like Macca.

Flinch drives slowly through the town, along the beachfront road and up the hill towards the pastel house, windows wound down, savouring the familiarity of the journey, the grainy afternoon light, the eucalypts and banksias and horsetail oaks shadowing the road. When he pulls up outside the pastel house, Milly whirrs contentedly, as if she too recognises the place as home.

The door to the pastel house is rarely locked, but Flinch had bolted it when he left, after Karma said she wouldn't be staying. The lock is stiff, he has to lean against it, grunting, to unlock it. The door swings in rapidly when it opens and sends Flinch stumbling into the kitchen. He has to steady himself by grabbing the table. He pushes back the curtains, opens the windows. Outside he can hear the ocean roaring as it charges the shore. He gets himself a beer from the fridge — he had been sure to leave a sixpack in stock for his return — and settles himself on the couch. It is almost six pm. He turns on the radio. Static rolls like waves over the voice reading the news. Flinch sips at his beer. A goat wanders in the open door, takes a long look at Flinch and leaves again. Only halfway into his beer, Flinch settles into the couch and sleeps and sleeps and sleeps.

In the early hours he does not dream but is haunted by the reflections of his journey; an old man dying unseen, kewpie dolls in pink tutus, the sour scent of lantana, young Nate in sepia, the shadow that he cast over brown-grey fur as he lifted a rock above his head, the green blur of cane fields through a window. They run over and over like a reel of film, flipping in and out of order. He wakes still exhausted.

Even during wakefulness, without desire or conscious effort, he finds himself replaying the trip to Duchess in his head, scripting alternative endings, endings in which he confesses, in which the mother hugs and forgives him, in which the grown Eleanor arrives at the door and he is able to explain everything to the family with perfect clarity. Frustrated at the futility of these imaginings, he slips into the habit of waking up angry and staying that way for the entire day. When Milly won't start, he gets out and kicks her tyres. He chases the goats away with a rolled-up news-paper, and doesn't offer them the scraps from his meals anymore. When he leaves the house, they no longer follow him around the yard. They stand at a distance and stare at him with disapproving yellow eyes.

After dinner one night, he throws his plate across the room and it shatters against the wall, leaving a splatter of tomato sauce like the blood stain from a gunshot against the pale pink paint. He sits on the couch, stunned by his own action. Sauce dribbles thickly down the wall. Sharp-edged chunks of the plate lie upside down on the carpet. The house smells like burnt sausage.

He realises he is indulging his anger. Like Audrey did.

He had watched the anger and regret consume her as if she were its prey. Piece by bloody piece of her, ripping its way through bone and marrow. And he can feel the same things starting to consume him, in the same way. His heritage, the inherited failure. As if he is genetically predisposed to sorrow, the same way others end up with black hair or big ears.

He doesn't know what to do about it.

He contemplates, some nights, returning to Duchess and giving it another go — telling them, the ageing mother, the lost, whimpering father, that their son is dead. He wonders what Nate would have wanted. He flips open his copy of *Moby-Dick* the way faithful Christians flip open their Bibles, looking for hidden answers in the text, a message from Nate on the other side encoded in the prose.

On the first page he opens, he reads the lines: *Now, in general,* Stick to the boat, *is your true motto in whaling; but cases will sometimes happen when* Leap from the boat, *is still better.*

He thinks about this for a while, but can't work

out what it might mean. So he opens another page, and reads *But no more of this blubbering now, we are going a-whaling, and there is plenty of that yet to come.*

He has a sneaking suspicion that, even from beyond the grave, Nate is poking fun at him. He gets angry at that, too.

Flinch is not ready for her when she arrives bruised and swollen on his doorstep. He had slept in, woken thick-headed, the tang of last night's rum and cola still on his tongue. Made a cup of tea, wrung the tea bag out over the sink in a way that allowed him to feel like he was strangling it. He had chased the goats down the hill with yesterday's rolled-up newspaper. Lay around in the dinghy for a while in the middle of the day when the sun was at its wretched worst, his hat over his eyes, allowing lethargy to set in. Sun-dazed and burnt, he'd headed back into the house and was napping on the couch, the radio buzzing in the background, when she knocked.

'What happened?' His eyes crusty with sleep and sun, the afternoon hum of the hangover still in his head.

'Jed.'

'I thought he wasn't around much. I thought you didn't see him anymore.'

'Can I come in?'

She looks like she's been caught in a storm. Hair in knots, the pale lines of old tears still glinting metallic on her cheeks. Her left eye is swollen shut, the bruise around it no longer the blue-purple it would have been a few days ago. Now the green of mushy peas and hail clouds.

'Of course.' He steps back to let her through, and as she passes he feels the weight of her and more, how small she is, and brittle.

'What happened?' he asks again, though he can guess enough.

'We had an argument.'

'At the commune?'

'Yes.'

'Where were the others?'

'We were in my tent.' She sniffs and he hands her a tea towel. She blows her nose in it. Apologises.

'Why?'

'We kind of got back together. I thought he might have changed. I'm an idiot.'

'It's not your fault.'

'I, of all people, should know better.'

She is crying properly now and he is at a loss. This isn't like Audrey crying. She doesn't seem to want anything from him. At least, she's giving him no clues.

'Cuppa?' he asks finally. 'I'm making one.'

She nods.

'It's just plain old tea,' he says.

She offers a weak smile. 'That's okay,' she says. 'Thank you.'

He makes up the bed in Audrey's room, taking care to shake the dust out of the blankets and smooth down the quilt, but when he sneaks a peek through the crack in the door later in the afternoon, he can see she has collapsed on top of all the covers, fully clothed, one sandal hanging off her foot.

Flinch has been getting by on toast and potato chips for dinner, washed down with a tall bottle of beer. He has been eating out in the yard, sitting on the grass, looking out to the ocean as if scouring the horizon for some passing ship that might sail in and rescue him. Sometimes, in the fading light, he has seen the fins of sharks rise and sink mechanically like submarines, their dark shapes slide by the surfers out near the breaks. He doesn't call out to the surfers. They wouldn't hear him anyway. Perhaps wouldn't care. They sit astride boards with legs dangling, laughing and talking until a set rolls in and delivers them in a white foam closer to shore. Some of them get dumped, sprain ankles and wrists, but while Flinch watches there are no attacks, nothing happens.

He has, sometimes, thrown his leftover chips to the gulls that crowd around him, bickering and jostling like old pub brawlers for the best position. He's only done it a few times but they seem to know already to congregate around him when he comes out at that time in the evening.

Karma, he is sure, will want more than bread and fried potatoes for dinner. He scans the cupboard for supplies. There's a tin of baked beans and he figures that's about as good as it will get. When he hears her stir, he puts a saucepan on the stove. She emerges from the bedroom looking dazed, though she's brushed her hair and pulled it back into a bun at the nape of her neck.

'Beans on toast,' he says. He puts the plate in front of her, steam rising from it, and hands her a knife and fork. She eats without saying anything, scrapes the plate clean. He watches her from across the table.

'Aren't you eating yours?'

'Yeah, just waiting for them to cool a bit.'

She shrugs. 'That went down a treat. Thank you.'

'No worries,' says Flinch.

She goes to the bathroom. Flinch hears the toilet flush, then the shower running. She walks back through the kitchen wrapped in a towel, her bare shoulders glistening with drops of water, and Flinch can see she is hunched around herself, concave, her collarbones protruding. She shuts the door to Audrey's bedroom.

Flinch eats his beans. Retreats to the couch. He unscrews the cap from the rum bottle but doesn't pour anything into the tumbler. The radio whines with old songs of heartache. Somehow the house feels empty. Haunted, perhaps. And it is, thinks Flinch; but aren't all houses, sometimes even by the living?

Karma spends most days sleeping. She shuts Flinch out of the room, and Flinch, his ear pressed to the door, hears her crying softly, or snoring. He dutifully makes her breakfast and dinner, which she eats mechanically, always thanking him politely and then retreating into the shadows of the bedroom. She doesn't come out for lunch.

Forced out of his own funk of temper tantrums and frustration, Flinch is resentful, in a way, that she is the one who gets to be like this and that he has to look after her. He hadn't finished, with the anger, with the regret. But he suspects that if he doesn't feed her, she'll starve herself. He can see it in her, the determined apathy. Flinch runs out of bread and milk and beans and drives into town to buy some more.

He bumps into Macca at the store. He's buying bait. Lazy old bastard, thinks Flinch. They used to laugh at the out-of-towners who did that and it was an unspoken assumption that real fishermen found their own bait.

'G'day, Flinch.'

'Yeah, g'day, Macca.'

'Rumour has it you got yourself a girl.'

Flinch is startled. But it's a small town and he guesses Karma must have passed through here on the way to the pastel house, maybe asked for a ride. He hadn't asked her how she got there. He'd assumed she'd walked, but maybe she wasn't up to it.

'Not really.'

'What's *not really* mean? You either got a girl or you don't.'

'She's a friend,' says Flinch. 'She's just staying with me until she finds somewhere else.'

Macca gives him a knowing wink. 'Yeah, righto, mate.'

Flinch shifts his weight, feeling awkward, his back and shoulders suddenly aching with his involvement.

'Going fishing?' he says eventually.

'Yeah, y'know. Just getting out of the house. The missus.' Macca doesn't elaborate.

'What'd ya get?'

Macca looks embarrassed, as if he's been caught perusing the aisle that holds the porn magazines and condoms.

'Squid.'

'Aw, right. Heard where they're biting?'

Macca scratches his bum with his spare hand. 'Nah. Just thought I'd chuck a line in. Y'know.'

Flinch knows. In his self-imposed isolation, he has missed that sense of calm, the connection from self to the vast ocean by a near-invisible thread, casting as if to propel a life's worries into the waves, to be taken out on the tide. He guesses Karma would call it a cleansing ritual.

'Good luck, eh. Say hi to Mrs Mac.'

Macca snorts. 'Yeah, righto. See ya.'

On his way back through the town, Flinch notices a few changes. The hardware store has reopened as a surf shop. Sleek, gleaming boards are lined up neatly like soldiers inside the window. Most of the surfers who drive to the bay are from the cities down south. Articulate suburban boys with blonde fluff over their lips and on their chins. Uniformly sporting unbrushed hair to their shoulders, tight T-shirts and a well-rehearsed air of nonchalance. Wearing Speedos and thongs into the grocery stores when they get to the coast, as if this might help them fit in to the fishing villages. Blaring the Bee Gees and Neil Sedaka and the Rolling Stones from crackling car radios. Flinch avoids them. In the town the division between locals and tourists is as solid as a wall and both sides regard the other through peepholes in it. There are more people out on the street, peering in shop windows, eating ice-cream, laughing, holding the hands of children in swimming togs, plastic buckets and beach towels hung over arms and shoulders.

There's a breeze blowing in off the ocean and as Flinch looks around the streets he feels a slight shift, in himself maybe, or in the town, or both.

But on his return to the house, all he can sense is the staleness of her sorrow. The doldrums is what Nate used to call it. 'Slightly north of the equator,' he had said. 'Right smack bang between two trade winds.'

'I'm just a bit stuck,' Flinch had replied. Another exhausting round with Audrey the night before still upon him, wearing the blame like an overcoat, unable to shrug it off.

'Too right, and no wonder,' Nate had said. 'The doldrums are noted for extended periods of calm, when the winds completely disappear and sailing vessels are trapped for days, even weeks.'

'I'll be right,' said Flinch.

'You will,' Nate had said, leaning closer. 'Because despite overcast skies and high humidity, the pure discomfort of the place, hurricanes originate there. Big, powerful storms that churn away over entire oceans, and everything in their path is shattered by their might. That could be you, Flinch.'

Flinch didn't see it, but had nodded anyway.

'Cheers,' said Nate. 'Here's to the wind picking up.' They had clinked their beer glasses.

'You're in the doldrums,' he says to Karma that night when she is eating the dinner he's made her.

She pauses midway through her mouthful and looks up as if noticing him there for the first time. 'How funny that you should say that. Yes. Yes, I guess I am.'

Flinch grins. He can't help it. It's the most she's said to him in a week or two.

'Do you want to listen to the radio after? When you've eaten?'

'Okay,' she says. 'Can't hurt, can it?'

The radio has been on the same station all of Flinch's life. When Audrey was around, and since.

Flinch knows the schedule, when to tune in to get the news, the tide times, the golden oldies.

'Bit dull, isn't it?' says Karma, when Flinch has turned it on. She kneels in front of it and starts fiddling with the dials. The radio squeals and hisses and Flinch feels something akin to panic.

'Oh,' says Karma, homing in on a new station, 'Simon and Garfunkel. I love them, don't you?'

'Yeah,' says Flinch. 'They're great.' But he's not sure who they are or whether he loves them.

They sit sipping tea for a while, Karma cross-legged on a cushion on the floor, staring through the window at the darkening sky, Flinch slumped awkwardly on the far end of the couch.

'I had to leave, you know,' she says, when the song on the radio ends. Flinch turns down the volume. 'Did they ask you to?'

'They? The others? No. I just couldn't stay.'

'Because of Jed? Was he still there?'

'No. He was asked to leave and he won't ever be welcome back. Violence is frowned upon, it's against the general community philosophy. Most of us ended up there in the first place because of shared anti-war sentiments. We knew violence was not a solution, on a personal or a political level.'

'So he was banished.'

'Yes,' she laughs. 'I guess you could say that. We were both forced out of Eden. Your garden variety, modern-day Adam and Eve.'

'So why did you go?'

She sighs. 'I guess because I realised that there will be no safe haven for me there or elsewhere until I understand what it is that makes me put myself at risk. Do you know what I mean?'

'Kind of,' says Flinch. 'I always did think you were hiding out there.'

She smiles. 'I was, in a way.'

'And why did you come here — I mean, to my place? Don't you have anywhere else to go?'

'Do you mind?'

'No. It's just … don't you have any other friends?'

She looks away from him. Rocks gently in time with the music, her arms encircling her knees. 'I do. But not around here. All my other friends are still at the commune. I want to stay in the bay for a while. I just don't feel ready to move on yet. Are you sure it's okay?'

'Yeah,' he says. 'It's okay. Till you, you know, find your feet.'

'Hoping to find more than that.' She sighs and smiles at him but he can't read what she is feeling. Flinch decides against asking her what it is she is looking for.

Outside, a wind picks up and rustles the leaves of the trees near the house so that they sound like they are gossiping in whispers. The radio hums quietly to itself.

'There was a rumour,' she says. 'After you left. Someone said you killed a man.'

Flinch takes a long hot gulp of his tea. Instantly feels sweaty and dizzy, as if he's suffering some kind of flash fever.

'But it was probably rubbish,' she says quickly. 'The source wasn't exactly reliable.'

'Drew,' says Flinch.

'Yes. He left as well, by the way. Reckoned he'd seen a bull or something in the bushes near the cow paddock. We checked with the farmer next door, in case one had got out, but there are only cows in that paddock. Drew ended up burning all the shrubs along the fenceline near his tent. We caught it just in time, before it did any damage. He took off the next day, anyway. Don't know where he went.'

A window in the kitchen slams shut in the wind.

'Sorry,' says Karma. 'That was stupid. I shouldn't have brought it up.'

'But I did,' says Flinch. 'He wasn't lying.'

Karma is silent. She's staring at him and Flinch can feel the heat of that old curiosity, the same as he used to feel when passing other locals in the grocery store or on the beach soon after Nate's death.

'Why?'

'It was an accident. He was a friend.'

'Oh.'

'I think about it every day.'

'That's what it is that is still hurting then, inside you? That's what I sensed?'

'Guess so.'

The light has faded completely. They sit silently in the shadowy room, listening to Karen Carpenter proclaim that she is on top of the world. Flinch feels as if he's breathing it in, the darkness, filling his lungs until they're black, like Audrey's were when she died. Or so the doctor said, after that many years of sucking the tar down her throat, heels yellow from stomping out cigarette butts. Flinch, at the time, thought uncharitable thoughts about the colour of her heart.

'Well I haven't killed anyone,' Karma says, almost a whisper, after what seems like a long while. 'But if it makes you feel any better, there have been moments in my life when I've wanted to.' She lifts the teacup to her face, leans her bruised forehead against the warm china.

Flinch is frying eggs in the morning when she wanders in, freshly showered and smelling of lavender, and declares that she's decided to start the healing process.

'That's good,' says Flinch.

'Yes,' she says. 'And I have a plan. We're going to the beach today.'

'We?'

'Yes.'

'Why?'

'Why not?'

'I'll take my line,' says Flinch.

Karma sniffs and looks away. 'I guess you could do that,' she says after a while.

'Bloody oath,' says Flinch. 'No point going to the beach without it.'

He takes her to Tallow Beach.

'What a beautiful name,' says Karma. 'Almost sounds like *mellow*.'

Flinch decides not to tell her that it was named after real tallow. Animal fat. Casks lost in a shipwreck, washed onto the beach. Some had exploded in the surf, smothering the shore with the hard fat of horses, cattle and sheep, the beach allegedly reeking for weeks afterwards, enticing black clouds of flies.

Karma spreads a sarong on the soft white sand and Flinch sits down next to her, fiddling with his fishing line and hooks. He hasn't been fishing for a while and he is almost shaking as he ties a knot in the line to secure the sinker, hearing all the while the ocean whispering its promise of bounty.

Kneeling in the shallows, it takes him a little while to bring a worm to the surface. Karma is nearby, wetting her ankles in the bubbly waves that rush up the beach. He finally spots his prey, and pulls the worm writhing and coiling from the sand.

'Far out!' says Karma.

'Cool, eh.'

'What are you going to do with that?'

'It's bait.'

'But it's alive!'

'Not for long.'

The worm bites him hard on the soft flesh between his thumb and forefinger. 'Shit!'

'Serves you right.'

Karma flicks her hair over her shoulder and retreats to her sarong, where she lies face down as Flinch snaps the worm's head off and baits the hook. He wonders how she will react when he brings the first fish, flapping and gasping, back to the bucket that he has placed near their things.

'If it makes you feel better, I lose a lot of the bait to fish that get away, so I feed more fish than I reel in.'

She doesn't answer, but shifts her weight slightly on the sarong, and he figures this is as close as he's going to get to a blessing from her.

Flinch is usually lucky with fish. On the boats, they sometimes joked he had an unfair advantage, being the shortest on board and therefore closer to the water. Nate told him that his knack for fishing was a gift.

'The universe responds to you, Flinch,' he had said. 'Fishing is a spiritual activity. Christ proved himself time and again by fishing. Island religions tell of their deities fishing their islands out of the water, dragging them out of the depths to form landmasses. In many eastern cultures, fish were the embodiment of gods and spirits, and made deals of fortune with the men and women who caught them.'

'Guess I had to be good at something, eh,' Flinch had replied.

But today they're not biting. Flinch catches a few small whiting but throws them back into the waves because they wouldn't be worth the effort of filleting. Karma watches him from the shore and he wonders if she thinks he is throwing them back in to please her. After a while, he sees her sitting cross-legged, her hands upturned on her knees, meditating. Flinch catches one decent-sized dart and decides to leave it at that, considering he's the only one who will eat it and Karma will be disapproving anyway. He figures he won't be able to convince her to hold the bucket on the way back, so when it's time to leave he balances it in the middle of the spare tyre in the tray of the ute, like he usually does.

As they are driving up towards the pastel house, Karma spots a whale out at sea and Flinch pulls over to the side of the road so that they can get out and watch its progress, the steady rise and fall of its massive back, appearing like a metallic island in the middle of the deep blue, then disappearing again as if the ocean was swallowing it like some rock of Atlantis.

'They're amazing,' Karma says. 'You like them too, don't you? You keep mentioning them, anyway.'

'They remind me of things.'

'What things?'

He shakes his head. 'Another lifetime really.

I used to be up close to them all the time. It was my job to spot them. Then we'd harpoon them. It would have been the worst job of my life, but it was really the best 'cos of my mates.'

'You killed the whales? What? Around here?'

'Yeah. We'd bring them up on Belongil Beach.'

She is silent. Flinch can feel her struggling with the concept. She doesn't move but leans slightly away from him.

'I don't know how you did that,' she says finally.

'Neither do I really. It was just a job. Like any butchery. Like killing cows for supermarket meat.'

'But the whales are so huge, and wonderful, and special! It's not like killing a cow.'

'I doubt the cow would share that opinion.'

Karma smiles despite herself. 'No, probably not.'

They stand quietly and watch the whale sink out of sight. The dart in the bucket thrashes against the plastic as it dies.

When there was an argument on the whaling boats, about anything, Nate was sure to be involved. His knowledge seemed to cover most topics. Either that or he just managed to sound authoritative. But Flinch had seen the amount he read, the intensity with which he pursued even the most obscure topics, and he believed every word Nate said.

'Fuckin' know-it-all,' Macca would growl, signalling an end to any conversation. Knowing but not admitting that he had been outwitted.

On the days when the sun shone crystalline through the water, splintering into shards below the surface, and the ocean was almost still, Flinch would wish they could just ignore the whales, call off the search, so that they could drink cold beer and lie on the deck in the warm morning sun, daydreaming and dozing to the lull of the sea.

'Not likely, mate,' Macca had said when Flinch suggested it.

'Unless there's a mass beaching,' said Nate. 'Then we could just drag them up off the sand.'

'Why do whales beach themselves?' Flinch had asked.

'There are a number of theories, actually, but it remains a mysterious phenomenon.'

'Christ, listen to it. Don't get him started, will ya?' Macca had pulled his hat low over his ears, spat overboard and wandered off.

'All cetaceans can strand themselves ashore.'

'All what?'

'Cetaceans. Whales and dolphins.'

'Oh. Yeah, right.'

'There have been countless theories put forward. Acoustic testing that stuffs up their sense of distance and direction; parasites that clog the inner ear, meaning they can't navigate by sound, which is how they usually

work out where they're going; magnetic field anom-
alies; social bonds in pods that dictate following a sick
or dying animal to shore. Nobody knows for sure,
really. But toothed whales strand more frequently than
whales with baleen, so our humpback friends are
usually okay.'

'So we probably won't get a day off then?'

'No.' Nate had smiled. 'Probably not.'

As the whaling boat made its way back to the
station, sailing parallel to the shoreline, Flinch could
make out the top half of the Surfside Hotel over the
dunes, the blurred pastel dots of scattered weatherboard
cottages on promontories, the slender trunks of the
coastal pines. That was all there was of the town. Since
so much of the industry had shut down, it seemed to
him that the town itself was beached here, had landed
on the promise of greener pastures and was stranded
now with no way back. Being slowly crushed under
the weight of its own ambition.

Flinch used to despair sometimes for the fate of
the bay, and he wondered whether it would ever
recover, if people would ever again picnic on its beaches
and share jokes with strangers in the local, like they did
all those years ago when the pier was still standing and
the big ships would cruise in and draw the crowds.
Long before the blood of whales and farm beasts red-
dened the ocean and the whole place smelt like offal.

Nate wasn't so worried. 'Life works in cycles,
Flinch. Things will pick up.'

But he didn't sound convinced to Flinch, especially when the whales started to disappear, and the men spent the days of that last season pinned down by the unforgiving heat of the sun, the glare reflecting off their wristwatches when they checked to see if the time was passing any quicker.

Flinch is glad to see the whales back. He decides that it's a good sign for all of them.

THIRTEEN

After that first trip to the beach, Karma leaves the house more often. Flinch lets her take Milly, and sometimes she's gone by the time he gets up, and doesn't get back until he's fallen asleep on the couch listening to the six pm news.

'I've got a job,' she says one morning.

'Where?'

'The surf shop. I'm working behind the counter.'

'How'd you get that? What do you know about surfing?' He remembers the first time he saw her, her complete inability to read the wave and the dumping she received as a result.

'Nothing. But I don't have to. I just find it easy to hook into the whole vibe, you know. The surfing subculture is not unlike that of a nomadic community; it embraces the concepts of freedom and connection to the planet, and I can dig that.'

Flinch looks at her, how lean and nut-brown she is these days, her eyes bright with health and enthusiasm, and figures they hired her because she is, as Nate would have said, one hot tamale.

'And I know you're low on money, so I'm going to start paying you rent.'

'You don't have to. You're a guest.'

'You've been very kind, Flinch. But I want to. I want to be independent.'

'Okay,' he shrugs. 'Your choice though.'

'Yep.' She smiles and brushes the hair from her face, pulls it back from where it is caught in her beaded necklaces.

'And,' she says, 'check out what I bought. A little pre-emptive since I don't get paid until next Thursday, but as it will contribute to the healing process, it is a justifiable purchase.'

From her shoulder bag, she produces a large sketchbook, a palette, tubes of oil paints and brushes.

'I haven't done this for ages, but I used to sketch and paint quite a bit when I was a child. At one stage I dreamt of being an artist.'

'That's nice.'

'You should try it too. Very therapeutic.'

'Nah,' says Flinch. 'Don't need to while the fish are still biting.'

She shrugs. 'Suit yourself.'

On the speckled laminex of the kitchen table,

Karma cuts the paper into even rectangles and folds them in half.

'Greeting cards,' she says when she sees Flinch watching her. 'They said I could put a display up in the surf shop and see how they went. There are a few tourists and backpackers passing through these days, so you never know.'

She starts first with pencil sketches. Soft grey lines trace the outline of the lighthouse, the curl of a wave.

'That's wrong,' says Flinch, when he looks over her shoulder at her sketch of a whale. 'The pectoral fin is too high.'

She rubs out the fin with her eraser.

'Here?' she asks, her pencil poised further down the body of the whale.

'Yeah, and make it a bit longer.'

'Hey, you're right,' she says. 'Thanks.'

From then on she shows him her sketches before she fills them in with colour. Dolphins, sea turtles, manta rays, gulls and the whales. His days out on the boat, spotting, are put to use again as he recalls the observations he made out on the ocean, remembers the lessons the sea taught him. After he talks her through the details, he can taste salt water in his mouth.

Flinch counts the number of whales she draws. She's up to eleven. With each one he helps her shape, he feels he is restoring one that he spotted, har-pooned. Recreating them. He feels a small chunk of his guilt break off and crumble into nothingness. The lightness that follows is disproportionate. He feels as if he could float.

The cards sell well.

'You wouldn't believe how many people are coming into town these days. Young people!' Karma tells him over their evening meal. 'You should come into town on a weekend. It actually looks a bit alive.'

'Yeah, I might,' says Flinch. But he stays in the pastel house, travelling only to the beaches to fish and, often, to lodge the handle of his rod in the wet hard sand and stare out at the sea, as if he is expecting a bottle to wash up at his feet with the answer to his life rolled up inside it. He has stayed away from the town, he's had no reason to go there. He hasn't even needed to go to the store since Karma started picking the groceries up.

'You've got a great eye for detail. You really should paint something.'

She pushes a piece of paper in his direction. He ignores it and goes into the living room to sort through the household bills he's been avoiding for as long as possible. Later, when she has gone to bed, Flinch picks up a brush and looks at the paints in front of him. The images of sea creatures disappear. All he can see in his mind is a broad red canvas, the colour of old blood.

Karma seems to fill the house, be around every corner, turning up the radio when Flinch is trying to sleep and locking the bathroom door when Flinch needs to get in — he pisses outside in the yard, against the shrubs at the edge of the garden, the goats nuzzling the backs of his knees. Flinch finds himself wishing she would leave when she is around and missing her when she is not. He does nothing all day, but is exhausted. The shape of his prone body is moulded into the couch, and once there he is as immovable as a stain. When he wanders around the house alone he feels like a bucket full of water, sloppy and weighed down, reluctant to move with speed lest something inside him spills over.

Karma makes him herbal tea.

He empties it down the sink when she isn't looking.

'You look terrible,' she says.

'I'm fine,' he replies.

She raises her eyebrows but he gives her nothing more to go on.

'You look like you need something to shock you into action. Bring you back to life. You've been walking around in a dream, Flinch. Why don't you do something? Your life isn't getting any longer, you know.'

To find some peace and space, and to make Karma think he's out doing something useful, he starts taking walks to the lighthouse in the afternoons, following the goat tracks that start at the edge of Wategos

Beach to the top of the cliffs, stumbling over rocks and the roots of trees, throwing himself into the wind that gusts up over the headland. He walks to the edge of the outcrop that extends from the mainland like some thin knobbly limb, and lies face down in the pebbles of goat droppings, his head over the edge, relishing the dizzying vertigo, the feeling of temptation and imminent flight. When he stands up and rubs his face on his jacket sleeve, his eyelashes and brows are caked with salt.

At the lighthouse he rests, leans against its cool cream base and feels the solidity of it, the reliability, its straight-backed resilience to storm and sea. Unflinching. Throwing light out across the whitecaps at night, over the decades, first by wick, then mantle, then electricity. The lantern itself composed of more than seven hundred pieces of crystal, floating in a pool of mercury. The crystal brought out from France, loaded precariously onto small boats so that it could be brought in to shore. On the fishing boats, Flinch had always looked for the red beam that lit up Julian Rocks, that one consistent stare from the lighthouse while its other huge eye blinked light and dark, awake and asleep.

He has been inside the lighthouse once, on a tour, when it opened for visitors on a Sunday. There had been a church community picnic at the headland, and Audrey had taken him. While she snuck sips from the flagon she had packed in their basket, he had joined the end of a guided tour group. Inside the eye of the lighthouse, the glass looked fractured, incapable of the single, pure beam of light he was to see from offshore years later. When he looked skyward, he saw shattered clouds, shards of sky, fragments of rainbows. Out on the balcony that surrounded the lamp room, the ocean stretched in a huge arc. The whistle and breath of the wind in his ears whispered wild half-formed secrets to him. He leant his weight against the white railings and hung his clumsy braced leg over the edge.

'Oh, be careful Flinch!' one of the church women said. And he was enveloped quickly in a flapping paisley housedress, his arm held firmly in the clutch of white gloves.

'You would think his mother…'

'She wouldn't even know he was up here.'

'Someone should say something…'

The sighs, then, that sound he was to hear like some intermittent soundtrack throughout his life, the little exhalations of pity.

But he didn't mind. 'Did you see the dolphins?'

'No, darling, I didn't see dolphins. Did you, Fran?'

'No, I didn't. But if you say you saw them, Flinch, we believe you.'

He knew they didn't. But that was still at the stage where they'd say that sort of thing. Because of the leg, and because they thought, even though he had often spoken to them, that he had a mental impairment as well.

'They're always such happy souls though, the slow ones, don't you find?' The women would say it out loud, when he was in earshot.

'That's their blessing, really.'

Murmurs of agreement over cups of tea and spongy slices of cake.

He stands up and scans the ocean now for movement, the flash of silver in the curl of a breaker. But there is nothing. The ocean is quiet. The whales, too, are long gone. Back to the cooler waters, having birthed and fed their young in safer tropical bays. Deep, still sea nurseries off Tonga and Niue, places Flinch has seen only as a cluster of dots on sailing maps.

As dusk settles around him, he can hear the coo of a cuckoo dove, the honeyeaters and wattlebirds, the shrill screech of a white cockatoo. The ocean, too, its long sighs into the early evening as it rolls towards the cliffs. He heads for home.

'The thing is, Flinch, I think you're getting worse.'

This conversation again. Flinch busies himself with washing up.

'Look, I've done some reading. I think you're still grieving for your friend. Some people say there are seven stages of grief, some nine, but to compact it a little, I've decided to go with the theory that claims there are five.'

'It was a long time ago.'

'My point exactly. I think you're stuck in one, or maybe across a few, of the stages.'

Flinch doesn't say anything. He's learnt that sometimes, if he lets her lecture for a while, she'll feel satisfied and leave him out of it.

'Okay, so, like, first there's denial, then anger, then bargaining, then depression, then acceptance. You're not in denial. But I think you've folded anger, bargaining and depression into one big stage, and you're not ever going to make it to acceptance unless you try to move through that.'

'What about you?' he says. A last-ditch attempt. 'Are you feeling *healed*?' The word hisses and fizzes, acidic on Flinch's tongue.

Karma frowns. 'There's been a *shift*, Flinch. I can feel it. I feel almost … reborn.'

'I haven't noticed any difference.'

She is quiet for a little while. He can feel her watching him and he keeps his back to her, busies himself with drying a saucepan. He knows he's struck at her with his words. He didn't mean to, but he feels trapped, hemmed into a corner.

'It doesn't matter whether *you* have or not,' she says finally.

She leaves the room.

In the middle of the night, Flinch lies on the floor of the living room. The lights are off. The moon splays dull silver through the window. On the radio, the weather report and tide times and shipping forecasts are being read like poetry, in half-sentences, a line at a time, updated constantly with reports from vessels in the region.

Gale Warning NSW coastal waters south of Broken Bay.
Strong Wind Warning.
On the synoptic, a low 992 hPa located about 300 NM
ESE of Gabo Island is moving slowly ESE.
SW wind up to 30/40 knots, tending
southerly in the afternoon.
Sea 4 to 5 metres in south and offshore.
Swell S/SW 2 to 3 metres, increasing to 3 to 4 metres.
Broken Bay to Tweed Heads:
SW wind increasing to 25/33 knots and tending
southerly in the afternoon.
Sea 2.5 to 3.5 metres. Swell 1 to 2 metres increasing to
3 metres later in the day.
Wind clockwise around low 30/40 knots increasing to
40/50 knots over the storm area on western flank of low.
Very rough to high sea.
Moderate to heavy swell.

In the words, Flinch can feel the pitch of the ocean, the rise and fall of a vessel. Knows the sailors will be pulling beanies down over ears; saying to each other, over lukewarm instant coffee, *No sleep tonight, mate, not with those seas ahead of us.*

'Pray to the sea gods,' Nate would say when they struck high water, rough sea.

'What sea gods?'

'Neptune, Nerid, Poseidon, Triton, Aipalovik, Njord. The Saxons sacrificed humans to Aegir for good sailing. Solinthar was the patron god of mariners, according to the Titans. Or you could try the gods who came from the sea as half-fish, half-man. Vishnu did, and the Babylonian god Oannes.'

The names would wash over Flinch and away with the water that flooded overboard. He listens carefully now to the forecast, focuses on the sounds of the words, hoping to feel similarly gutted, washed away.

The following afternoon, a storm rolls in from the ocean, thick and dark green, flashing lightning, exploding above the bay with a furious roar. The windows of the pastel house rattle in their sills. Karma is still at the surf shop. Flinch takes his bottle of rum and heads out to the dinghy. He sits on one of the bench seats as the lightning sears the sky around him and thunder threatens to split his eardrums. The dinghy fills with dirty grey water that rises to mid-calf. Flinch screws the lid on the rum bottle between nips so that it isn't watered down.

He has heard that once, during storms like this, two lighthouse keepers were struck by lightning in the same week. Both survived. One was left unconscious, recovered black and bruised and disoriented, and was never quite right afterwards — though nobody could put a finger on how he'd changed. The other was struck quite unexpectedly, as the skies were clearing; the paper he was reading set alight in his hands, his fingers charred. Smelt like burning human hair for weeks afterwards.

Flinch waits impatiently for a bolt to set him alight where he sits, but the storm dries up and the lightning fades to flashes over the hinterland. The dinghy empties of water through a hole near the stern.

'Next time,' he says to the goats as they wander back into the yard from their shelter under the awning.

FOURTEEN

A thump that makes the wall paint flake off in scabs.
And again and again. Flinch awakes from an afternoon
slumber thinking some part of the roof has finally
caved in. Realises through a numb haze that it's someone at the door.

'Who the hell?' He says it out loud, hoping
whoever it is will decide to go away before he gets to
the door. Karma has a key. The door unlocked anyway.
Audrey, once, spying men, starched white shirts and
black briefcases, making their way up the gravel driveway, flung the door open just before they knocked.
Stark naked except for feathery pink slippers, fanning
herself with a soft-bound hymn book she'd pilfered
from a church outing. The men, red-faced and wet
through their shirts with the effort of climbing the
driveway, hands poised in fists, turned around without
saying a word. Audrey had put her dressing gown back

on, filled a glass with cask wine and poured Flinch a cordial and they toasted the success. It was one of the good afternoons.

Flinch squints as he opens the door. Macca, clutching terry-towelling hat in hands. A couple of goats have wandered up behind and are staring at him, as if he should have asked their permission to enter the garden. And now here he is already at the front door. The audacity. They move away bleating, black tongues out.

'Mate, you look like shit.'

'Thanks, Macca, good to see you too.'

Macca starts to laugh, stops, sniffs. Wrings the terry towelling as if trying to squeeze drops from it.

'You want to come in?'

'Yeah, thanks, mate.'

Flinch wonders what brought on this visit. Macca hasn't dropped around much since the failed attempts at bringing Flinch out of his isolation after the accident, visits involving warm beers and stilted conversations that ended in an awkward inertia. Now Macca only ever visits the pastel house to drop off the odd bit of news, and pick up tackle he borrows and perhaps one day intends to return.

'Beer?'

'Yeah, could do with one alright. Thirsty weather, eh?'

'Yeah, too right.'

The fridge has to be peeled open from the side.

Closes with a thunk and hums like a plane taking off. They take long swigs. Let out sighs, both of them, after.

Macca clears his throat, leans forward over the table, hairy hands clutched together as if in rough and ready prayer.

'So, I'm startin' a business.'

'Really? What?'

'Sailing. Fishing. For the tourists. Charter boat stuff.'

'Why?'

'Whaddaya mean why? I've been out of work since they let that lot of us go at the meatworks. Like to say I put aside a nest egg that was big enough to keep us going till we carked it, but all I got really is the old place and the shirt on me back. Need something to live on, eh?'

'Yeah, s'pose you do.'

'Anyway, I was wondering … Maybe you'd like some work? I know you're always keepin' an eye out. I can't pay you much to start, but I've got to get my old boat in working order. Set it up all nice and cushy for tourists.'

Flinch shrugs. 'Not much good at that. Fixing stuff.'

'Wouldn't need to be, mate. I just need another pair of hands really. I'd direct ya. Then maybe later you could take out some of the charters and stuff. Must be itchin' to get your feet on deck again, eh?'

The afternoon light pounds hot through the

window onto the laminex of the table. Warms the beer in their hands. The bubbles dull.

'Can I think about it, mate?'

'What's there to think about? Thought you'd jump at the chance. Would do you some good.'

'How do you reckon?'

Macca pauses. Scratches at the sweat forming on his brow. 'Well, I met your lady friend the other day.'

Flinch groans. Plonks his beer on the table. Froth rises to the top, dribbles over. 'So she's got to you too?'

Macca fidgets in his chair. Scratches his thigh, readjusts his privates.

'Oh, Macca.'

'No, mate, it's nothing suss. She just said she's worried about you. Says you're sleeping all the time.'

'Yeah, well I'm tired, mate. Really tired.'

'She says you yell out in the night. Have night panics. She said you call out stuff about drowning.'

Flinch winces. Sinks back. The vinyl of the kitchen chair brings a sweat to his back.

'She reckons it's about Nate. She reckons you never got over it.'

'Yeah, I know.'

'How much have you told her about it?'

'Nothing. She just knows it happened.'

Macca sighs and rubs at the sweat that has dripped stinging into his eyes. 'She's an interesting one, that's for sure.'

'She's fixated on healing me, whatever she means by that. She's like a bloody terrier. Won't let it go.'

They sip at their beers in silence. Belch and sniff, listen to the radio hissing the coastal forecast in the background. The humidity of the day dissolves around them. The sun shifts across the room.

The chair creaks as Macca stands. Downs the last of his hot beer.

'Yeah, well. The offer's there. And even though your lady friend suggested it, it is genuine. Could really do with a hand. The old lady would be pleased to see you again. You know how she is. Needs to dote on someone when she's had enough of me. And she's always had a bit of a soft spot for you, mate.'

Flinch takes a final swig of his beer. 'Yeah, righto, mate. Look, I'll think about it. Get back to ya. Ta.'

Outside the afternoon is bruising blue to night, cooled by a wind that flutters in over the ocean. Birds call out to each other from overhead, in the shrubbery, as if passing on news of the day, the evening headlines.

'Great spot up here, eh?' says Macca, stretching his arms, back cracking like a nut. The ocean sprawled before him to the horizon.

'Yeah, good view anyway.'

A goat starts towards Macca with its head lowered, ready to butt. He shoves a boot in its face.

'Feral bastard. Pity they don't make good eating. You'd have to stew 'em for days and then they'd still taste like me thongs.'

'Yeah, I guess.'

'I'll see you around then, son.'

'Yeah, Macca. See ya.'

Karma comes home late. Slams the door, trips and laughs out loud.

'You high on something?' Flinch smoulders quietly in the doorway to the kitchen, preparing to get mad at her for interfering, not really knowing how to vent his irritation.

'Life, Flinch. High on life.'

He takes a step into the kitchen and sits opposite her. She's grinning at him, eyes like a dozing cat.

'Smells more like bourbon to me.'

'Yeah,' she concedes, stretches lazy arms across the table and rests her head. 'Could be a bit of that. Friday night drinks. A tradition, I have been told.'

'You shouldn't have talked to Macca.'

'It's a free world, baby.' She looks up at him through a mesh of hair. 'Anyway, he approached me. Well, kind of. Came into the surf shop to see if he could bring in flyers for his fishing thingy when it's up and running. Seemed right up your alley. So we had a little chat.' She yawns. Flinch sees her tonsils. 'I'm so sleepy I could nap here all night. But I think bed is a better plan. See you in the morning, darl.'

Flinch, alone, wonders what to do with his

annoyance. Whether to bring it all up again in the morning. Instead, he does the dishes that have been left stinking in the sink for three days. Somehow ends up washing the energy to discuss it all down the drain with the suds.

Flinch catches himself daydreaming about stripping the paint off Macca's old boat. Setting it newly sealed and freshly painted out onto the ocean and pushing it off like some majestic creature he's releasing back into the wild.

When he finds himself going through his tool-box, fingering the paint scraper and screwdrivers as if they were musical instruments, he figures it's probably inevitable. The return to water. His love affair with the docks and with leaving them for the wild blue.

'Yeah, alright,' he says. Throws his shadow over Karma as she sunbathes in the garden. Over the faded yellow and white plastic foldout sunbed she had found at the back of Audrey's cupboard.

'Yeah, alright, what?'

'Yeah, alright, I'll do it. I'll help Macca with his boat.'

She smiles, lies back, spreads a magazine over her face.

'Yeah,' says Flinch. 'You knew I would.'

The boat tilts to one side in the dry dock that Macca has fashioned in a shed in his backyard out of broken-up leftover pylons from the jetty. Looks like a dying beast, slumped at that angle, ribs exposed on one side, flaking wood elsewhere, metal all over rusted dark brown, staining Flinch's hands the colour of dried blood when he touches it. An old sail is clumped in the corner in a rippled pile of grey.

'She's a beauty, though, mate, I can tell ya. I saw her in all her glory, before she went under. A real classic yacht.' Macca swollen and buoyant like a new father with his firstborn.

'Where did she go under?'

'Weathered every storm this bloody coast could whip up then went down in the slip, would you believe it?'

'How?'

'Fire. Some idiots shootin' off fireworks one New Year's Eve. They never caught the culprits. She didn't burn much but enough to take out some of the wood down one side and send her down. She stayed half afloat, anyway. The owner was devastated. Hadn't insured her. He sold her to me wailing like a baby. Felt bad takin' it from the man. Apparently it was the last straw after a rough divorce. The missus said his wife had taken off with another woman, would ya believe.'

Macca raises his eyebrows. 'Bloke shot himself eight months later.'

Flinch looks at the boat, sees the wet charring at the edge of the boards, and feels cold.

Macca shakes the gloom off like a wet dog. 'Anyway, she's destined for greater things than fillin' up a shed in my backyard, don't ya think?'

'Yeah, mate. Sure.'

The boat has to be stripped bare. Foam swollen thick with sea salt and reeking has to be torn from cabin bench seats. The masts are gone, eaten away by termites while the boat awaited repair in the shed. She's a funny old thing, thinks Flinch. Part wood, some sections a sort of ill-moulded iron. It looks like she's been revamped once or twice, probably when the previous owner could afford it. Or when Macca had a bit of time and a brainwave, in Flinch's experience of his mate a risky combination at the best of times. Parts that were almost right have been battered into shape then drilled together like Frankenstein's beast. Flinch is not surprised to hear from Mrs Mac that Macca retreats to the shed when he's in a temper.

'You'll fix it up, though, won't you, Flinch?' Mrs Mac stands outside the shed door, hands on hips, housedress flapping in the wind, clinging to reveal pot belly, trunks for thighs.

'Yeah, I'll give it a shot.'

'You'd be good with your hands, wouldn't ya?'

Flinch nods in what he hopes is a non-committal

manner. He knows she didn't mean it, but he can hear the echo of Audrey in her voice.

'Leave him be, woman, he's trying to work!' Macca, damp fag hanging from the side of his mouth, calls from his position on the foldout chair in the shade. Grunts and sucks at his stubbie.

'And what are you doin' then?'

'Supervisin'.'

Mrs Mac turns back to Flinch, rolls her eyes. 'I'll save you an extra chop at lunchtime, love,' she hisses towards him. 'Goodness only knows his lordship over there doesn't need it.' She walks past Macca, nose in the air, sniffs loudly as she passes.

'Yeah, orright,' he says.

'Face like a slapped arse,' he yells across to Flinch when she is inside. Mrs Mac's face appears briefly at the kitchen window then disappears. A saucepan clangs loudly against the stove.

'Thanks, doll, love ya,' Macca calls in the direction of the noise. Then winks at Flinch, and chuckles.

Days in the shed bleed together in the fug of a humid summer. Mrs Mac brings Flinch lemonade and ice water on a tray during the morning, beer after midday. Beads like sweat form on the cold glasses. The afternoons buzz with mosquitos and midges that hover like dark halos over the men as they work.

Macca helps with some of the harder stuff, peeling back boards, removing the rust and ill-fitted shell until the boat is bare bones.

'Contacted some guy in Lismore about replacement pieces. I'm splashin' out,' he says. As the boat takes shape in Macca's imagination, he starts to call it The Yacht. Flinch, more familiar with the bullish shape of trawlers, isn't sure exactly what she is.

'She has sails, mate,' says Macca. 'That makes her a sailing yacht. She's a Waterwitch.' Runs his hands down the long iron ballast keel as if he is stroking her into submission, calming some wild horse.

'See that, look at that,' he says, almost a whisper, the voice he uses in church. 'That design translates to steadiness at sea.'

'You'll have to think of a name for her,' says Flinch.

'Yeah, reckon. Later though. Let's get her in one piece first, eh?'

As Flinch lies in bed each night, aching and satisfied with the day's work, possible names for the old vessel flap through his head like bats. Regal options like *Pacific Diva*, *Wind Dancer*, *Silver Lining*, *Pacific Perfect*. Or like some of the boats he has seen around the region crewed by the weekend boaters, sporting the good old Australian tradition of piss-take monikers, *Wet Dream*, *B-Anchor-upcy*, *Seas the Day*, *Knotty Buoy*.

He hasn't landed the right one yet, but he hopes to before the boat is ready to be named. He imagines mentioning it to Macca as if it had just popped into his head, and Macca grinning in that sly old way and saying, Perfect, mate.

'Bit of history,' says Macca. Hands Flinch a book with a hard green leather cover. Pages tattered at the edges, yellowed to brown. A quick soft creak as Flinch flips it open. *Kathy Anne*, it reads on the top line, handwritten. Excessive use of curlicue. *Voyages and History to Date.*

'Kathy Anne was the leso wife, from what I know. Called the boat after her, the poor bastard.' Macca sighs and shakes his head. 'He didn't write down what she was called before he got her, but he recorded where she'd come from. Must have been copied from an older logbook. Thought you might be interested.'

Flinch thinks of the previous owner, pouring his love and dedication into a vessel named after a woman who betrayed him, feeling abandoned twice-over when the boat burnt up. A life even emptier of his beloved Kathy Annes.

Flinch takes the book home and studies it. The last owner had sailed it almost every weekend at one point, taking it out around Yamba and Coffs Harbour. Once to Sydney. A couple of trips to the Whitsundays in the temperate tropical winter. Nothing too adventurous. Flinch wonders if that was why his wife left him. Whether she got bored with sandwiches and beers on the deck every weekend, bobbing about unable to share in her husband's enthusiasm, cruising into the same old harbours.

The boat had been built in Rhodesia in the mid-sixties. Flinch looks up Rhodesia in his old school atlas. He notes that it is landlocked. He imagines the boat being shaped under dark African hands, by workers who had probably never seen the ocean. *Water traps abounded, design faults*, written in a following paragraph.

The boat spent the first few years of her life cruising the Seychelles and Mauritius on the warm, glassy currents of the Indian Ocean, before being shipped to Scotland, where she was tossed and battered by the wild, icy northern seas. She bore down through high, torn water around the Outer Hebrides, survived ice-slicked fogs and pitching water only to be sold later to a man who sailed her up the River Dart and there let her rest, becalmed and pitiful, until she rotted through in places under the dampness of his lost enthusiasm for weekend boating.

Shipped to Antipodes, very poor condition on arrival, page four. No explanation of why she came all this way, to end propped up on rotting jetty wood in Macca's back shed. Flinch suspects an enthusiast, an obsession. There are bucket loads, he has noticed, when it comes to boats and water.

Most of the pages of the logbook are empty. On the inside back cover, the boat's dimensions are recorded, in a different, far blunter hand than the writing in the front.

4 berths, 2 cabins
Length: 33 ft
Beam: 8 ft 6 ins
Draft: 3 ft 3 ins
Displacement: 6 tons in full cruising trim
Hull: 15 mm marine ply on mahogany frames
Decks: 12 mm ply, cabin trunking 18 mm ply
Doghouse: varnished teak

Then, underneath, *Happy Birthday Greg. Love, Kath.*

Flinch closes the book with a snap.

A crash from the kitchen, exaggerated whispers and Karma giggling like a schoolgirl. A man's voice, the door to her room dragging across the floor then silence. It's not late but Flinch, the skin on his hands and knuckles raw and arms and legs heavy with hard labour, is already in bed. He lies awake listening for more but even the thin walls will not betray any secrets.

In the morning she wanders out of her room buoyant and dishevelled and flushed and grinning. When she has left for work, Flinch peeks through the crack in her doorway to see crumpled sheets, pillows on the floor, a burnt down candle and the muddy prints of a man's sandshoes near the bed. Flinch winces. Hot pang of something close to jealousy. He's thought about this since she moved in and, apart from a couple of inevitable schoolboy fantasies, realised he doesn't really desire Karma. She's not a partner. She's more like family. And besides Macca, she's his only real friend. All the same, he doesn't know if he's up to sharing her so soon. To the possibility of losing her. A worn sarong has been tacked up over the window that looks out over garden and ocean. Flaps careless hot pink in the breeze, catches the scent of the frangipani blooming virulent just outside.

'Are you going to move out?' he asks her later, over dinner. He thinks she looks as smug as a cat. Shovelling pasta into her mouth while she reads a newspaper.

'What? Are you thinking of evicting me?'

'No,' Flinch says, louder than he means to. 'No, I just thought that you might be thinking of it, since you have a boyfriend.'

Karma pauses. Yawns. Ties her hair back in a knot. 'He's not a boyfriend.' Through a mouthful of pasta.

'Oh,' says Flinch. 'I thought…'

'Nope. He's just passing through. From Holland. He leaves tomorrow, I think.'

'Oh.'

Pasta grows cold on Flinch's plate and starts to coagulate. He separates it with a spoon and fork. Karma has finished hers quickly. She simply has an appetite for everything, he thinks.

She leans back in the chair and stretches. Creaking vinyl. Contented sigh.

'How's the boat coming along? Out on the water yet?'

'No.'

'Why not?'

'There's still quite a bit to be done. Macca wants to restore it traditionally. Lots of bronze and varnish.'

'Ah, right.'

'You don't just make something like that sea-worthy overnight.'

'My mistake.'

Silence hangs in the air, a remnant of something else, like the smell of a burnt dinner. Even the chewing noises gone. Cutlery resting on plates. Flinch puts the kettle on, hovers over it while it boils, his back to her.

'Flinch?'

'Yeah?'

'What makes something "worthy of the sea"?'

'It's just a term. It just means she'll float, I guess. That when we push off from shore she'll deal with whatever the sea hurls at her.'

'Flinch?'

'Hmm?'

'I love you, you know. You're the best friend I've made in a long time.'

She slips her arms under his armpits and hugs him from behind. The kettle blows a shrill whistle. Steam dampens his cheeks. His heart thuds as if he's been struck in the chest.

'I'll have chamomile, ta,' she says. Releases him and strolls humming into the living room to turn on

the radio. He stands for a long moment clutching at
the kitchen bench for support, reeling, unsteady in the
wake of her affection.

FIFTEEN

Stripped back, naked and sanded, the wood feels like silk. Flinch strokes it and thinks of skin. Some days he almost convinces himself the boat is starting to breathe again, in between the buzz of saws and the thump of hammers he hears its soft moans, catches the scent of the sea in its exhalations. He tells Macca.

'It's the echo of the tools. They're ringin' in your ears. And the heat. You might be spending too long in the shed, mate. It's like a sauna.'

Macca buys Flinch a new pair of earplugs. Flinch takes his shirt off when he's working and steps outside every hour to cool his sweat.

Macca has been researching, contacting old boating and fishing mates, swapping stories of catches and information on where to get pieces for the boat. He appeals to their sense of shared passion. Puts in the time on the phone, long distance, discussing Friendship sloops, American sharpies, pinkies, bugeyes, skipjacks, coasting schooners, Chinese junks. Debating the merits of gaff cutters, yawls, ketches. There's a huge phone bill at the end of each month, but it pays off. Bronze-rimmed portholes arrive from Broome for the cabin. Smooth, solid foredeck beams, strapped together with masking tape, land with a clatter outside the shed, post-marked Hobart. A letter from someone they've never met describes the best way to build a self-draining cockpit. The letter folded neatly around a photograph of a small weathered man in a beanie, beaming to reveal teeth like rotting stumps, standing on the deck of a beautifully polished yacht. *My* Bella Donna *on completion, 1973*, scrawled on the back of the photo.

The boat remains a hollow animal, bare to its glistening mahogany ribs. On the wall of the shed, written in chalk, is a list of things that have to be done, which they seem to add to each day, even as they patch parts of the boat and cross items off. Almost everything needs restructuring or regalvanising or some sort of touch up before she'll be ready for launching. The whole transom, the main bulkhead, the bridgedeck structure, the port and forward cabin trunk, the beam shelf.

Flinch feels a little like a surgeon, some days more like a witchdoctor, working and observing her slow and careful resurrection.

'And she's beautiful, underneath. I mean, she's not, she looks kind of strange at the moment, you probably wouldn't see it, but she has an internal beauty,' he enthuses to Karma while they drink beer and watch the sunset from the garden. Sitting in the dinghy, pushing the goats away with gentle shoves when they come too close.

'You know what it sounds like to me?' Her head to the side, hair falling over her eyes.

'What?'

'It sounds like you're rebuilding something else, Flinch.'

'What?'

'Yourself.'

'Aw, shit, woman, not that again.'

He hides his recognition of the truth in a long, cool swig of his stubbie.

'Wood's still the best stuff for boats, y'know,' says Macca. He stands back from the frame of the boat, snaps the measuring tape back into its container. 'Has one of the highest stiffness-to-weight ratios of any material in the modern world. Graphite is rubbish to work with in comparison. It's just that wooden yachts are hard to mass-produce, that's why the big shipyards don't use wood anymore. But that's why this old girl is going to stand out from the crowd.'

Flinch suspects Macca has done some reading beyond the racing guide. The way he talks reminds him of Nate, the confidence that comes from spouting something that he has seen written down in black type.

While Macca does some of the hard grind, Flinch practises tying sailing knots with pieces of leftover string. The slippery hitch, rolling hitch, figure eight, bowline, sheet bend, reef knot. Occasionally gets one right. More often, ends up with the string tied in inexplicable loops around his thumb or fingers. Has to cut his left hand free of it at least once with his pocket knife. He takes a few feet of rope home to practise throwing a loop around a dock mooring, imagining himself bringing the boat in after a day at sea, something he was never in charge of on the fishing vessels. Waits until a night that Karma is out with friends from the surf shop. Recalling all too easily the embarrassment of forced participation in school sports days and his guaranteed ineptitude. He starts by aiming at a stump in his backyard. When he gets good at that, he tries lassoing the goats, to try his hand at moving objects. Manages to get the rope over the necks of a couple of the slow ones, until one of the bigger bucks turns on him and butts him in the kneecap. Later that night, he rests his foot on the couch, ice wrapped in a tea towel over a shining bruise. Drinks a cup of ginger tea, which has healing properties, or so Karma had told him once. He's unsure if it applies to bruises. Washes it down with rum, his own home medicine, just in case.

'Come to the pub for one?'

Friday. Macca finding tradition hard to break after years of a working man's shifts, the retreat to the bar, a few cold beers under the whirr of the fans, all the blokes at knock-off slumped forward on their elbows, smirking and sweating and grateful for the simple fact that it's a Friday afternoon, the demise of the working week.

'Yeah,' says Flinch. 'Yeah, can't see why not.'

They walk up Jonson Street under the shop awnings, snatching shade. The tar on the road shimmering like water in the heat of the afternoon. As they pass the grocer's, the air is dense and syrupy with the perfume of mangoes and bananas and pineapples, all ready to burst their skins in the heat. Expectant fruit flies hover. Someone is cooking a curry in a back kitchen. The breeze carries murky green scents of brine and seagrass. The whole afternoon overripe and soupy with humidity, the almost-tropics.

They pause at the end of the street, wordlessly climb the sand dunes towards the beach, sharing the sea-dog's lust for a glimpse of the ocean. Main Beach, its sweeping arc, the crests of waves as they roll to shore streaks of white. Some way out Julian Rocks, the spray as the ocean flattens itself against them. And the sky, enormous and smooth blue, the horizon the promise of things eternal.

A Nankeen kestrel wheels graceful circles above them, wings outstretched and perfectly still. A pelican soars steady and low and purposeful over a dark gutter in the ocean, its head tucked back into its body, reminding Flinch of a big old warplane, a fish–focused B52. The gulls at their feet gather, appraise them with a canny eye for the possibility of food or bait.

'Seems almost too good, some days,' sighs Macca.

The back room of the pub, cool and dark with shadow, smelling like stale beer and ashtrays. A radio behind the bar cracks and whistles with the comment-ary of summer cricket matches.

'Score?' Macca takes a seat on a stool.

'Three for seventy. Chappell out for thirteen.' The barman snaps the tap on the barrel and plonks two small cold glasses of beer in front of them.

'Shit.'

'Reckon.'

'It's recoverable.'

'Could be.'

As shadows elongate in the late afternoon, the torpid weight of the heat lifts and with it Flinch's mood. People trickle in and out of the bar. The workers down the first few glasses then take their time, sip at the cold froth, chew their gums and offer opinions on the match. Flinch knows he's a part of this. The back–slap greetings, the casual, friendly ribbing of each other, the shared anticipation of a long, lazy weekend of sunshine, of fiddling with boats and cars and gutting fish and napping on the couch to the drone of the cricket commentator on a flickering TV or radio. Weekends around the bay.

He arrives home to find the house in darkness, a goat curled like a cat asleep on the welcome mat. He gives it a shove with his boot and it bleats, levers itself to its feet, shakes and wanders off.

In the kitchen, he switches on the fluoro and it flickers a couple of times before settling into a bright hum. He sees evidence of the beginnings of a meal. Raw chopped onions and garlic pungent on the bread-board. A saucepan on the stove, the oil in it glistening clear and cold. The cutting knife is wedged upright in the lino floor, vertical from the tip like a fallen arrow. Flinch bends to dislodge it.

'I have to go home.' Karma has moved to the doorway as quietly as a gust of wind. When she speaks she gives him a fright and he drops the knife again and it clatters on the floor.

'Matt dropped by a while ago. They received a message at the commune, from my folks. Some bad news. I'm needed.'

She looks hollow, as if some part of her has caved in. Flinch picks up the knife very slowly and puts it on the bench, steps back as if expecting it to launch itself through the air again. He's still wary of knives.

'I'm going to be gone for quite a while, I think.'

Flinch nods. 'Do you need anything?'

'A ride to the bus stop tomorrow?'

'Sure. Of course.'

'Thanks. I've packed up the room. Leaving some things, though — you don't mind, do you?'

'No, no. So you're coming back?'

'Yeah.' She smiles, small, with effort. 'This is where I live now.'

Flinch breathes out, tastes relief. He doesn't know what he'd do without her just yet. Feel less guilt eating red meat, maybe. But he suspects that's only the tip of it.

They almost miss the morning bus. Milly, baking in the heat of the morning, her paint cracking, doesn't make a sound when Flinch turns the key. He stomps on the clutch, sweat dripping onto the collar of the fresh new shirt he selected especially to say goodbye. Eventually the ute gives in and Flinch floors it all the way into town, to the bus stop, pulling up in a cloud of dust as the bus engine starts.

Karma grabs her rucksack and is out the door before Flinch has even turned off the engine.

'Bye! I'll see you in a few months. Look after yourself, won't you?' She says it as if it were an instruction on a list of things that needed doing, a list that might also include remembering to turn the iron off, watering the plants. She waves to the bus driver to wait, and leans through the open window on Flinch's side of the cabin to kiss him goodbye. Her lips on his cheek soft and wet and quick.

'I'll miss you, Flinch. Take care.'

'Yeah,' he says. 'Reckon.' Words failing him, as they do. She smiles and jogs off towards the bus. The doors close behind her. The bus emits a loud creak as its brakes are released, and rumbles away.

Flinch, the engine still running unsteadily, sits in the cabin looking at the empty spot next to him. The weight of her is still imprinted in the seat, the sagging foam and vinyl slow to resume their shape. He places his hand on the seat to feel her warmth. Such a sudden goodbye. He is unprepared. For a second, he convinces himself that she has just vaporised into thin air and almost panics. Instead, he revs Milly until she whines like a lost dog, turns into the white light of the morning, and heads for home.

The house, empty before when Karma wasn't around, seems even emptier still, in a way he did not realise it to be before she came to live with him. Bristling and hot with guilt, he creeps into her room and runs his fingers over the things she has left behind. A few tattered books he wonders if she has read. *Das Kapital, To Kill a Mockingbird*, a compilation of short stories by Hemingway, something to do with the Third Eye, a Steinbeck.

There are bands for her hair, long light-brown strands woven around them. He flicks them between his fingers and stings his thumb when they snap. When he wraps himself in the sarong that she uses for a curtain, he smells incense. Lemongrass. He takes a candle from the room, places it on a saucer, and puts it in the dining room, in the middle of the coffee table. At night, he will light it. It's a little morbid, he realises, but he hopes that rituals and routine will sustain him while she is gone.

And, of course, filling the long hours, there is the boat. He finds himself thinking about her, the curve of hull and keel, the long, smooth planks for decking, her bumps and hollows, as if she were the object of a schoolboy crush.

Macca, known for mismatched red and orange socks, lurid T-shirts sporting logos like *Aussie Blokes are Big Down Under* alongside pictures of well-hung kangaroos, sauce and oil-stained King Gees, has, for some reason, been taken with the idea of painting the boat in traditional colours.

'Understated,' he tells Flinch. 'Classic.'

Flinch wonders if Mrs Mac has had a say.

'I want the deck wood polished and varnished. The outside, though, I'm going to do white. Well kind of white. More like cream. Kind of.' Macca spreads small cardboard paint samples like a pack of cards in front of Flinch's nose, like some magician.

Flinch takes them in his hands and reads the

names on the back. *Desert Glow. Jasmine. Porcelain. Bleached Blossom. Ice Glaze. Whitehaven. Foam.* All slightly different, but each one on its own looking, well, white.

'I never knew there were so many types of white,' says Flinch. Lays them out on the table in front of him to see if he can distinguish the difference from further away. Reminded of the snowy bellies of seagulls in flight, whitecaps near the Wreck, a grain of sand.

'Me either, mate. I imagine it's the well-kept secret of painters and brides. I can't decide, so I'll leave that one up to you. But I did receive this yesterday. I ordered it months ago. Told you I was splashing out.'

Macca unties string from around a huge column covered in brown paper. Unravels the bolt of sail material and shakes it out, floods a brilliant blue over the floor of the shed. Flinch has to catch his breath. Is taken quickly by images of the ocean on a clear day, sun-streaked and glossy with brilliance, a feeling of abundance, of purity, of an absolute carelessness.

'Pretty nice, eh?' Macca runs his hand down the sailcloth where it creases and prepares to roll it up again. Flinch, feeling tears hot behind his eyes, bites his lip. Sniffs. Macca pauses.

'You okay, mate?'

Flinch nods. 'It's just a beautiful thing.'

Macca sighs. 'Yeah, I know.'

Knowing that the house is empty, Flinch spends more time in the shed, working on the boat. Summer bleeds away slowly as the humidity drops off and autumn reveals itself in the crisp mornings, on the ocean breeze, in the cool, dark, silky layer that lies beneath the white sand on the beach.

Parts continue to arrive from all over the country, dumped outside the shed by couriers. Flinch arrives at Macca's place to find ropes coiled like snakes basking on the lawn. Rolls of thick wire glinting silver. Boxes of bolts and fittings that rattle and clank as Flinch moves them into the shed. Each day that Flinch opens the doors to let the light and air stream into the boat shed, he is taken aback by the difference the work is making to the appearance of the boat now, after months of reshaping the internal structuring but seeing no real change in the boat's formation. Each morning, he can see the evidence of the previous day's work and it is as if he has forgotten overnight what she looks like. It makes the boat appear as if it were coming together by some kind of magic. He opens the small window on the side of the shed to let that blue smell of ocean and sky in, the same way a horse trainer might let the smell of turf into a stable to comfort the beast.

For the outside of the boat, Flinch chooses a crisp white paint that reminds him of the bellies of the humpbacks when they roll under water. When he has finished painting the final layer, he and Macca stand back to observe his work.

'Startin' to look like the real thing,' says Macca.
'Think that deserves a beer.'

Over the next few months, the varnishing is completed, masts and sails and lines put on and fixed into
place, bronze fittings attached. Macca does up the
inside as well, fits out a small galley and the cabins.
Flinch watches on like an anxious parent at a dentist's
office as an electrician and a plumber drill through
the walls down below. Mrs Mac sews cream and light-
blue striped material over the new bench seats for the
cabin, buys toilet paper printed with small blue
starfish for the head.

'That's a nice touch, love. The tourists will think
they're on a luxury liner,' says Macca. Puts a sweaty
arm around her shoulders and squeezes, plants a kiss
on the side of her head. Mrs Mac smiles, coy, blushes.
Flinch catches a glimpse of the way she must have
looked in her youth.

A letter arrives from Karma. It sits in the letterbox
for three days before Flinch discovers it there. By the
time he retrieves it, the envelope is soggy due to
afternoon showers, the postmark and his address
completely blurred. He is unused to receiving anything
more than utility bills and envelopes from Readers'
Digest telling him he could already be a millionaire,
remnants of a one-off subscription of Audrey's that

expired decades ago. Flinch admires their persistence. He's never the millionaire.

Darl!
Wish I could say I was having a wonderful time, but sadly that's not the case. I hate this place and long to breathe the fresh sea air into my lungs. Have to stay a little longer to sort out some family business but will be home before you know it. How's the boat going? I can't wait to see it, I bet it will be beautiful. Please drop into the surf shop and let them know that I'll be back in time for the school holidays. Pat the goats for me.
Miss you. Love, Karma.

Flinch reads it twice before he folds it into his pocket. Three times more before he goes to bed. Again upon waking.

Macca catches him with it flattened over his knee during a break for lunch.

'Letter from your girlfriend?'

'She's not my girlfriend, Macca.'

'What is she then? She lives with you.'

'She sleeps in the other room. She pays rent. It's not that kind of thing.' Flinch folds the letter, shoves it into a back pocket. 'It's a friendship. A really close one.'

Macca raises his eyebrows. 'She's a bit of a doll.'

'Yeah,' says Flinch. 'She is. But she's kind of like my sister. Y'know. You'd give your life for 'em, but you just can't feel that way about your sister.'

'Fair enough,' says Macca. 'Guess you'll never fall out that way.'

'Yeah,' says Flinch, flooded warm at the thought. 'I guess not.'

At night, Flinch lights the candle that he has taken from her room. Its flame, almost imperceptible under the stark white light of the fluoro, flickers large and brilliant when he turns out all the household lights. He lets it burn down, peels the hot wax from its sides as it drips and cools, and moulds it into a small ball that he flicks across the table and into the sink.

Later, he takes out *Moby-Dick*. Reads, *We felt very nice and snug, the more so since it was so chilly out of doors; indeed out of bed-clothes too, seeing there was no fire in the room. The more so, I say, because truly to enjoy bodily warmth, some small part of you must be cold, for there is no quality in this world that is not what it is merely by contrast. Nothing exists in itself.*

Flinch can't say why, but the passage seems to him more like a parable. No warmth without cold. No joy without sorrow. No sense of freedom without imprisonment. No resurrection before death.

In the morning, he wakes up knowing what he wants to name the boat.

SIXTEEN

The final coat of paint on the boat dry, Flinch puts the name to Macca.

Westerly.

'*Westerly*? Doesn't sound as slick as I was hoping. I was thinking more along the lines of something … posh. Imposing. At least meaningful.'

'But it is,' Flinch protests, almost desperate. 'Think about it. The westerly is the wind that will take us out to sea. Out to the big blue.'

'Rotten wind,' snorts Macca. 'Blows a bloody gale in winter. Carries the flu and the smell of cow shit from inland.'

'Not out on the ocean.'

Macca's mouth screwed up as if with the taste of something sour. 'I don't know, mate. Why do you like it?'

'It reminds me of good things. Being out on the

ocean and knowing we could drift on that wind to the horizon. And of ... other things.'

'*Westerly*. West. Nathan West, you mean.'

Flinch nods.

Macca can see the tears brimming and Flinch's nose turning red. Doesn't have the heart to say no. 'Alright, then. In honour of that mate of ours, a windy bloody gasbag himself, we'll call her *Westerly*.'

They sit back on foldout chairs on the grass and look up at the bow. A shaft of sunlight catching the brass trim of the boat, glinting like gold. The lawn crisps brown in the heat.

'He was a good bloke, wasn't he?' says Macca, after a while.

'Yeah,' says Flinch. 'He was a good mate.'

A fly buzzes thick and dull around them in lazy circles. They take turns brushing it from their faces.

'Well, better get on with it.' Macca grunts as he stands. 'I'll call a sign writer today. Running writing, you reckon?'

'Yeah,' says Flinch. 'With curly bits on the ends of the letters, like they do.'

'I get to name our next one, y'know.'

'Yeah, alright, Macca. The next baby's yours,' Flinch concedes. Hides a smile behind his hand.

On the way back to the pastel house, Flinch buys a single white bed sheet and some blue paint in a large tin. At home, scatters old blankets and crusty fishing gear onto the floor in order to retrieve Audrey's sewing box from the back of a cupboard. She'd used it once, to sew a button onto one of Flinch's thread-bare school shirts after a concerned teacher had sent a letter home suggesting a new one might be in order. Flinch had hung onto the sewing box after she died, used it a few times over the years to sew patches over worn pockets and to alter the hems of trousers to fit his shorter leg. The leftover fabric and the thread in the sewing box were rarely the right colour for his purpose. He left the house some days knowing he looked like a rag doll. A clown. All bits and pieces, uneven and uncoordinated. Learnt to shrug off with good humour the comments from the others in their blue overalls. Secretly thought the patchwork suited him.

He takes a measuring tape and measures twice, to be sure, a perfect square. On hands and knees, cuts it out. Drags the furniture to the edge of the living room and covers the floor with newspaper, so that he can lay the square flat. From Karma's room he takes the largest paintbrush he can find, and the big, dull pencil she uses for drawing before she paints.

In the centre of the square sheet he draws another careful square. The outer square he paints bright blue. When it dries, turns the sheet over and does the same again.

He leaves the windows open, but paint fumes waft in to his bedroom on the night breeze and he wakes with a headache.

Unrolls the flag in front of Macca and his missus the following day.

'A Blue Peter,' chuckles Macca. 'Bloody genius.'

'It's so everyone will know she's ready to sail,' says Flinch. Feels a little swell of pride at his handiwork.

'It's very pretty, Flinch.' Mrs Mac, in the tone of a benevolent teacher.

Buoyed by his success with the flag, the following night he takes a sheet of paper and the paints from Karma's room. Sits, pencil in hand, unmoving. Later, pins and needles through one leg and his hip and spine aching with immobility, and the paper still blank, he gets up and makes himself some toast. Eats without tasting. The night ages pitch-black, barren of moonlight. Eventually he gives in to the colour rising inside him. Adds black to the fire-engine red of Karma's palette until it is dark, streaky scarlet. Paints quickly and furiously, overcome with fervour to have it out, covers every square inch of paper red and leaves globs of the colour drying on the kitchen table and floor like some gruesome crime scene. He goes to bed in the early hours and dreams of a harpoon exploding, a cloud of whale blood rising to clot the ocean surface. The lighthouse keeper, propped against the closed door of the lighthouse, shakes his head.

The next letter from Karma is a postcard. A grainy photograph of a kangaroo with a joey in its pouch on the front. Blurry orange background. AUSTRALIA'S OUTBACK, it says in yellow letters above the kangaroo's head. The roo looks perplexed. Flinch empathises.

Darl, heading home AT LAST. Will be on Thursday bus. Arrives about 11 am. Can I bum a lift, if Milly is cooperating? If not, will hitch to the house, no worries. Hope all is well. Love, Karma.

Wednesday night he hardly sleeps. After the dreams he's been having, it doesn't bother him. He's awake before the birds' dawn chorus, makes himself a cup of tea and sits sipping it in the dinghy as the sun rises over the ocean. Tries to convince himself he'll miss the quiet solitude. He irons a shirt. Rubs Brylcreem through his wet hair and pats it down. A recalcitrant cowlick flicks over his forehead. He remembers Audrey's spit on his scalp as she tried to tackle that one. 'Useless,' she'd say. And he'd know she meant him. He decides to leave it there, where it wants to be.

At quarter past ten he's at the bus stop. He sits in the ute for half an hour listening to radio talkback, tries to muster a vague interest in the discussion. Refugees from Vietnam. Arriving on the nation's doorstep, pretending to be workers but covertly planning to turn the country a commie shade of red — according to the bloke who's called in, anyway, some croaky-voiced old codger. A whining housewife agrees, says she's worried about the kind of nation her kids will grow up in. She's trying to sound polite. Just simply concerned. The real displeasure bleeds through in her tone. The talk show host neither agrees nor disagrees, sounds like he'd rather be elsewhere. He has a polished English accent.

Flinch switches the radio over to a music station promising hard rock, delivering advertisements for car insurance and discount clothing stores and white-goods. After an hour he needs to pee, but doesn't want to walk down the street to the pub in case the bus arrives and Karma doesn't see Milly there and hitches a ride home. He looks up and down the street. A few shoppers wandering in and out of doorways. Seagulls settling in a grassy patch in the median strip. The publican cleaning the windows of the Great Northern. He ducks behind a tree in the nearby park when the street seems emptiest. Tries to look casual on his way back to the ute. Hands in pockets. Whistling.

The bus arrives at quarter to twelve. Flinch has fallen asleep to the drone of the radio, head lolled back over the seat, mouth open. Drooling onto his shirt collar. The squeal of the bus's brakes wakes him with a start that results in mild whiplash. He wipes his mouth on the back of his arm.

Doors hiss open. A young couple, tanned, wear-ing silver bracelets and anklets and carrying backpacks, are off the bus first. They walk past him, a map open between them, speaking a language Flinch can't identify. Then an older man, short sleeves, a bow tie, a fedora, a small checked suitcase. Flinch watches him as he waves to the driver, heads straight across to the pub. The bus doors remain open. He can see a figure standing in the aisle. He tries to make out if it's her, his heart thudding in his chest. He feels strained with impatience. Finally she steps off. The doors make a clunking sound as they close behind her.

He is out of the car, rushing towards her as if propelled, near her, embracing her.

'Well,' she says, kissing him on the cheek. 'You missed me after all, eh?'

Flinch steps back, wipes his wet nose on his palm and runs his hands down the front of his shirt. 'Yeah.'

'So everything is still good?'

'Yeah.'

'House still standing? Goats still perpetually hungry?'

'Yeah.'

'The boat's coming along?'

'Yeah.'

'And you're still fishing?'

'Yeah.'

'Barbarian.' She gives him a shove on the shoulder. He stumbles back, grinning.

Milly is compliant for a change, and once on the road Flinch finds the words that he thought he had misplaced. Months' worth of news is uncorked and tumbles forth from him as if he is an upturned pitcher. He tells her about the boat, how he chose the colours and the name and that the blue of the sail moved him to tears and about the starfish on the toilet paper and the blue-and-white striped seat covers and the Blue Peter that he painted. It is only when they reach the pastel house that he realises his mouth is dry from so much talking. Karma has barely said a word. She has been nodding, and laughing in all the right places, but as they pull up in the driveway he looks across at her and notices that she looks as if she is sagging. She has dark circles under her eyes. She is paler than when she left.

'What about you?' he asks.

'Me? Oh, you know, I'm fine.' She pats his knee. A couple of firm slaps that are meant to be reassuring.

'Your family okay?'

'Not really. But they never were.'

'Oh.'

'It was the end of an era,' she sighs, a small shudder. Her hand moves lightly to her breastbone. 'I had some things to sort out. But it's good to be home.'

'Yeah,' says Flinch. 'I know what you mean.'

She sleeps all afternoon. Flinch roasts her every vegetable he can find for dinner. Zucchini, beetroot, sweet potato, carrots, onion. She laughs when she sees the offering.

'Flinch, you are a darl.' She wipes tears from her eyes with the base of her palm.

They sit in the dinghy in the evening and drink beer and watch the moon tinge the whitecaps the silver of mercury.

'What did you have to go home for exactly?' Flinch asks her.

Karma yawns. 'There's too much to explain. I'll tell you some other time, okay?'

Flinch feels a little sting in the avoidance. 'Okay,' he says quietly.

She puts her arm around him and rests her head on his shoulder. Wisps of her hair blow across his face like web.

'The stories of our lives reveal themselves in all sorts of ways, Flinch. They don't always make sense to tell.'

Flinch thinks of Audrey and the stories that she told over and over, compounding her despair and bitterness with the retelling. In the end that is all she was, all she amounted to. A collection of anecdotes from her own past, a series of half-truths and exaggerations and justifications invented after the events. Drawing targets belatedly around the bullet holes. He wonders if the truths of her life came to her on her deathbed, as she lay hawking up the black bile, as the effort of breathing became too tiresome. The simple truth of her love and hate of him, and his of her. He wonders if she reconciled. If anyone gets that chance.

In the glimmer of the morning they stand on Macca's struggling, dew-soaked lawn and admire the boat. Macca has loaded her onto a trailer and wheeled her out into the sunlight. The white gleams bright and crisp, the brass glinting gold. Flinch believes there is something of the divine about her.

'She's beautiful!' says Karma. Looking at the boat, and realising the truth of her beauty and completion, Flinch feels like he's won the lottery, fathered a child, discovered a cure.

'Bloody oath,' says Macca. 'Didn't pour blood, sweat and tears into her for nothin', eh, Flinch?'

'Did you see the inside?' Mrs Mac, hovering with a teacup and saucer.

'I did,' says Karma. 'It's gorgeous. A beautiful selection. It really complements the whole thing. They really make it, don't they, the little touches.'

Mrs Mac, having initially raised eyebrows and pursed lips at the sight of Karma with her unbrushed hair, bare feet, no bra, beads and hemp-weave singlet, softens. 'Yes, you and I know it takes a woman's touch to finish things off properly, doesn't it, pet?'

Macca nudges Flinch in the ribs and they both twist the grins off their lips.

The ocean breeze blows inland and the sails, strapped to the masts, billow in the places they are a little loose, as if catching scent of the sea, eager to unravel.

Tea and homemade pumpkin scones in the McTavish's kitchen. Flinch notices Karma screw her nose up at the huge side of meat defrosting on the sink, blood running into the drain, and is glad she refrains from saying anything.

The kitchen is overwhelmingly orange. Orange laminex cupboards, orange plastic tap handles, orange vinyl padded chairs around a small table. A cream blind above the window has a citrus fruit print.

'We had the kitchen redone recently,' Mrs Mac says to Karma. 'These fruity colours are all the rage at the moment. I got the ideas out of the *Women's Weekly*.' Mrs Mac surveys the kitchen with what Flinch decides is pretend modesty, wipes at an imaginary stain on the bench top with a tea towel.

The others look on in silence. Mrs Mac fills the kettle again.

'Karma likes orange,' says Flinch, uncomfortable in the dull quiet that has thickened in the room. 'It's her favourite colour. Her whole tent at the commune was orange, hey, Karma?'

Karma shoots him a quick look that he can't decipher.

'Really?' says Mrs Mac. Puts the kettle back on the stove. 'Well, I guess you young people are up on all the trends, after all.'

'Actually, it's an eternal colour,' says Karma.

'Buddhists have believed for centuries that it has energising properties.'

Mrs Mac looks sideways at Flinch and her husband.

Macca grunts and clears his throat. Starts to say something but ends up scratching the back of his neck instead.

'That's nice, dear,' Mrs Mac says eventually.

Leftover pumpkin scones harden. A fly lands in the whipped cream and drowns.

'Look, mate, I'm taking the missus away for a little holiday.' Macca is standing out in the yard with Flinch. The women inside rinsing the cups and saucers. Through the open window, the occasional bleating of Mrs Mac's schoolmarm voice. Karma's polite laughter.

'Well, the boat's done.'

'Yeah, that's what I reckoned.'

'Where are you off to?'

'The in-laws. Live up in Maryborough. Maybe get in a bit of deep-sea fishin' off Fraser Island if I'm lucky. Her brother's a good bloke and the ladies like time alone to natter. There's a good run of tailer off the beach up there too sometimes. Might be wrong time of year, but.'

Macca walks over to the *Westerly*. Pats her side. 'Shit, she's come up nice though.'

'I'll check in on her, mate, if you want.'

'Yeah. Can't put her back in the shed so I'm going to throw a tarp over and park the trailer under the tree. But if you could come around, check up on the place, I'd be grateful.'

'No worries.'

'Thanks, eh, Flinch. We'll be back in about a week. Some things are best in small doses, if you know what I mean. Then we'll take her out.'

'Lookin' forward to it.'

'Bloody oath.'

Before returning to the pastel house, Karma wants a swim at Wategos Beach. Flinch parks Milly in the shade and they slip down onto the beach through a tangle of tree roots and rocks. The dry white sand reflects glare like a mirror in the midday heat.

The surf in this bay has no urgency, no purpose. Cupped by headland, the waves that roll in peak slowly, dissolve into foam. The tidal drag and rip of the more open beaches break and weaken. The water most days as clear as a resort pool, just the inkling of something wild in the taste of the salt spray. In the early mornings, the fins of dolphins appear close to the shore. Flinch has been in the water a few times and glimpsed a steely tip nearby, each time holding his breath, his mind snapping immediately to an image of hundreds of jagged teeth, but each time the fin has risen again and curved in the graceful arc of the dolphin, been joined by another almost in unison. In those moments, Flinch felt full gratitude for his existence.

Today the ocean rises and falls, gentle as a melody. They lie on their backs in the water, float like driftwood. Flinch looks skyward. There are no clouds. Nothing but blue. He realises that he is entirely sur-rounded by blue, above, below, beyond. He imagines this is what the afterlife must feel like. Still, boundless, bright, motionless, quiet, weightless. The colour of the sails of the *Westerly*.

That night, still thinking of the afterlife, Flinch reaches for his copy of *Moby-Dick*. He is about to flick it open, find some passage that he hopes will be a message from Nate, when Karma knocks on his door. He shoves the book under the covers.

'Saw your light on,' she says as she leans her head in. 'I'm making a cuppa. Do you want one?'

'Um, I'll skip it. Thanks anyway.'

'Okay,' she says. 'See you in the morning then.'

'Yep. Night.'

'Night.'

Flinch reaches for his book, puts it in the drawer of his bedside table. He turns off his light. It is hard to consult the dead when the living are asking you questions. He decides to leave the drawer shut, the book unopened. At least for a while.

Karma goes back to work at the surf shop, back to feeding the goats and using all the hot water when she showers and turning up the radio in the mornings. Charred lentils burnt onto the bottom of saucepans most evenings. Flinch resumes his meaty breakfasts, burying the T-bones in the backyard so that Karma doesn't complain about the smell of cooked meat when she opens the bin.

He drives down to Macca's daily to check on the *Westerly*. He peeks under her tarp as if he's lifting a skirt. He starts to believe she is impatient for the ocean, that she's whispering it to him when he turns his back. He puts his ear to her broad wooden hull but she tells him no secrets.

'Soon,' he tells her anyway. He imagines Nate's laughter in his head and he knows he's a bit of a crazy, sentimental bastard.

'Macca and the missus are back tomorrow.' Flinch tries to sound casual. The week has felt like a month. Afternoon beers in the dinghy, the sunset blazing red and auburn overhead. Karma looking tired. They haven't been saying much.

'Are you going to take the boat out then?'

'The yacht. Reckon he might need a day to settle in.'

'Yeah, probably. Not long now though until you're behind the wheel, or rudder, or whatever it is.'

Flinch takes a swig of his beer. 'I'm not sure if I'll go out, but.'

'What? You've been obsessed with this thing.'

'With rebuilding it, yeah.'

Karma rests her stubbie on the lawn next to the dinghy. Turns to face him. 'Okay, what's going on?'

'What?'

'Why wouldn't you go out? The main reason to rebuild a yacht is so you can sail it, Flinch. Otherwise you would leave it to rot.'

'Not necessarily.'

'Whatever. You know I'm right.'

He takes a deep breath. He admits it in the exhalation. 'I'm scared.'

'What of? Drowning? Sinking?'

Flinch thinks for a moment. 'My destiny.'

'How can you be afraid of your destiny? How do you know what it holds? Are you a psychic now? Thought you were sceptical of all that cosmic stuff. It's not destiny, Flinch, it's just plain old cowardice. That's what is holding you back.' She won't look at him.

Flinch is surprised by the strength of her annoyance. 'But I've proven it,' he struggles to explain. 'In the past.'

'The past, my arse. You only have the moment. You don't own yesterday or tomorrow, you only have today.'

They sit in silence. Around them a couple of goats bleat and bump heads before curling up near the dinghy. The afternoon slides blue towards night. Flinch can hear the waves crashing against the cliffs like some kind of repetitive taunt.

'I have an idea,' she says later. They have moved inside. Even though they have been in separate rooms, Flinch resting feet up on the couch, listening to the weather reports, Karma pacing between her room and the kitchen, Flinch has felt her brewing and is not surprised. 'We did this once at the commune. It's a burning ceremony, to release us of the past. In all honesty, I need to do one too after the last trip home. We could do it right now.'

'Now? A burning ceremony?'

'Yep. It's a great way to shake off old demons.'

They had skipped dinner in lieu of a sixpack of beer, and Flinch is hungry. He thinks of the sausages he has tucked away in the back of the fridge and has a sudden hankering for a couple of them barbecued over an open flame.

He shrugs. 'Guess it couldn't hurt.'

They set up a fire in a ring of stones. Flinch burns his sausages. Eats them ash-black on white bread with butter and sauce. The smell of smoke and burnt meat reminds him a little of Audrey, but he dismisses the thought of her quickly.

'How are they?' asks Karma, standing upwind of the smell of the burnt fat in the flames.

'Delicious,' says Flinch. 'Perfect.'

Under Karma's instruction, Flinch has gathered a small pile of belongings for burning.

'Not everything from your past,' she had told him, 'but tokens representing incidents or memories or feelings from which you'd like to free yourself. It's a symbolic ritual.' She had shown him her collection. A string of beads that had been a gift from Jed, which she'd worn only once. The stub of a bus ticket from Canberra to Sydney, a trip to see him. A school exercise book filled with coloured writing. A black and white photograph of a bullish-looking man with a scar over his eye. Flinch hadn't asked.

Flinch had rattled stiff drawers, looked under his bed, raided his tackle cupboard and had come up with a few things. An old cigarette packet of Audrey's that he'd kept after she died, one bent cigarette still in it. A fishing rod he'd snapped in two when he couldn't find the words to voice his feeling of entrapment. Audrey's pale pink scarf. His dark red painting.

'When did you do that?' She is surprised when he produces it.

'While you were away.'

'Explains why my red tube is almost empty. What is it?'

'The colour of my guilt.'

'Wow, Flinch. That's deep. Excellent work.'

Flinch collects a few more large chunks of dry wood from around the edges of the yard. They stoke the fire until it's blazing, sparks shattering against the black night.

'You first,' she says.

'But you know how to do this. Why don't you go first?'

'I'll guide you through it. Go on.'

Flinch takes the cigarette packet and throws it into the flames. It crumples with a hiss.

'Hang on,' says Karma. 'What are you freeing yourself of? You have to think about it, then speak it out loud as you throw the object towards the fire.'

'This is why you should go first.'

'No, it's cool, you can do it properly for the next thing.'

Flinch inhales, raises eyebrows. The smell of the lone cigarette is lost in the smoke.

He picks up Audrey's pink scarf. 'This,' he says, 'is my mother's disappointment in me.'

The scarf catches alight while still in his hand and he releases it quickly towards the flames. It flutters ablaze for a second before shrivelling into ash.

'Oh, cool, I want a go,' says Karma. She holds the beads over the flames. 'This is *Brother* Jed's hypocrisy.'

She drops the beads into the fire where they crackle and pop like corn. 'And this,' she takes the ticket stub, 'is his disrespect.' The paper burns quickly and disappears. 'I hereby declare that those things are gone from my life and I will never be subject to them again.'

She stands back, hands on hips, smiling, her cheeks flushed from being so close to the flames. 'Okay, you go again.'

Flinch picks up his broken rod. 'Here's goodbye to the anger I inherited.' The rod smells toxic as it burns.

Karma holds the school exercise book over the fire. 'Here's goodbye to my childhood plans of running and hiding.'

The fire emits a brief roar as it consumes the pages. Flinch imagines it hungry for the offerings. He unrolls his red painting in front of him, in the light of the flames. Feels the colour still surging through him. As he holds it over the fire, the paper curls upwards towards his hand, as if recoiling from the heat of its fate.

'It was an accident.' He almost whispers it. Drops the painting into the flames.

The fire leaps high into the night. Flinch can see the paper coil in on itself, holes appear through its centre, the edges disappear, and it is gone. He doesn't know why he feels like crying all of a sudden.

'Good, Flinch.' Karma has her hand on his shoulder. 'Let it go. You can't carry it around anymore.'

Flinch steps back from the heat. He realises he is sweating and wipes his brow with the back of his hand.

'Almost done.' Karma looks for a long time at the black and white photo. 'Goodbye, you old bastard. May there be a type of heaven for you and your kind.' She kisses the photo. As she throws it towards the fire, the flames seem to leap to consume it.

They sit in the dirt and watch the fire as it dies down to small flickers and coals. The night around them cools.

'Feel any better?' she asks.

'A bit. Yeah.' For once, it's the truth.

'Me too.' She puts her arm around him and kisses him on the forehead. Leans back on her hands and sighs. 'My father is dead. He died while I was at home. The doctors knew his time was just about up.'

Flinch is quiet. He never knows what to say in these circumstances. He thinks he should touch her hand, or shoulder, or hug her, even. The moment passes and he cannot bring himself to move.

'He was a useless drunk. He used to bash me. Us. The family. I had all these things I was going to say to him,' she says. 'But I didn't. By the time I got there, he was as weak as a child. He didn't recognise me. But he hugged me and sobbed and looked so … so grateful. It was pathetic. I couldn't say the things I'd rehearsed.'

She picks up a twig and draws circles in the sand.

'We buried him and I thought that was that. But,

tonight I realised that I still pay tribute to his legacy of abuse.'

'Because you went out with Jed?'

'That, but I won't do that again. I'm aware now of repeating the cycle.'

She wipes the scrawling in the sand clear and starts drawing again.

'When I left home, I discarded the name my father called me and made up a new one, because I thought if I didn't use that name, then I would be a new person, I wouldn't be his daughter, the girl who was abused. But it wasn't that easy. I still was that girl. And I've only just realised that it's okay to be that girl, because she became me. I can accept my past and its lessons and rise above it. Overcome it. So I think from now on, I'll start using the name I was born with. People who loved me called me by that name as well, after all.'

She finishes her scribbling, breaks the twig in two and throws it over her shoulder.

'There,' she says.

Flinch looks down at what she's drawn. Sees the name etched in the sand. The name etched in his head.

Eleanor.

SEVENTEEN

A blur of images in Flinch's head as he hurtles towards the beach, Milly's engine whining torture. The name in the sand, *Duchess 4825*, a dead kangaroo, kewpie dolls, a lantana bush, the photograph of a man with a scar above his eye, thrashing white water, flames, flames, Nate's hair sticky with whale blood.

He had made it to the ute before she had realised he was leaving, and now he was driving, her voice the wind in his ears, calling his name. *Flinch, Flinch, come back, what's the matter? Come back.* Pieces of the puzzle fall into place like pointed shards into soft flesh.

Off Main Beach he parks the ute and stumbles down to the shore, the sand a disintegrating cold blanket, the night blackest around the piercing single light of a distant trawler out at sea. He makes his way to the water. The lighthouse sweeps its gaze high over the beach and disappears. The water around his ankles is cold, forces an involuntary gasp, but still he sinks to his knees and sits with it swirling around him, his teeth chattering, until he is numb, feels nothing but the sea and the night air and each pure breath in his lungs.

Dawn, the water swelling around Flinch turns liquid silver. The tide has stolen in like some wary visitor and Flinch sits up to his shoulders in sea water. He hasn't moved. The water has carved a hole in the hollows beneath his body and built dams of thick sand up against his torso and he feels embedded. A couple of surfers have wandered past, asked *Are you alright, mate, do you need a hand, shit how long have you been there?* Flinch has ignored them. They have taken their boards into the surf, the lure of the waves curling into tubes too tempting, promising if he's still there when they get out they'll be taking him into town, to the doctor, to the police station.

The promise reaches Flinch from some distant place and he realises he has to move. His legs are numb, stretching them out brings tears to his eyes, the pain like some slow tearing. His skin is wrinkled taut, soft and pasty as dough. When he licks his lips he tastes the crusty layer of salt that has formed around his mouth. His tongue thick with thirst.

He drags himself out of the water with his arms. Lies on the dry sand as the sun rises, waits for the heat to melt the pain in his body, to warm his blood. The light hardens bright white. He lies with an arm slung across his eyes. The darkness has a red glow to it.

When he feels he can, he sits up. Almost collapses again with dizziness. He squints and sees that the ocean in front of him is clear today, unhurried, unchurned, just … waiting. A quiet swell beckons. It is pale, aquamarine, glittering as if diamond-encrusted. He can make out with ease the dark patches of rock further out, gutters of deep sapphire.

It is a perfect day.

Any other day, he would feel glad just to be alive.

Today, he decides, there is no escaping his destiny. Karma, Eleanor, his message from Nate. A revenge, Flinch thinks, from beyond the grave. To have and to know and then to lose. Again. He has not been for-given. Leap from the boat, he hears Nate say. Cases will sometimes happen when *Leap from the boat* is still better.

Feeling even more the cripple, he retreats slowly from the beach. Each step sends sharp spikes of pain up into his ankles and knees. He makes his way to the tap in the park and there drops to his knees, drinks with his tongue out like a dog, gulping the water down.

He drinks until his stomach is engorged with water. Feels at that moment entirely fluid. Back at the ute, he crawls across the hot vinyl and with some effort starts the engine. He sees he is almost out of petrol, but he will have enough, he estimates, for what he has in mind.

At Macca's, the house is still locked up. Windows shut, dead flies lining the sills inside. The lawn overgrown where it doesn't bald to dirt. The *Westerly* is there, dormant under the tarp, waiting too, Flinch feels now, for this moment. He releases the ropes and the wind lifts the tarp partly off the boat, revealing a bright wink of metal along the edge of the deck. Flinch drags the rest of the tarp off so that she is laid bare.

It takes him twelve frustrating attempts before the ball of Milly's towbar is lined up properly underneath the trailer. The trailer itself is rusted, and for the half hour that Flinch struggles to release the old brake and the jockey wheel, he begins to doubt whether this is what he is meant to be doing. But as he is about to give up, it snaps into place, and the trailer sinks onto the towbar.

He knows of a disused concrete ramp and jetty that is a short drive out of town. Only the occasional hobby fisherman uses it now. Flinch is betting that on a day like today there'll be one or two out there. No crowds, but he'll need a hand with the launch.

Milly groans and rattles like a sick old mule all the way. Flinch checks his smeared rear-vision mirror every minute or so. The *Westerly*'s massive bow fills the frame, bulging white. She stays steady on the road behind him, following like some faithful steed.

Near the jetty, he spots another ute parked in the shade, an empty trailer hitched. He turns a wide circle and inch by careful inch backs the trailer up the jetty, towards the ramp. Sweat drips into his eyes, he's licking it off his lips by the time he reaches the edge. Two men stand on a boat tied to a pylon, watching Flinch's slow progression, their eyes fixed on the yacht as if it were some street carnival float. Flinch watches the *Westerly* lower towards the water as the ramp dips towards the sea. He stops, pulls with all his might on Milly's handbrake, and gets out.

'Oi,' says one of the men on the boat, 'need a hand there, mate?'

'Yeah, thanks,' says Flinch. 'Was meant to meet someone here but they cancelled last minute.' He wonders if he sounds convincing. He's never been any good at lying. But the men nod and climb onto the jetty.

'She's a lovely vessel,' says one. 'She yours?' Flinch can hear the suspicion. Decides that if he tells another lie, he won't sound believable.

'I wish,' he says. 'I've just been helping restore her. She's McTavish's. He's been away for the week and I thought I'd have her in the water before he gets back. Sort of a surprise. He's been a bit down, you know, since the lay-offs.'

The man nods and sighs. 'Yeah, it happens to the best of us.'

Flinch guesses that they probably know of Macca, but even if they don't, every worker from the bay to the mountains knows the state of the industry, knows someone who has been sacked, knows of the struggle to provide for your kids and hold onto your land and your house and keep your chin up despite it all. The men start unhitching the boat from the trailer.

The *Westerly* sinks into the water with what Flinch imagines is relief. Small waves lap at her sides.

'Will you be right now?' asks one of the men.

'Yeah, ta,' says Flinch. 'I can manage from here.'

'Good on ya.'

The men wave as they motor off into the distance. Flinch watches them until their boat is a small white speck on the watery blue landscape. After checking the ropes that tie the yacht to the pylons, he climbs back into Milly, wrenches the handbrake loose and drives back up the jetty to park under some low-hanging tree branches. When he turns back towards the sea, he forces himself to take a deep breath. The walk up the jetty like the walk to an altar, the first few steps towards his destiny.

On the boat he clings white-knuckled to the handrails. The rhythm and sway of the ocean beneath him rocking unsought memories to the surface. The dead-fish stench of a slippery panic. A chunk of blubber carved off a ribcage that curves almost as tall as he is. Pages of one of Nate's books lost overboard, dissolving in sea water.

It takes him almost half an hour to will himself to let go of the handrail. With small steps he makes his way to the side of the boat and releases the knots that bind the *Westerly* to the dock, and makes his way to the motor. As a wave rolls in, the boat lists sideways, a slight tilt, but enough to cause Flinch to land hard against a railing. He cusses, but only quietly. His heart's not in it. He has never expected to arrive at his destiny unscathed.

The motor starts with an easy snap, purrs steadily. Flinch would expect nothing less, knowing the care Macca has taken. Fortuitous, he thinks, that there will be no stalling now that he is facing up to the ocean. He sits down on the bench, grabs hold of the tiller as if it were the horn of a bull and guides the *Westerly* away from the dock.

It takes him a few minutes to remember the feel of the sea, the roll and pitch and the churn, the flatline consistency of the horizon, the expanse of it all and the sound of it smashing against the bow, coiling foam at the stern. The yacht is steadier than the old trawlers on which he started his fishing career. She slices through the swell barely heaving.

Flinch motors out until he can no longer see the dock. The shoreline, too, a distant streak of rock. He can just make out the peak of Mt Warning cut sharp against the sky. He turns off the engine. He longs to unravel the sails, to set the boat free on the wind to take him where it may, but his experience on fishing and whaling vessels hasn't prepared him for sailing. He had read carefully Macca's books on forestays and shrouds and kickers and jibs and mainsheets and clewstraps when they were rebuilding the boat, but out here the location and use of each makes no more sense to him than surgical implements, or saddlery, or even the parts of Milly's engine.

He feels thirsty all of a sudden and wishes he'd thought to bring a water bottle. He leaves the rudder and lets the boat drift, and makes his way below. Mrs Mac's cushions are tied to the bench seats with tiny neat bows. A cupboard door swings open on its hinge. Flinch makes a mental note to put a bolt on the door at some stage. He doesn't think through to when. He doesn't yet know what he is going to do, or where exactly he is headed.

He opens the small fridge and it hums bright but there is nothing in it. The cupboards, too, empty of food or drink. He will have to face his fate on an empty stomach.

As the boat drifts further out to the open sea, Flinch allows himself to be rocked towards daydreams under the long straight shadow of a mast. The water at the sides of the boat makes licking and sucking noises, wet noises, as if suckling. The sun reflecting off the water scatters patterns through the shadows on board. If he could just sleep and wake up in some other place, in some other existence. One in which friends survive to squabble over space on park benches in their old age. One in which bodies are strong and useful, in which the land remains bountiful, in which lessons can be learnt the easy way. He shuts his eyes and wishes for such a place. Appeals to the wind gods to blow him in that direction. He realises he needs Nate around to tell him their names.

The slight breeze that had cooled Flinch as he lay in the shadow dies away. The boat barely moves on the swell. There is a stillness in the air that seems to Flinch ancient and elemental and ominous, like the eye of a tornado, the calm before a storm. Squinting, he scans the sky for clouds, but it is a huge blank blue canvas. He can almost see the curvature of the earth. He imagines what he would look like from space. A crooked little man on a boat, adrift in the midst of so much open water.

The sound of a bellow, of a watery, guttural exhalation, shakes him from his sleepy contemplation. It's a sound he knows well. A sound his ears strained to hear in days past, now like some trumpet blast announcing a victorious homecoming, his return to the sea. He moves to the side of the boat and leans over the rail. There's a footprint on the surface, the flat watery sphere left by a diving whale. Flinch waits. In a few minutes he hears the blast of another blow. He turns to the other side of the boat to see fine spray like a mist dispersing, and then the back of the whale, a humpback, emerging from the water like a gleaming revelation. Next to the whale, a small replica of the perfect arch appears and Flinch realises it is a mother whale and her calf. Both move, arch and sink, with unhurried grace. Flinch hangs his head over the side of the rail and sees a dark shadow slip beneath the boat;

they have an escort, a male humpback. In the old days, that would have meant two kills instead of one, the escort occasionally following the corpse of its mate nearly all the way to shore. The boat would harpoon the female, unload at the jetty and turn around to seek out the male. Flinch felt sorry for them then, and is filled now with a regret that weighs down his heart and limbs like lead in his veins. The whale in front of him hasn't moved. She's hanging in the water, her nose sticking out slightly above the surface. She is only a few metres away. He can make out the length of her, the bulk, the streaks of white along the top edges of her fins. The calf has disappeared.

Flinch watches, expects the whale to lower her head into the deep blue and pass by, but she doesn't move. She must be resting. Letting the calf suckle, probably. An easy target. He wishes he could stop thinking such thoughts.

The escort pops his head up some distance away, a spy-hop, the huge dark glassy eye and ribbed lower jaw, the long-lipped grin. Flinch knows he's being assessed. A gentle observation. He cannot imagine the wrath of Melville's white whale in this species, with their haunting, elegant songs and fins like snow-white wings. These whales may have passed through this region during the harpooning seasons, may even have been pursued by the whaling boats and eluded them by diving, camouflaged by the darker depths. Perhaps these ones are the offspring of those that managed to escape his keen sight. Yet they return to their timeless path harbouring no fear or malice, as if they know that their long, slow journeys are part of some eternal plan.

He longs to know their secrets.

He slides down the railing and lies flat on his stomach, his face over the boat's edge, so that he can look deep into the water. The glare off the surface a bright white shield. Spray up the sides of the boat when the swell rises. Flinch tastes salt water and licks his lips. He tries to think about what Nate would want from him. How to reconcile. He tries to recall the prose on the pages at which his worn copy of *Moby-Dick* fell open. Only one sentence returns to him.

Now, in general, Stick to the boat, *is your true motto in whaling; but cases will sometimes happen when* Leap from the boat, *is still better.*

Another loud blast of sea water from the whale startles Flinch, and he slips a little towards the ocean. Seeing the watery chasm beneath him, feels something akin to vertigo, temptation, lust. His hand is slippery on the railing, the sweat on his palm like a lubricant, making the slide towards the surface all the easier.

He hangs his head further over. His hair and scalp wet as the current licks the side of the boat. It fills the cavities in his ears with watery whispers. *Good, Flinch. Let it go. You can't carry it around anymore. Leap from the boat is still better.*

The calf rises to the surface and lets out a soft wet breath, like the sigh of a child. Flinch lets go.

The immersion, the sudden chill of the water sucking the breath from his lungs, white foam and bubbles and his shirt billowing around his neck. Flailing he bursts to the surface, paddles in circles until he sees the whale, the black boulder of her head just visible. She hasn't moved. His performance nothing more to her than the splashing of some insignificant fish. He realises that he is probably smaller than some of the remoras that attach themselves to her belly, hitch a ride with her through the waters of the Pacific.

He treads water for a while, just watching her. Every now and again he allows himself to sink under the water and he hears the song of the male, feels it resonate in his bones, the pitch and volume rising and falling like the swell of the ocean itself. The water still and glassy. Even from under water he can make out the grainy outline of the whale, her dark shape at an angle, her tail stretching into the depths. A smaller shadow, the calf, slips in and out of sight, circles her, retreats below to suckle, rises again to lie across her back and on her head. As curious and playful as a puppy.

The current leans on the *Westerly*. She drifts very slowly further away from Flinch. His legs and arms grow tired, he begins to feel he is churning through mud instead of sea water. Lets his head sink a little lower, the water rise a little higher, so that it is at his chin line. His shirt bubbles in front of him. He plunges beneath the neckline and shimmies out of it. Sheds his shorts as well. He feels a little lighter. His clothing sinks slowly beneath him. He holds his breath to watch it disappear into darkness, as if it is falling in slow motion down some deep well.

His arm and leg movements slow. He tilts his head towards the sky. The water laps around his cheeks and scalp. Water and whale song fill his ears. He takes one large breath and sinks below the surface. He hangs in the water, allows himself to float, to rest his heavy limbs. He scans the water in front of him for the whale and calf. They are gone. He allows himself to sink further. From above, shafts of sunlight slice through the water like blades. This is his journey, he tells himself. His lungs tighten. That old, familiar taste of sea water, the element of his destiny, seems to well up from the inside.

Right in front of him, a small dark shape rises vertically, propels itself upwards. It hovers before him, pectoral fins stretched wide in a gesture that looks like a welcome. The calf. It circles him slowly, hovers beneath him. The sun through the water revealing it to be grey, almost black, the colour of wet stone, a broad patch of white on the underside of its tail when it rolls and tumbles in front of him as graceful as a dancer. It comes almost within touching distance. Flinch knows himself to be a curious thing, even more so in this underwater universe, to this young creature.

The mother's shadow looms large in the distance. She draws nearer, growing ever larger. Flinch's mind cannot comprehend her size; he feels as if he is watching her gradual approach through a lens.

As she glides in front of him, the calf returns to her side. She passes so close to Flinch that he sees her eye, the size of a saucer, roll slowly over him, and he knows she is watching him, watching her. Recognises the protective mother, the sea monster. The eye is soft and knowing. A huge fin like the wing of some angel passes over his head. She glides by him, a wall of speckled grey. He sees nothing else beyond her. He forgets, momentarily, that he cannot breathe under water. He is left in a stream of bubbles, in the wake of one long slow undulation of her tail.

His lungs ache with a sudden piercing pain and with some effort he struggles towards the sunlight, fingers spread, legs churning. He bursts to the surface and gulps down the air, panting and shaking. Above the water, the same warm stillness as before, the arcing sky.

Flinch floats for a moment while he catches his breath, then remembers the glassy-eyed sharks that used to follow in the paths of whales and their calves, hoping for an opportunity to attack the young and the weak and the weary. Spluttering, he swims in the direction of the *Westerly*, half dog paddle, half freestyle, all churn and white water and rising panic. He stops every few metres to check his direction. The boat is drifting slowly away from him, but he propels himself forward, imagining behind him the ruthless curve of a shark's metallic fin, and makes up the distance.

By the time he reaches the stern, he is exhausted, wheezing like a dying man. He can hear the whistle in his own breath. His lungs burn, he can feel his heart beat in his temples and vague, dark patches blur his vision. He manages to haul himself from the water and onto the deck. He covers his eyes with his arm. He feels touched by the divine. As if he's been witness to something mortals were not meant to see.

With the last of his energy, he sits up and drags himself over to the motor. It switches on, uncomplaining, chugs patiently. He grasps the tiller. As Flinch points her towards shore, towards the distant speck of Mt Warning, the *Westerly* turns neat against the current, bounces slightly over her own wake.

NATE

I am beginning to peel away from my body.

But my anger is heavy and it grounds me to the flensing floor. It is thick and sticky like syrup. It traps me here. There is no way to escape it but to plunge through.

Through the days I loved you.

At the end of our street of dirt and gravel, in the dust of a vacant block, a cricket ball thuds against the earth and knocks over the aluminium rubbish bin and it rolls clanging towards the road.

'What a shot,' you say, and laugh and tuck the bat under your arm, and Eleanor beams from behind our makeshift wicket because I beat you, I got you, and you're proud of me for doing that, for once.

Through the days I hated you.

Home from school, through the front door, the torn fly-screen, the shattered cup and a fresh cut across Mum's cheek, the bruise around her eye spreading before my eyes like a blossom. Your spoor. I could track you by the destruction you left in your wake. The mantelpiece cleared with one backhand sweep.

The smashed radio won't speak.

My model airplane in pieces nearby. I had known better than to grow attached to it but I feel a bit of myself break off regardless.

The stains left inside me by you now rise to the surface like oil on water, leaving splotches that I fear will reveal themselves through my skin as rashes. I am so cold I feel ensconced in ice. When I open my eyes I see my hand on my chest has turned purple, each finger a bruise. Inside I burn hot and white like seared metal.

'Consider yourself lucky,' you would say, panting. Exhausted after another lesson. My nose bleeding.

My nose bleeding. My breathing does not sound like my own. Wet, choked. I might be crying.

You weren't a drunk who slurred your words. They were always as clear as cut glass, razor sharp at the edges, aimed precisely to slice through our confidence. If you kept us weak, you had us.

I cannot feel my hands or my feet.

You had a tough life, you old bastard. Your own father used to beat you around, knock sense into you, you said. It was the way things were done back then. You would joke about it and Mum would offer a silly little chuckle and leave the room. You kept a mental record of your scars and what you'd learnt while your skin was healing over. You pointed them out and described them to us as if they *were tattoos you'd picked up during adventures at sea. You never tried to understand it, just accepted it as the way life turned out.*

You never stood a chance.

I think.

I don't think.

I don't think you meant to hurt us.

At thirteen years old, I recognised the self-hatred in your eyes as you tore up my favourite book. At that age, I could still feel pity.

And now that I feel myself eking away like the waning tide, I don't know why I wished death upon you. It is not the punishment I imagined it to be.

With each slippery minute it feels a little more like freedom. As it would have been for you. The perfect escape, quick and clean and final, leaving no scar of the life you lived, leaving behind the things that haunted you like belligerent old ghouls. That monster in the bottle, the dreams like shipwrecks, your own grotty past where the kid deserved what he got, the bullying and the fisticuffs and the small part of yourself that remained, that place you retreated to, crying with regret, when the anger subsided and your family lay all around you in tatters.

I wonder if you are dead. King-hit in a pub brawl, hitting the curb at a bad angle. A mining accident. Your car wrapped around a tree on the way back to Mum's on a Friday night. Heart or liver packed in.

Will you be waiting for me, then? They say a family member waits to greet you, some ghostly welcome party, on the other side, wherever that is. I've seen no tunnel, no bright light. Maybe I'm not going anywhere just yet.

Flinch is back. I can hear him sobbing my name into my ear through a fug of darkness and I feel his forehead resting on mine, and as he rests his hand on my shoulder, I can feel him quivering as if he were cold.

I am sinking, I tell him. I sink to a seabed that is murky with forests of kelp and as I swim among it the kelp tangles around my ankles and hands and throat and the blood that gushes behind me leaves the water dark in my wake. When I spin around, I am engulfed in this darkness and I find myself more tangled than before.

Looking up towards the surface I see Flinch leaning over a boat, reaching down into the water, his hand reaching for me, so far over that the boat is tilting. I reach upwards and our fingertips brush but I can't hold on.

I can't hold on.

I yell it at him.

He yells something back at me but the water in my ears distorts his voice.

· I can't hold on.

The words come out of my mouth as bubbles that pop when they reach the surface.

EIGHTEEN

Flinch lies in his bed shivering, fading in and out of consciousness. He feels the talons of a fever clutching him like a brace around his torso. Through half-opened eyelids, the room appears to be filled with mist, sea spray, frequented by visitors. Audrey in a bright red dress, leaning over him, unsmiling. Nate, by the window, looking out at the view through the part in the curtains. The lighthouse keeper standing in the corner of the room, smoking a pipe and rubbing his eyes. Karma, sitting on the edge of the bed, looking concerned.

'Are you hot or cold, Flinch? Hot or cold?' she asks him.

Flinch doesn't answer her, partly because he can't distinguish how he feels and partly because explaining that is too exhausting.

In the sticky blackness that is sleep, Flinch dreams

feverish dreams. Whale song fills his ears, mournful resounding bellows that he thinks will split his eardrums. Then wind whistling in and out of his head, the roar of the ocean as it crashes over him, a murky underwater dream where he is entangled in a net, only to realise that it is made up of bluebottles that sting him over and over.

He opens his eyes for a second to see Karma dabbing him with a warm cloth.

In a quieter moment, he is standing on the cliff near the lighthouse. The waves lap at the rocks below and, except for the lull of the sea, everything is still, silent. He hears someone cough behind him and turns around to see the lighthouse keeper, rubbing his eyes, never removing his hand from his face, as if sand were lodged permanently into his sockets. Without looking at Flinch he walks straight up to him, grips him by the wrist, and takes him to the doorway of the lighthouse. Flinch thinks he is going to take him up the stairs, to the top, but instead the keeper points to the door. Flinch sees letters etched into the glass there, something is spelt out, but he can't read it. The lighthouse keeper opens the door to the lighthouse and enters, and when Flinch tries to follow he slams it in his face. Flinch wakes up with his heart pounding to see the door of his bedroom creaking open and slamming in the breeze.

He is aware of his surroundings only long enough to notice that he is in his bedroom in the pastel house, but he can't recall how he came to be here. When he shuts his eyes he glimpses images that seem more like shards of some other reality. Macca and Karma standing on a jetty, waving him in. Blue. Blue. Blue. Being rolled back and forth on the hot vinyl in the cabin of a ute. White walls of a room that is not his own. The watch-ful eye of a whale under water.

The lighthouse keeper taps on the glass panel of the door to the lighthouse. Flinch inhales the smoke billowing from his pipe and coughs up something wet.

'For Christ's sake, get over it would you, boy,' says Audrey.

Nate, sitting slumped against a wall, looks up from his open copy of *Moby-Dick* and chuckles.

A woman's hand warms his own.

'Karma,' he says.

'Eleanor,' the reply.

He remembers that there are things he would rather forget.

He wakes hot and perspiring with the sun in his eyes, feeling as if he has been dragged up from some deep, dark cave. He listens for signs of movement in the house. Hears nothing but the waves below and the cries of gulls swept to silence in the wind.

He sits up slowly, lowers his feet to the floor. His head spins with the effort. Using the wall as a support, one careful step at a time, he makes his way to the kitchen. Pots and pans have been recently washed and are lined up drying on a tea towel. In the living room, the couch has been covered by a colourful throw. A rug that looks vaguely South American lies over the worn patch in the carpet. Touches of Karma's. No, he thinks. Eleanor's. He shakes his head, tries to clear the confusion that surfaces when he thinks of them, the two women. Of her.

He goes into her room. It smells of her, of incense and frangipanis. There is the hint of chaos that seems to float around her like an aura, the unmade bed, clothes in small colourful piles on the floor. He stands in the middle of the room for a while and holds his breath.

The grunt and churn of Milly's engine as she pulls up. He hurries back to his bed, his knees and back and hip joints creaking like rusty hinges. Pulls the covers up, panting with effort. Keys clink on the kitchen table. He hears footsteps approach and faces the wall. His door creaks slightly as it is pushed open. Hears her sigh, move to the edge of the bed. He squeezes his eyes tight as the bed sinks with her weight and his blanket tightens around his shoulders. She heaves him into a sitting position, his back against the bed rest.

'Flinch?'

He says nothing. Holds his breath.

She slaps him hard across the face. He moans and recoils but he keeps his eyes shut. Slumps back across the bed. She is bawling, he can hear her struggling for breath in between each wet gulp.

He thinks, *I am under water. I am safe and still and deep under water.*

She moves away.

He pretends for days. Acutely aware of where she is in the house, what she is doing each moment, the rhythm of her existence. The scrape of the front door, keys clicking over the latch. She goes to work every day. He lies listening to goat bleatings and the squawking gossip of birds. To the rise and recession of the tides. To crickets in the shrubs. Chorus of frog and toad after an afternoon shower. The wind singing secrets below the cliffs. She returns each night with the same question in her voice.

'Flinch?'

He doesn't know how to answer her. He pretends he is asleep. She makes herself dinner, turns on the radio, sighs often and sings less than he remembers, and, quite a few times, she sobs. She helps him to the toilet each night when she gets home and before she goes to bed and he pretends he is groggy and unseeing. He doesn't open his eyes. She leaves him in there with the door slightly ajar. He wonders how much of him she has seen, before now. Stripped down to who he is, the crooked body, leg, the hated half of himself. Naked, he feels he is only a shred of a human. She makes him sit up and feeds him soup.

'Good boy,' she says when he swallows. Like a pet.

She has one-sided conversations with him before she leaves each day.

'Wake up,' she tells him. She runs a warm washer under his arms and over his chest. He allows his head to roll backwards. Arms limp as a rag doll's.

'Come back to us, Flinch. We have a lot to talk about.'

That we do, thinks Flinch. All the things he cannot say make his chest ache. His throat parches dry at the thought.

Macca comes around once while she is out. Flinch has to hide the evidence of his mobility, a piece of bread and butter he had fetched himself from the kitchen, under the sheets. Lies limp on his side.

'Hello, mate.' Macca is quiet, as if he's in confession. 'How you feelin', eh?'

Flinch has to focus to lie still.

'The boat is goin' so well, got people lined right up some weekends for fishin' and sightseeing. Eleanor painted us some special brochures and everything. She's a lovely yacht to sail, but you'd know that. Would love to talk to you about her maiden voyage.' Macca lays a hand on Flinch's shoulder. 'Cheeky bastard,' he says. 'Later, eh.'

Reaching for his snack after Macca leaves, Flinch feels the butter like a paste against his palm.

He can't pretend for much longer. He wishes he had Audrey's strength of conviction in fictional realities. His mother has disappeared from his dreams. She stormed out in a gust of wind and dust and slammed the door shut behind her. Nate has left too.

Faded into the wallpaper where he was sitting. The copy of *Moby-Dick* that he was reading lies open and face down on Flinch's bedside table. The lighthouse keeper returns during pasty daytime dreams, tapping away on the door of the lighthouse like some demented woodpecker. Flinch tries to speak to him.

'I don't understand,' Flinch tells him, trying to still his rapping hand.

The lighthouse keeper coughs. 'Olim,' he splutters. Flinch wakes, the word in his head like the rusted key for some padlock he has long ago misplaced.

Flinch picks up *Moby-Dick*. On the page on which it was lying open, he reads: *And the drawing near of Death, which alike levels all, alike impresses all with a last revelation, which only an author from the dead could adequately tell.*

He throws the book spinning across the room. Pages flap once like broken wings.

It's the routine of ablutions that forces him to admit his awareness. She comes home one day looking exhausted. Circles shadow her eyes. She doesn't say hello to him, just shakes him a few times and attempts to hook his arms over her shoulders, sit him up.

'C'mon,' she says. 'You must need this more than I do.'

He resists.

'Come on Flinch. A quick trip to the loo then you can go back to bed. You know the routine.'

'Karma,' he says quietly. 'Eleanor.'

She springs back from him. 'Flinch?'

'Yes.'

'When did you…?'

'Come back?'

'Yes.'

'A little while ago. Not long.'

She wipes her eyes with the base of her hands. 'We've all missed you, you know, you silly bastard.' She doesn't try to stop herself crying. 'We didn't know where you'd been or what happened to you out there.' She sniffs, looks at him in a way that makes him feel like hiding. 'What *did* happen?'

Flinch thinks of the underwater, the airless, blue peace, the wings of whales.

'I fell overboard,' he says.

She strokes his fringe from his face. He turns his head away and she lowers her hand.

'I must have suffered lack of oxygen to the brain.'

She doesn't look convinced.

'You still got the *Westerly* home. Lucky you did, too. Macca knew where to find you.'

'I had to bring the boat back. Macca would have finished me off for sure if I didn't, eh?'

'Near drowning or not, I suspect.'

The humour a welcome diversion. As thin and brittle as paper.

They eat dinner in silence. He looks up from his plate a few times to catch her staring at him with the wide-eyed curiosity of a cat. She starts to say something but stops herself. Takes their empty plates to the sink and runs the tap, leaves the water gushing over her hands even after she's rinsed the crockery. As if she's trying to dilute something, the memory of some incident, thinks Flinch. Cooling what is burning. Flinch fingers a pile of brochures left in a small stack on the table. On the front cover of each, a beautiful, hand-painted portrait of the *Westerly*. Desire and shame rise in him spontaneously, feeling acidic.

'Come outside,' she says. 'It's a full moon.'

They sit in the dinghy.

'Funny,' Flinch pats the side of the boat. 'We've spent a long time in this little boat that goes nowhere.'

'Don't know about that,' she says. 'Not all journeys are physical.' She's not looking at him but there is a message for him in the words. They cause a ripple through Flinch like a stone thrown into a pond.

'So, who are you now?' He asks to distract her. To shift focus.

'What do you mean? I'm me. You know me.'

'I mean, what do you call yourself — are you Karma or Eleanor?'

'Eleanor,' she says.

'Oh.' Even now, when she says it he feels as if it is being scratched afresh into his mind. He thinks of the little girl with the blonde pigtails in the photo on the mantelpiece in a decrepit weatherboard house in Duchess.

'Do you remember everything? Like, do you remember our bonfire night?'

'Yes,' says Flinch. He can say nothing more. He knows he will give himself away. He tried and failed to hide himself from Audrey, who accused him of wearing his heart on his sleeve as if it were an embarrassment, a foul stain.

'Flinch, I want you to listen, and not say anything. Even if you think you need to. Can you do that?'

He hears the tone in her voice that sounds like panic, the waves splintering against the rocks and dissolving. The wind picks up and he is cold, suddenly, immersed in something he doesn't understand. But he nods. His teeth rattle in his jaw.

'I didn't know why you took off that night. I thought maybe you were just really into it and had gone off to … I don't know, reflect. I didn't follow you. When you didn't come home the next day, I looked all over town for you, and then I went to Macca's place to see if you'd stayed there, but Macca was only just back from his trip. I told him you'd disappeared and then he saw that the boat was gone. Some fishermen thought they'd seen you at the old jetty so we went out there, and we found Milly. We waited for hours. You were a mess when you docked. You couldn't speak. You were spluttering half-sentences, throwing up sea water.'

'I don't remember,' he says.

'You weren't yourself. You looked like you'd been struck by something. Blinded, almost. You were unseeing.'

She rubs her eyes with her fingers. Flinch can't work out whether she's crying again or whether she's just exhausted.

'You were in hospital for a while, and we had to have a nurse here as well for a bit. Then I took over. I decided to read to you, in case it made you feel better. Brought you back. I read you stories of healing from some of my alternative medicine books. I even read to you from a Bible I found on your shelf. Book of Revelations. There's this quote in there that says something about the prayers of the saints being delivered to God on the smoke of incense. So I burnt some for you in your room.'

'The smoke,' says Flinch. 'Audrey. The lighthouse keeper.'

'What?'

'Nothing,' says Flinch. 'I dreamt a lot.'

'You did. You talked, too. All sorts of rubbish. I kept listening for a sign that you were on your way back to us, but I couldn't make sense of any of it.'

She takes a deep breath. Flinch notices that the moon above has paled silver from gold. Paves a brilliant white streak across the dark ocean.

'I got tired of reading my own books to you. I went looking for something else. A couple of weeks

ago, I opened your bedside table and found a copy of
Moby-Dick.'

The chill sets in his bones. He feels himself plum-
met from a great height. The strength and solidity of
the board on which he is sitting dissolves beneath
him. He feels himself land with a thud but he hasn't
moved. He looks up at the moon through a translucent
surface, as if from the ocean floor.

'I read the inscription. I know who you are,
Flinch. I know what you did.'

He is shaking, being hauled up into the cold.
Exposed and pale and naked.

'And you know who I am.'

Flinch's shirt is wet. He doesn't realise he is
sobbing until he exhales and a blubbering, wet sound
bursts out of him.

'Eleanor.' It's all he can say.

'Yes.'

He wants to collapse, faint, disappear. She sees
him slipping away again. Sinking under. Before he
can, she takes him by the hand.

'Come inside,' she says. 'I have something to
show you.'

She sits him on the couch. Hands him a double
shot of rum. He drinks it with one wide gulp and it
burns quickly through him, but the warmth does not
last. She goes into her room and he can hear her shuf-
fling around, opening and closing drawers. He thinks of
Audrey's ability to escape in this very spot. Slide into

oblivion in the velour and return only when she felt fit enough to face her life again. He thinks about a glazed-eye retreat, but there is a pull like a lunar tide to stay, and he anchors himself to the moment. Eleanor returns to him with a piece of paper that looks as ancient as parchment. There is a fine fur along the edges where it has been folded so often. A tear in one corner.

'I didn't come to the bay by accident,' she says. 'The commune was convenient. It made it easy to reinvent myself and travel to where I was headed. A happy coincidence, you might say. But really I came here because Nate told me about this place. He sounded happy here. I didn't know what had happened to him, but I knew something must have.'

She hands him the folded piece of paper.

It is a letter.

Flinch unfolds it. His hands shake. The paper falls open along its creases.

He recognises the hand in which it is written.

Dear Eleanor,

I am sending you some of my beloved books. Please look after them, you know they are my best and oldest friends and I hate to think of them mistreated. I've decided recently to unload them, a painful but simultaneously rewarding process. I am thinking about moving on from this place, as beautiful as it is, but when I tried to pack my rucksack I had no space for clothing, thanks to all my tomes. I figure you can hold on to them for me until I see you, that way I will be able to rejoice in a double reunion. I've handed some of my other books around to various people who I think will appreciate them.

I've given a friend of mine here my copy of Moby-Dick. *You know it's my favourite, and I know you would look for it in the pile I am sending you. But this friend, El, is deserving of my prized possession. He is such a gentle soul. He's weathered a terrible childhood (like ours, though not in quite the same way) with a calm dignity — in him I see the kindness and optimism and love for what could still be that I wish I could have retained under the pressure of our upbringing.*

He has been like a brother, and I have grown to love and respect him more than anyone else I have met since I left home.

In some distant future, perhaps we could all meet up here in the bay. We'd walk up to the lighthouse just before dawn (you'd love the sea and sky, sis) and we'd toast the sunrise. We'd be the first people in Australia to see it. Nothing like the promise of a new day, as we both know. Miss you, as always.

Love, Nate.

'It was his last letter to me,' says Eleanor. 'No more ever came.'

Flinch notes the date. 'It was sent the week before the accident ... before I...'

'I know. When I found the book, I caught on to why you took off that night. Who your dead friend was. And realised your terrible guilt. I worked out the big picture. Macca confirmed the details.'

'I'm sorry.'

'I went to the graveyard and found where you'd buried him. I gave him flowers and I had a long chat to him. I read to him, too.'

'I'm so sorry. So sorry.'

Flinch folds the letter. Places it on the arm of the couch and shifts away from it.

'Did you know that he was gone?'

Eleanor's blank stare. 'There was nothing. He just stopped writing.'

'We sent a letter. The priest.'

She shakes her head. 'Nothing ever came. I think my mother had a suspicion but I'm not sure. She locked herself away from us a long time ago.'

'You must hate me,' he says. 'You will want to leave.'

'I did.' As a sigh. 'Hate you and want to leave. At first. I even packed. But I couldn't go. I read that letter again and again after I found out, and I realised that Nate would have wanted me to forgive you. He loved you. You clearly loved him as much as I did. It was an accident. And Nate would have wanted you to forgive yourself for that as well, Flinch.'

Flinch lets the words trickle through him like water.

'You were meant to see this letter. I was meant to find you. And you were meant to restore me to who I was, who Nate knew me as. We're like a gift to each other, from Nate.'

'That sounds like Karma talking.'

She allows herself a small smile.

'Yeah, well, I know you think it's all a bit cosmic, but it's amazing how often she's right about these things.'

Flinch breathes and it feels like the first breath he's taken in years. As if he's reached a fresh surface. It almost stings his lungs.

'I named the boat after him, really.'

'I know. Macca said you were insistent.'

'He was my best friend.'

'He was mine too.'

Eleanor turns on the radio. It is fixed on the weather station. She leaves it there, the snap and crackle of static and snatches of conversations about winds and seas somehow comforting to them both.

'Hear that?' she says, listening to the words being spat out amid the white noise. 'It's been a full moon. A high tide. A perfect time to wash away all old sins and start again. A clean slate.'

'You reckon?'

'I reckon.'

Flinch shrugs.

'It's true,' she says.

'It'll be good fishing anyhow.'

Eleanor slaps him on the knee.

A waft of sea wind smelling of brine and tasting of salt lifts the curtains. Nate's letter flutters to the floor but neither of them notices. The radio weatherman, preaching like an evangelist, predicts fine sailing in the days to come. In the kitchen, the brochures advertising the *Westerly* lift from the table and dance around the room like carnival confetti.

NINETEEN

Over the white foam the *Westerly* pitches and falls and Flinch, riding the rhythm, leans over the railing scanning the horizon for the familiar bellow and spray.

'There,' he says, pointing. 'Macca, starboard. There.'

The tourists on board cluster to one side and the *Westerly* keels slightly.

'I don't see,' says one of them.

'Over there,' says another.

Where Flinch has pointed a whale breaches suddenly, propelling itself skyward and landing again in an eruption of white water.

Since they've been taking the boat out on the sightseeing charters, they've seen a few whales. Flinch observes their shapes, fin indentations, mottled colouring, in the hope that he will recognise the whale he met under water, but so far he hasn't seen anything that jogs his memory. Like a half-remembered dream, his recollection of the moment is blurred, but when he thinks of the encounter, a feeling of peace drifts through him, soaks through to his core.

Mrs Mac feeds the tourists on finger sandwiches of crustless white bread filled with ham and mustard, chicken and mayonnaise, soggy cucumber. Lukewarm mini sausage rolls with a glob of tomato sauce on the pastry. Eleanor makes up a tray of felafel balls and salsa and marinated olives and Turkish bread with hummus. Mrs Mac moves that tray to the back when Eleanor looks away to pour the tea and coffee for the passengers. When Flinch catches Mrs Mac's eye, she gives him a *well, honestly* look that forces him to conceal a grin.

On the deck, the sails bubble and flap as the *Westerly* is turned towards the shore. Flinch has grown to love the sound, the sight of the sails flailing then filling like lungs, bloated with the sea breeze. The English passengers, mostly backpackers with anklets and necklaces dangling seashells and St Christopher medallions, lie charring their bodies in the fierce afternoon sun. On the headland, the lighthouse pricks the horizon, its white trunk visible even from this distance.

'The most easterly point of Australia,' says Flinch, pointing.

The passengers lying on the deck lift their heads briefly, nod politely. A few come out from the cabin to take photographs. Flinch wonders if any of them see it, the shoulder of the land lying prone in the water, the limb outstretched, beckoning him home.

Mrs Mac and Eleanor clean up the leftovers and pour the tea leaves overboard.

Macca downs sails. Flinch scrubs down the deck with Mrs Mac's kitchen mop.

'So, day off tomorrow,' says Macca. 'But full boat the next day.'

'Yeah,' says Flinch. Concentrates on working the mop back over his uneven foot prints.

'It's all goin' good, eh.' More question than statement. Macca is checking on him.

'Yeah, mate,' Flinch responds. 'It's going great.'

Eleanor has packed a small bag with some frozen juice and sandwiches, a thermos of tea.

'Breakfast,' she says. 'I'll carry it.'

The winding road up the headland and then down again to Wategos Beach flickers black and white in front of Milly's one fading headlight. They park at the far end of the beach. With the tiny single beam of Flinch's camping torch, it takes them a while to find the entrance to the path up the cliff, but eventually Flinch pushes through the undergrowth and over some rocks and they find it, set off uphill. Eleanor stays behind Flinch. He slips, sends small rocks scuttling down the hill behind him.

'We'll miss it,' he says.

'We won't.'

The sky lightens pale violet. The colour of pre-dawn that Flinch has seen so many times before at the end of long all-night shifts of trawling, a time that now seems as hazy and pastel in his memory as the light itself.

The last section of the track to the lighthouse a steep ascent. The ocean is moving, shifting, drawing back and forth over the rocks, mumbling gently of the dawn. The birds startle as they pass, flutter out of bushes with a whirr of whistles. They get to the top as the horizon starts to shimmer orange.

Flinch leans against the base of the lighthouse. Cool, pristine white, solid against his back. Eleanor pours them a cup of tea each and they sit and watch as the sun flickers a small arc above the horizon.

'To Nate,' says Flinch, raising his cup.

'To a new day,' says Eleanor.

The ocean has depth and colour that Flinch has not previously noticed. Ripples mauve and gold. Chameleon colour changes that flash brilliant, almost blinding, as the sun hovers on the horizon. Clear of its watery birth, the new sun brightens white and Flinch can no longer look at it. The ocean settles into its varying shades of blue. Seagulls take flight overhead, wheel out over the cliffs in search of their first meal of the day.

'We had a saying at the festival,' Eleanor says.

'Kind of like a benediction. We said, "May the long time the sun shine upon you." When you see it like this, you realise why that's such a generous blessing.'

She puts her arm around Flinch's shoulder. There is a calm, a stillness, around the lighthouse that settles upon Flinch like a warm blanket.

'Come on,' she says. 'Let's go back down for a swim.'

'Wait,' says Flinch. 'There's something I want to see.'

He walks around to the door of the lighthouse. He tries the handle. The door is locked.

He feels a strange sense of disappointment. The disappointment of the lighthouse keeper, who struggled through his dreams to bang his fist upon this door.

'Hey,' says Eleanor, behind him. 'I've never really looked at that properly before.'

'What?'

'That. The etching on the glass there.'

Flinch looks closely. It is difficult to make out in the shadow, the new dawn still brilliant on the opposite side of the lighthouse. He sees some kind of flower. A lion. A banner, depicted as if caught in a breeze. The words etched across it make no sense to him.

'*Olim Periculum, Nunc Salus*,' reads Eleanor.

'What does it mean?' asks Flinch.

'It's Latin,' she says. 'I took Latin for a semester at university, though that was a few years ago now.'

'Can you read it?'

'Yeah, hang on a sec. *Olim Periculum. Periculum.* Okay. Um. Yes. Yes, that makes sense.'

'What does it mean?' Flinch feels anxious all of a sudden. Thinks he catches a waft of pipe smoke on the sea breeze.

'It means "Once Perilous, Now Safe". Referring to the ocean and the ships when the lighthouse was erected, I guess.' She picks up her pack and starts making her way down the hill. 'I'm too hot now, I need a swim,' she calls over her shoulder. 'I'll meet you down there.'

Flinch, standing alone, stares fixated at the door. Understands what the lighthouse keeper was trying to point out. Not the staircase, or the brilliance of the lighthouse bulb, or the exposure and freedom of the view from the top, but this message etched so delicately in glass.

And Flinch, since childhood cast adrift, sailing towards his destiny on a turbulent sea of emotion, realises the truth. That understanding and forgiveness and friendship and love can smooth the roughest waters. That the ocean that is in his blood, the ocean upon which he has claimed his destiny, once perilous, is now safe.

NATE

This is where the wind blows me.

It sweeps over the red and brown plains of my childhood.

Like some phantom through a wall I pass through my mother and father, see in intimate and brilliant detail into their individual lives and loves and losses. I understand, I whisper into their ears. All is forgiven. My mother pulls her dressing gown tighter around her throat with a shaking hand. My father awakens from some afternoon half-dream with my voice in his ear. He rolls over and goes back to sleep, his mind a fog. I wonder if he will remember later.

It propels me towards Eleanor, through her blood and bone, through her pulsing, living heart and its fear and confusion and glory and wonder. I float over her as she runs down the steps to the lantana and stands staring at its secret entrance.

It dusts me over Flinch, here with me. I settle over his shoulders hunched and shaking with his grief and I wonder if it will scatter me further but I stick to him like glitter. Don't grieve, I tell him. He stops crying.

He has taken comfort in my voice, but he is still staring at the lips on my body and I fear he has not heeded what I have said.

Revelation has been described as a dawning. But that is not the case with me. On me it lands solid, with a thud, like an anchor. It is grey and blue, the colour of a bruise, the twilight, the moon, and as tall and wide as a wall.

I feel trapped by it at first but then it lifts, and it takes me with it. Slowly. Slowly. Into the blue sky. Heavenward. I cling to the sea breeze with a desperation that only the dying understand.

From high above, I am a spectator watching from the sidelines that complicated game of my life.

Run faster, *I holler at my young self.*

Stay, steady on, *I tell my older self.*

Hang on, please Nate, please, *says Flinch.*

A watch ticks. A soaring kestrel flaps its wings. A boat on the ocean crashes against the bulk of a freak wave. A whale breaches. A car collides with a street sign. A page of a book is turned. A young girl sighs. A jellyfish is washed ashore. The tide turns. A heart beats and slows.

Ah. So. This is how long it takes for a man to die.

Long enough to regret.

Long enough to reconcile.

Long enough for revelation.

Long enough to be … reborn.

ACKNOWLEDGEMENTS

For assistance with the research for this novel, I thank passionate whale lovers Rae Gill and Annah Evington, and the wonderful Aquarians, Graeme Dunstan and Paul Joseph. For first readings and advice, gratitude to Jen McKee, Nicole Carrington and Lyndal Vermette. For editorial support, thanks to Annette Barlow, Christa Munns, and for her insightful words, Ali Lavau. Mum, Dad, Glenn and Lyndal, thanks, as always, for the constant flow of love and encouragement. Thanks also, with all my heart, to my husband, Miles Gillham, for his love and unfailing belief in me — without his support these stories would remain lodged in my imagination.

Thank you to Northwestern University Press for the permission to reprint extracts from *Moby-Dick, or, The whale* by Herman Melville, Penguin Books, New York, USA, 2003 edition. And thank you for permission to reproduce lyrics from 'The Lion Sleeps Tonight' on p. 121 by Luigi Creatore, Hugo Peretti and George D. Weiss © 1961. Renewed 1989 and Assigned to Abilene Music administered by Memory Lane Music Ltd. Reprinted with permission. All Rights Reserved.